glimmerglass

glimmerglass

jenna black

St. Martin's Griffin   New York

This is a work of fiction. All of the characters, organizations, and events portrayed in this novel are either products of the author's imagination or are used fictitiously.

GLIMMERGLASS. Copyright © 2010 by Jenna Black. All rights reserved. Printed in the United States of America. For information, address St. Martin's Press, 175 Fifth Avenue, New York, N.Y. 10010.

www.stmartins.com

Library of Congress Cataloging-in-Publication Data

Black, Jenna.
  Glimmerglass / Jenna Black.—1st ed.
    p. cm.
  ISBN 978-0-312-57593-9
  1. Teenage girls—Fiction. 2. Magic—Fiction. I. Title.
  PS3602.L288G57 2010
  813'.6—dc22

                             2009046746

D 10 9 8 7 6 5

To the Deadline Dames—Devon, Jackie, Kaz, Keri, Lili, Rachel, Rinda, and Toni—for support above and beyond the call of duty.

acknowledgments

A novel is rarely written in a vacuum, and this one is no exception. Many thanks to my critique partner, Kelly Gay, for all the valuable input she gave me along the way, and for reading multiple drafts without a word of complaint. Thanks also to Dame Kaz for helping me make sure my Avalon Fae didn't speak too much like transplanted Americans, and to Lauren Abercrombie for helping me make sure my teens came out sounding like teens. Thanks to my editor, Jennifer Weis, and her assistant, Anne Bensson, for making this book possible in the first place. And last, thanks to my fabulous agent, Miriam Kriss, for believing in me, and for helping me believe in myself when my confidence wavers.

prologue

The absolute last straw was when my mom showed up at my recital drunk. I don't mean tipsy—I mean staggering, slurring, everyone-knows drunk. And as if that wasn't bad enough, she was late, too, so that when she pushed through the doors and practically fell into a metal folding chair at the back, everyone turned to glare at her for interrupting the performance.

Standing in the wings, I wanted to sink through the floor in embarrassment. Ms. Morris, my voice teacher, was the only one in the room who realized the person causing the disruption was my mother. I'd very carefully avoided any contact between my mom and the students of this school—my newest one, and the one I hoped to graduate from if we could manage two full years in the same location just this once.

When it was my turn to perform, Ms. Morris gave me a sympathetic look before she put her hands on the piano. My face felt hot with embarrassment, and my throat was so tight I worried my voice would crack the moment I opened my mouth.

My voice is naturally pretty—a result of my ultra-secret, hush-hush Fae heritage. Truthfully, I didn't need the voice lessons, but summer vacation was going to start in a few weeks, and I'd wanted an excuse that would get me out of the house now and then but wouldn't require a huge time commitment. Voice lessons had fit the bill. And I enjoyed them.

My heart beat hard against my chest, and my palms sweated as Ms. Morris played the introduction. I tried to concentrate on the music. If I could just get through the song and act normal, no one in the audience had to know that the drunken idiot in the back was related to me.

Finally, the intro was over, and it was time for me to start. Despite my less-than-optimal state of mind, the music took over for a while, and I let the beauty of "Voi che sapete," one of my favorite Mozart arias, wash over me. Traditionally sung by a woman pretending to be a young boy, it was perfect for my clear soprano, with the hint of vibrato that added a human touch to my otherwise Fae voice.

I hit every note spot on, and didn't forget any of my lyrics. Ms. Morris nodded in approval a couple times when I got the phrasing just the way she wanted it. But I knew I could have done better, put more feeling into it, if I hadn't been so morbidly aware of my mom's presence.

I breathed a sigh of relief when I was done. Until the applause started, that is. Most of the parents and other students gave a polite, if heartfelt, round of applause. My mom, on the other hand, gave me a standing ovation, once more drawing all eyes to her. And, of course, revealing that she was with me.

If lightning had shot from the heavens and struck me dead at that moment, I might have welcomed it.

I shouldn't have told her about the recital, but despite the fact that I knew better, there'd been some part of me that wished she would show up to hear me sing, wished she'd applaud me and be proud like a normal mother. I'm such a moron!

I wondered how long it would take the story to make the rounds of *this* school. At my previous school, when one of the bitchy cheerleader types had run into me and my mom when we were shopping—a task she was barely sober enough to manage—it had taken all of one day for the entire school to know my mom was a drunk. I hadn't exactly been part of the popular crowd even before, but after that . . . Well, let's just say that for once I was glad we were moving yet again.

I was sixteen years old, and we'd lived in ten different cities that I could remember. We moved around so much because my mom didn't want my dad to find me. She was afraid he'd try to take me away from her, and considering she isn't exactly a study in parental perfection, he just might be able to do it.

I'd never met my dad, but my mom had told me all about him. The story varied depending on how drunk and/or depressed she was feeling at the time. What I'm pretty sure is true is that my mom was born in Avalon and lived there most of her life, and that my dad is some kind of big-deal Fae there. Only my mom hadn't realized who he was when she started messing around with him. She found out right about the time she got pregnant with me, and she left home before anyone knew.

Sometimes, my mom said she'd run away from Avalon because my dad was such a terrible, evil man that he'd be sure to abuse me in horrible ways if I lived with him. That was the story she told when she was sober, the story she built to make sure I was never interested in meeting him. "He's a monster, Dana," she'd say, explaining why we had to move yet again. "I can't let him find you."

But when she was drunk out of her gourd and babbling at me about whatever entered her mind at the moment, she'd say she'd left Avalon because if I'd stayed there, I'd have been caught up in some kind of nasty political intrigue, me being the daughter of a high muckety-muck Fae and all. When she was in one of these moods, she'd go on and on about how great a guy my dad was, how she'd loved him more than life itself, but how her duty as a mother had to come first. Gag!

I wanted to slink away from the recital before it was even over, but I didn't dare. It was possible my mom was dumb enough to have actually driven here, and there was no way I could let her drive back home in the state she was in. I had the guilty thought—not for the first time—that my life might improve if she got herself killed in a car wreck. I was ashamed of myself for letting the thought enter my head. *Of course* I didn't want my mother to die. I just wanted her not to be an alcoholic.

Ms. Morris took me aside as soon as everyone was done, and the sympathy in her eyes was almost too much to bear. "Do you need any help, Dana?" she asked me quietly.

I shook my head and refused to meet her gaze. "No. Thank you. I'll . . . take care of her." My face was hot again, so I made my escape as quickly as possible, avoiding the other students who wanted to either congratulate me on my brilliant performance (yeah, right!) or try to get the full scoop on my mom so they could tell all their friends.

Mom was trying to mingle with the other parents when I walked up to her. She was too out of it to pick up on the subtle you're-a-drunk-leave-me-alone vibes they were giving her. Still feeling like everyone was staring at me, I took hold of her arm.

"Come on, let's get you home," I said through gritted teeth.

"Dana!" she practically shouted. "You were *wonderful!*" She threw her arms around me like she hadn't seen me in three years and gave me a smothering hug.

"Glad you enjoyed it," I forced myself to say as I wriggled out of her hug and began heading for the door with her in tow. She didn't seem to mind being dragged across the room, so at least that was a plus. *This could have been worse,* I tried to tell myself.

I didn't have to ask Mom whether she'd driven, because the minute we stepped outside, I could see our car, parked so crookedly it had taken up about three spaces. I said a silent prayer of thanks that she hadn't managed to kill anyone.

I held out my hand to her. "Keys."

She sniffed and tried to look dignified. Hard to do when she had to clutch the railing to keep from falling headfirst down the steps that led to the parking lot. "I am perfectly capable of driving," she informed me.

Anger burned in my chest, but I knew exactly how much good it would do me to explode, no matter how much I wanted to. If I could just keep pretending to be calm and reasonable, I could get her into the passenger seat and out of the public eye much faster. The last thing I wanted was to have a big shouting fight scene right here in front of everybody. Mom had given them enough to talk about already.

"Let me drive anyway," I said. "I need the practice." If she'd been even marginally sober, she'd have heard the banked fury in my voice, but as it was, she was oblivious. But she handed over the keys, which was a relief.

I drove home, my hands clutching the wheel with a white-knuckled grip as I fought to hold myself together. My mom was in the middle of gushing over my performance when the booze finally got the best of her and she conked out. I was grateful for the silence, though I knew from experience it would be quite a production to get her out of the car and into the house in her condition.

When I pulled into our driveway and contemplated the task ahead, I realized that I couldn't live like this any longer. Nothing could possibly be worse than living with my mother, constantly lying for her, trying to cover up that she was passed out drunk when she was supposed to be meeting with my teachers or driving me to some off-campus event. Ever since I could remember, I'd lived in mortal fear that my friends at school—what friends I managed to have when we moved around so much, that is—would find out about her and decide I was some kind of freak by association. A fear that, unfortunately, I'd found out the hard way was not unfounded.

I'd been the adult in this family since I was about five, and now it was time for me to take my life into my own hands. I was going to contact my father and, unless I got some kind of vibe that said he really *was* an abusive pervert, I was going to go live with him. In Avalon. In the Wild City that was the crossroads between our world and Faerie, the city where magic and technology coexisted in something resembling peace. Even in Avalon, I figured, I'd have a better, more normal life than I had now with my mom.

I've never been so wrong about anything in my life.

chapter one

My palms were sweaty and my heart was in my throat as my plane made its descent into London. I could hardly believe I was really doing this, hardly believe I had found the courage to run away from home. I wiped my palms on my jeans and wondered if Mom had figured out I was gone yet. She'd been sleeping off one hell of a binge when I'd left the house, and sometimes she could sleep for twenty-four hours straight at times like that. I wished I could be a fly on the wall when she found the note I'd left her. Maybe losing me would finally turn on the lightbulb over her head and she'd stop drinking. But I wasn't holding my breath.

I'd had no trouble finding and contacting my father. Mom would never have dreamed of telling me his name when she was sober, and he wasn't listed on my birth certificate, but all it had taken were a couple of probing questions when she was in one of her drunk, chatty moods to find out his name was Seamus Stuart. The Fae, she confided, didn't use last names in Faerie, but those who lived in Avalon had adopted the practice for the convenience of the human population.

In the grand scheme of things, Avalon is tiny, its population less than 10,000, so when I'd gone online and brought up the Avalon phone book, I'd had no trouble finding my father—he was the only Seamus Stuart listed. And when I called and asked him if he knew anyone by my mother's name, he readily admitted he'd had a girlfriend of that name once, so I knew that I'd found the right guy.

Before that first conversation was over, he had already asked me to come to Avalon for a visit. He'd even sprung for a first-class plane ticket into London. And never once had he asked to talk to my mom, nor had he asked if I had her permission to come visit him. I'd been surprised by that at first, but then I figured she'd been right that if he could have found me, he'd have spirited me away to Avalon without a second thought. *Don't look the gift horse in the mouth,* I reminded myself.

The plane hit the tarmac with a jarring thud. I took a deep breath to calm myself. It would be hours still before I would actually meet my father. Being a native of Faerie, he couldn't set foot in the mortal world. (If he'd decided to kidnap me, he'd have had to use human accomplices to do it.) The unique magic of Avalon is that the city exists both in Faerie and in the mortal world—the only place where the two planes of existence overlap. When my father stood at the border of the city and looked out, all he could see was Faerie, and if he crossed the border, those of us in the mortal world wouldn't be able to see him anymore.

He'd arranged to have a human friend of his meet me at the London airport and take me to Avalon. Only when I got through Avalon immigration would I be able to meet him.

I went through the immigration and customs process in London in something of a daze. I'd been too excited and nervous to sleep on the plane, and it was definitely catching up with me now. I followed the herd to the ground transportation area and started searching the sea of placards for my own name.

I didn't see it.

I looked again, examining each sign carefully, in case my name was misspelled and that's why I'd missed it. But the crowd of drivers steadily thinned, and nowhere did I see anyone holding up my name. I bit my lip and examined my watch, which I'd adjusted to London time. It was 8:23 A.M., and when I'd last talked to my dad, he'd estimated that if the plane was on time, I'd get through customs somewhere around 8:15. His friend should be here by now.

I took another one of those deep breaths, reminding myself to calm down. Dad's friend was only eight minutes late. Hardly worth panicking about. I found a comfortable chair near the doors, my gaze darting this way and that as I looked for someone hurrying into the terminal like they were late. I saw plenty of those, but none of them carried a sign with my name on it.

When 8:45 rolled around and still there was no sign of my ride, I decided it was okay to get a little bit panicky. I turned on my cell phone, meaning to give Dad a call, only to discover I couldn't get a signal. Belatedly, I wondered if American cell phones worked in London. I swallowed another wave of nerves. Dad had sent me a lovely getting-to-know-you gift, a white rose cameo, and I found myself fingering it anxiously.

I'd been in and out of a lot of airports in my life, and if the flight was long enough, my mom was invariably sloshed by the time we landed. Even when I was like eight years old, I'd been capable of steering my mom through the airport, finding our baggage, and arranging a taxi to take us to wherever we needed to be. Granted, the most exotic place I'd ever had to do it was Canada, but heck, this was England, not India.

Telling myself not to sweat it, I found a bank of pay phones. Because my mom couldn't be trusted to keep track of bills or anything, we'd arranged for me to have my own credit card, which I promptly used to make the long-distance call to Avalon.

I let the phone at my dad's house ring about ten times, but no one answered. I hung up and bit my lip.

I'd been nervous enough about this whole adventure. Now I was stranded at Heathrow Airport and my dad wasn't answering his phone. Add to that a crushing case of jet lag, and all I wanted to do at the moment was curl up in a snug, comfy bed and go to sleep. I swallowed a yawn—if I let myself get started, I'd never stop.

At 9:15, I had to admit that the chances of my dad's friend showing up were slim to none. My dad probably wasn't answering his phone because he was waiting for me at the Avalon border, as he'd promised. So okay, all I had to do was get a cab to take me to the border. It was only about twenty-five miles out of London. No big deal, right?

I exchanged some money, then got in one of those enormous black cabs they have in England. It felt really weird to see the driver on the wrong side of the car, and even weirder to be driving on the wrong side of the road.

My driver drove like a maniac and talked nonstop the entire way to Avalon's Southern Gate. I don't know what his accent was, maybe Cockney, but I only understood about a third of what he said. Luckily, he never seemed to require a response aside from the occasional smile and nod. I hoped he didn't see me flinching and wincing every time it seemed like he was about to squash someone into roadkill.

Like everyone else in the universe, I'd seen lots of pictures of Avalon. You could find about a thousand guide books dedicated to the city—I had two in my luggage—and just about every fantasy movie ever made has at least one or two scenes that were filmed on location in Avalon, it being the only place in the mortal world where magic actually works. But seeing Avalon in person kind of reminded me of seeing the Grand Canyon for the first time: no photograph on earth could do it justice.

Avalon is situated on a mountain. Yes, a real, honest-to-goodness mountain. The thing juts up into the sky out of the flat, green, sheep-dotted countryside, and it looks like someone grabbed one of the Alps and haphazardly dropped it where it most definitely did not belong.

Houses and shops and office buildings had been built into every square inch of the mountain's slopes, and a single paved road spiraled from the base to the castle-like structure that dominated the summit. There were lots of lesser cobblestone roads that led off that main one, but the main road was the only one big enough for cars.

The base of the mountain is completely surrounded by a thick, murky moat, the moat surrounded by a high, electrified fence. There are only four entrances to the city itself, one at each point of the compass. My dad was supposed to meet me at the Southern Gate. The taxi driver dropped me off at the gatehouse—a three-story building about a half a block long—and I felt another pang of apprehension as I watched him drive away. It was possible for cars to pass through the gates into Avalon, but the driver would have to have an Avalon visa to be allowed through. Backpack over one shoulder, I dragged my suitcase through a series of rat mazes, following the signs for visitors. Naturally, the lines for residents were all much shorter.

By the time I got to the head of the line, I was practically asleep on my feet, despite the anxiety. There was a small parking lot just past the checkpoint, and like at the airport, I could see people standing around there with placards. But as I waited for the customs official to stamp my passport, I still didn't see my name on any of them.

"One moment, miss," the customs official said, after having examined my passport for what seemed like about ten years. I blinked in confusion as he then walked away from his post, carrying my passport.

My throat went dry as I saw him talk to a tall, imposing woman who wore a navy-blue uniform—and a gun and hand-cuffs on her belt. It went even drier when the official gestured at me and the woman looked in my direction. Sure enough, she started heading my way. I saw that the official had handed her my passport. This didn't seem like a good sign.

"Please come with me, Miss . . ." She opened the passport to check. "Hathaway." She had a weird accent, sort of British, but not quite. Meanwhile, the customs official gestured for the next person in line.

I had to step closer to the woman to avoid getting trampled by the family of five that came up to the desk behind me.

"Is there a problem?" I asked, and though I tried to sound nonchalant, I think my voice shook.

She smiled, though the expression didn't reach her eyes. She also reached out and put her hand on my arm, leading me toward a key-carded door in the side of the building.

I tried to reach for the handle of my suitcase, but some guy in a coverall got there before me. He slapped a neon orange tag on it, then hauled it off behind the official's desk.

I wondered if I should be making a scene. But I decided that would just dig whatever hole I was in deeper.

"Don't be afraid," the woman said, still towing me toward

the door. Well, I suppose she wasn't really *towing* me. Her touch on my arm was light, and it was more like she was guiding me. But I had the feeling that if I slowed down, it wouldn't feel like guiding anymore. "It's standard procedure here to conduct interviews with a certain percentage of our visitors." Her smile broadened as she swiped her key card. "It's just your lucky day."

I was now hitting stress and sleep-deprivation overload, and my eyes stung with tears. I bit the inside of my cheek to try to keep them contained. If this was just some kind of random selection, then why had the official looked at my passport for so long? And why hadn't my dad told me it was a possibility? I certainly hadn't read anything about it in the guide books.

I was led into a sterile gray office with furniture that looked like rejects from a college dorm and a funky smell like wet wool. The imposing woman gestured me into a metal folding chair, then pulled a much more comfortable-looking rolling chair out from behind the desk. She smiled at me again.

"My name's Grace," she said. I wasn't sure if that was a first or a last name. "I'm captain of the border patrol, and I just need to ask you a few questions about your visit to Avalon; then you can be on your way."

I swallowed hard. "Okay," I said. Like I had a choice.

Grace leaned over and pulled a little spiral-bound notebook from one of the desk drawers, then readied an intricately carved silver pen over the paper. I guess the Fae aren't big on using Bics.

"What is the purpose of your visit to Avalon?" she asked.

Well, duh. I'm sixteen years old—I'm not here on a business trip. "I'm here to visit with family."

She jotted that down, then looked at me over the top of the

notebook. "Aren't you a little young to be traveling unaccompanied?"

I sat up straighter in my chair. Yeah, okay, I was only sixteen, but that's not *that* young. I was old enough to balance the checkbook, pay the bills, and drive my mother around when she was too drunk to be allowed behind the wheel. Grace's eyes flashed with amusement as I bristled, and I managed to tamp down my reaction before I spoke.

"Someone was supposed to meet me at the airport," I said, though that wasn't really an answer to her question. "No one showed up, so I just took a taxi. My father's supposed to meet me when I get through customs."

Grace nodded thoughtfully, scribbling away. "What is your father's name?"

"Seamus Stuart."

"Address?"

"Er, 25 Ashley Lane." I was glad I'd bothered to ask for his address before showing up. I hadn't really known I'd need it.

"Was he in the parking area? I can ask him to come in if you'd like."

"Um, I've actually never met him, so I don't know if he was there or not." I hoped I wasn't blushing. I don't know why I found the fact that I'd never met my father embarrassing, but I did.

She scribbled some more. I wondered how she could possibly be writing so much. It wasn't like I was telling her my life's history. And why would the border patrol need to know all this crap? I'd had to answer most of these questions when I'd applied for my visa.

"Am I going to get my luggage back?" I asked, too nervous to sit there and be quiet.

"Of course, dear," she said with another of those insincere smiles.

Just then, the door to the office opened. The guy in the coverall who'd taken my luggage popped his head in and waited for Grace's attention. She looked up at him with an arched eyebrow.

"It's confirmed," he said.

For the first time, Grace's smile looked entirely genuine.

"What's confirmed?" I asked, the genuine smile for some reason freaking me out even more than the fake one.

"Why, your identity, dear. It seems you really are Seamus Stuart's daughter."

My jaw dropped. "How did you *confirm* that?"

"Allow me to introduce myself properly," she said instead of answering. "My full name is Grace Stuart." Her smile turned positively impish. "But you may call me Aunt Grace."

chapter two

I'm sure I was sitting there like an idiot with my mouth hanging open. Grace laughed at the expression on my face as I tried to pull myself together and think.

For the first time since I'd laid eyes on her, I looked past her uniform and her imposing manner to really *see* her. She was tall and model-thin, her body almost boyish in its lack of curves. Sort of like mine. My hopes that I would one day fill out were dwindling. Her pale blond hair was thick and lustrous, pulled back from her angular face into a braid that trailed down almost to the small of her back. Blue eyes just like mine, except hers had more of an upward tilt. A *Fae* tilt.

"You're my dad's sister," I said, the words somewhere between a question and a statement.

Grace clapped her hands like I'd just performed a backflip. I felt my face steadily heating.

"Very good, my dear," she said in a tone of voice that suggested I was just a bit on the slow side. "Seamus is, shall we say, indisposed at the moment. But he charged me with taking care of you until he is able to do so himself."

I narrowed my eyes at her. "If this is your idea of taking care of me, I'm probably better off taking care of myself." I'm not usually that rude—certainly not to authority figures—but jet lag, stress, and confusion had combined to make my temper brittle at best. "You could have just introduced yourself from the start instead of scaring me half to death with your Gestapo routine."

Grace blinked a couple of times. I doubted she was used to having *anyone* talk back to her, much less teenage human girls. The smile faded from her lips, and an arctic chill entered her eyes.

"A girl no one's ever heard of comes marching into Avalon claiming to be the half-blood daughter of one of the great Seelie lords, and we're just supposed to accept you with no questions asked?" she said, her voice as frosty as her eyes. "Seamus had no idea he'd sired a child on your mother, and while he might have been quick to accept you into his bosom as one of his own, it was certainly conceivable that you were an imposter."

One of the great Seelie lords? My mom had said Dad was a big-deal Fae, but this sounded like more of a big deal than I'd imagined.

"While you and I chatted, my staff searched your bag for your hairbrush. They were able to determine that you truly are who you say you are."

The violation of my privacy pissed me off, but I was also puzzled. "You were able to do a DNA test in, like, fifteen minutes?" I asked incredulously.

Grace gave me another of those looks that said I was obviously a little simpleminded. "Not a DNA test, dear."

Oh. Magic. I'd kind of forgotten about that. My face heated with another blush. Grace was really good at making me feel like an idiot, and I was pretty sure it wasn't by accident. I didn't know what she had against me, but it was obviously something. My brain felt all fuzzy around the edges, and once again I longed for that cozy bed to curl up in. Despite my stress—and annoyance—a yawn forced its way out of my mouth.

Grace's expression softened into something concerned and almost sweet-looking. I didn't believe it.

"You poor thing," she said. "You must be exhausted after your long trip." She stood up, the movement inexplicably graceful. "Come." I wondered if she knew she said it like she was talking to her favorite pet. "We must get you settled in so you can get some rest."

I stayed seated, not sure what she meant. "So I'm free to go now?"

"I will arrange for another officer to fill in for me for a couple of hours," she said in another one of her non-answers. "I'll take you home. If you'd like to stop and grab something to eat first, just let me know. There are a number of lovely cafés very near my house."

My stomach gurgled, but I wasn't sure it was from hunger. One thing I knew for sure was I didn't want to go home with Grace.

"Can you just drop me off at my dad's house?" I asked, already knowing the answer would be no.

Grace made a sad face. "I'm afraid not, dear. He isn't home at the moment, and I don't have a key. But have no fear—you need only stay with me a day or two. Then your father will be ready to take you in."

It sounded like I wasn't going to have a choice in the matter, so I tried to resign myself to the idea. "Okay," I said, standing up and hoping I didn't sound too pouty.

"Splendid!" she said with false cheer.

Splendid? Who says "splendid" in this day and age? Of course, since Aunt Grace was Fae, I supposed she could be a zillion years old, even though she looked like she was in her mid twenties.

I followed Grace through a dizzying set of mazelike corridors. I couldn't help noticing the security cameras that spied on our every move.

She stopped by what I think was a break room, based on the microwave and vending machines. A small group of uniformed officers sat around a table. Grace barked some orders at them—arranging for someone to cover for her during her field trip—and then we were wending our way through the corridors again.

Eventually, we came to a key-carded door. Aunt Grace swiped her card, and the door opened onto the parking lot that I had spotted when I'd been standing in line. She guided me to an elegant black Mercedes. The car was so pristine she could have driven it off the lot five minutes ago. It had that lovely new car scent, somewhat spoiled by the tacky, rose-shaped car freshener that hung from the rearview mirror. At least it wasn't one of those pine-tree taxi-cab specials.

"Your bag is in the trunk," Aunt Grace told me before I had a chance to ask. Then she started the car and we were on our way.

The bridge over the moat was a narrow, two-lane affair, and the guard rails on the side looked kind of flimsy to me. Maybe that was just because the moat's murky, nasty water gave me the creeps.

Trying to ignore the water, I glanced over my shoulder—a bit wistfully—at the gatehouse that marked the border between Avalon and the mortal world. A part of me was already wishing I'd never set foot out of my mom's house. Yeah, it majorly sucked living with her, taking care of her, lying to all my friends about her. But at least she was the devil I knew.

A wave of nausea rolled over me, and my vision went momentarily blurry. I turned back around to face front.

"Is something wrong?" Grace asked.

I shook my head and swallowed past the nausea. "I'm just jet-lagged and stressed out and maybe even a little motion sick." I wondered if she'd mind me barfing in her shiny new car. I bet the answer was yes.

"What did you mean when you said my father was 'indisposed'?" I asked her as my stomach—luckily—settled down.

"He's had a spot of . . . legal trouble, I suppose you'd call it." The Mercedes began its smooth, effortless ascent of the steep two-lane road that spiraled up the mountain. "But don't worry. Everything should be cleared up in a day or two. And I'll take good care of you until he's home."

"Where is he?"

The corners of her mouth tightened, and she hesitated before answering. "Very well, if you *must* know," she said, making it sound like I'd been badgering her about it for hours, "he's in jail."

I gasped. Steering with one negligent hand, she reached over and patted my knee. I had to resist an urge to jerk away.

"It is merely a misunderstanding," she said in what was supposed to be a soothing tone. "He'll be seen by the Council tomorrow, or the next day at the latest, and he's certain to be released at that time."

My father was in jail. Of all the problems I'd imagined facing in Avalon, this wasn't one of them. My hand crept again to the cameo I wore, fingers nervously stroking the textured surface. Grace's eyes tracked my gesture. Her lips thinned when she saw the cameo, but she didn't say anything. I dropped my hand anyway.

I was bubbling over with more questions, but at that moment, Grace pulled into a tiny parking lot, big enough for maybe a half dozen cars at most. She was out of the car and popping the trunk before I'd managed to get a single one of my questions out. Again, I didn't think it was by accident.

I was too tired to deal with this now. After I'd had a nap and didn't feel so much like roadkill, I'd sit down with dear old Aunt Grace and have a long heart-to-heart in which she would explain what was going on with my dad. Like why he was in jail. And what was this Council he was going to be seen by? I belatedly wished I'd read up on the Avalon governmental system. All I could remember about it from civics class was that it was unlike any other government in the world, and the duties were shared equally between humans and Fae.

Grace opened the trunk for me, but she left it to me to do the heavy lifting. I sure was glad my bag had wheels. Without a word, she led me down one of the cobblestone side streets. The cobblestones weren't exactly easy on the wheels, and I struggled to keep the bag upright. And to keep it out of the puddles that gathered in the low spots, and the horse crap that gave the street a distinctively barnlike smell.

I must have been making some kind of face, because Grace actually volunteered information for the first time I could remember.

"The internal combustion engine does not function in Faerie," she explained. "Those who have reason to travel between Avalon and Faerie perforce do so on horseback, so you'll see a great many more horses here than you might in most cities."

This was probably fascinating information, and no doubt I should be gawking at my exotic surroundings. But the jet lag was too overwhelming, and I was struggling too hard with my stupid luggage to manage it.

I was relieved beyond words when we finally came to a stop in front of a picturesque stone row house. It was three stories high and rather narrow, but the old-fashioned, leaded-glass windows and the window boxes overflowing with white roses gave it a pleasant, homey look.

Aunt Grace muttered something under her breath, and the door made a series of clicking sounds before it swung open. No one had touched it.

Magic, my mind mumbled. But I was too tired and grouchy to be properly impressed.

I didn't get a good look at the interior, because Grace immediately led me upstairs to the third floor. And no, she didn't offer to help me haul my bag up the two narrow wooden staircases.

"Here we are," she said, opening the first door at the top of the stairs.

I hauled my luggage over the threshold, then dropped it gratefully. The room looked really nice, but all I really had eyes for was the huge, soft-looking four-poster bed. Never had a bed looked more inviting.

Grace smiled at my obvious yearning. "I'll leave you to get some rest," she said. "There's an en suite bathroom right through there." She pointed at a closed door at the other end of the room.

"Thanks," I said, my tendency toward politeness rearing its ugly head. I took a couple of steps toward the bed. I probably should have fished my toiletries out of my luggage and at least brushed my teeth before collapsing, but the lure of sleep was overpowering.

"Sleep well, dear," Grace said; then the door closed behind her and she was gone.

I had just reached out and put a hand on the bed to pull back the fluffy down comforter when I heard a distinctive click. I blinked. *Surely* I hadn't heard what I thought I'd just heard.

Alarm overriding my fatigue for the moment, I went to the door. I could hear Grace's footsteps retreating down the wooden stairs. I put my hand on the doorknob, hoping against hope I was wrong. But when I tried to turn the knob, it stayed stubbornly in place.

My dear Aunt Grace had just locked me in.

chapter three

Of course, I had to try pounding on the door and yelling, but I can't say I was really surprised when that didn't work. The only other way out of the room was the window. I had to climb up on a chair to look out, and what I saw was discouraging. I was on the third floor, so climbing out the window didn't seem like the best idea in the world—even if I could have gotten it open, which I couldn't. There was no lock that I could see, and it didn't look like it was painted shut, but repeated banging and prying got me nothing but a couple of broken nails.

Why, oh why, had I decided to leave home? I'd been dealing with my mom for my whole life; what would another couple of years have mattered? Hell, it wouldn't even have been a full two years—just this summer, my senior year at school (I'd skipped a grade in middle school, so I was generally younger than everyone else in my class) and then the summer that followed. After that, I'd be away at college, and I had every intention of going to school as far away from home—wherever that happened to be at the time—as possible.

My eyes were gritty and my head ached, but I couldn't imagine lying down and taking a nice little nap under the circumstances.

I found myself fidgeting with the cameo once again. Was my father really in jail? If so, what for? Mom had told me some terrible stories about him, but I was convinced at least half of them were lies.

But what if they weren't? What if he was in jail because he *belonged* there?

I shook the thought off. Aunt Grace had intercepted me at the border, bullied me, and then locked me up. I sat down on the edge of the bed and considered my options. Too bad I didn't seem to have any at the moment. About fifteen minutes later, I heard the sound of footsteps approaching. And voices.

One of them was Aunt Grace, and the other was a man—I hoped against hope that the man was my father. I couldn't hear what they were saying, and when they got close enough for the words to be distinct, they shut up.

The hair on the back of my neck prickled for no reason I could name, and I backed away from the door. I heard the soft mumble of Grace's voice, and the door unlocked and opened itself.

I'd said Aunt Grace was tall and imposing. She had to be at least five-nine, five-ten. But the man who stood behind her in the doorway was enormous. Well over six feet tall—probably more like seven—he'd have to bend over to fit through the door, and he was wide enough that I wondered how he'd made it up the narrow staircase. He looked like what you'd get if you crossed an NBA star with a non-green version of the Incredible Hulk.

Grace entered the room, and, thankfully, her giant friend stayed behind. Blocking the doorway, I suppose, in case I made a run for it. I crossed running for it off my list of options.

I had to fight down a shiver even as I tried to sound brave. "Where do you get off locking me in my room?" I demanded. At least, I *tried* to demand. I'm afraid "whimpered" might be a better description. Then I got a better look at her—and at the big bruise that bloomed on one side of her face. I gasped.

"What happened?" I asked, momentarily forgetting that she was the enemy.

She looked grim. "My brother was . . . unwise to bring you here."

"Huh?"

"You are in danger. Our family is one of great power and consequence. Now that Seamus has claimed you as his daughter and brought you here, there are factions who might see you as a tool to be used to control him. Someone must have seen me bring you here. I was attacked while I was unlocking the front door. I was lucky I'd called Lachlan and asked him to meet me. He chased them off before they could do too much damage. But this proves I was right: you aren't safe here."

"Tell you what," I said. "Why don't you let me go back to London? I can get a hotel room there and wait until my dad's out of . . . er, until he's available. That way I won't be putting you through any trouble, and—"

She shook her head. "The men who attacked me were human. I don't know who they were working for, but they could easily pursue you to London. No, we have to take you to a more secure location, at least until Seamus is free."

My head felt all fuzzy, like my brain had decided it couldn't take any more and was going on strike. Aunt Grace looked genuinely worried, and that bruise on her cheek was ugly. Still, just because someone attacked her didn't mean they were after *me*. I mean seriously, I'm a half-blood American teenager. How could any of this possibly be about me?

"Lachlan will take you to a safe house," Grace said, gesturing at the giant. "I might make a tempting target for attack, but he does not."

I looked at Lachlan, who still loomed in the door. I imagined bad guys would take one look at him and run the other way. His huge arms were crossed on the lintel, showing off his incredible height. He flashed me a smile that seemed to have a hint of warmth, but he was still one seriously scary dude. I kinda wanted to run the other way myself, but somehow, I didn't think Grace would let me get away with it.

"All right," I said, trying to act like I had a choice. "I'll go with Lachlan to the safe house."

"A wise decision," Grace said, doing a crappy job of hiding her sarcasm.

She crossed to a chest of drawers I hadn't yet bothered to examine, then rooted through them until she pulled out a long black cloak with a cowl-like hood. Very sinister-looking. She held it out to me.

"Put this on," she ordered, "and put the hood up."

The cloak was obviously hers, and was way too long for me. She frowned when she saw it dragging on the floor.

"Can't be helped," I heard her mutter under her breath. "Off you go, then," she said out loud. "You should be safe for tonight, and hopefully Seamus will be able to take over tomorrow."

I reached for my bags, but Grace shook her head. "I'll have them sent over," she said.

Shrouded in the cloak, trying not to trip over its hem, I made my way toward the door, where Lachlan awaited me. He didn't say anything, just nodded sharply and started down the steps. He had to stoop to get down them, and he walked kind of sideways to keep his shoulders from brushing the walls.

When we got to the ground floor, he led me out a back door. I felt ridiculous walking around in a black hooded cloak—like some kind of shrunken Grim Reaper—but at least it was warm. I tripped along beside Lachlan, trying not to step on the hem of the too-long cloak. The hood practically blinded me.

It was summer, but here in Avalon, a cold, gray mist floated through the streets. Even under the heavy wool cloak, I shivered in the chill.

"Don't worry," said a profoundly deep voice that apparently belonged to Lachlan. "We'll soon have you warm and cozy." His accent sounded like Grace's, only with a pleasant, soft burr at the end. Under other circumstances, I might even have said he sounded nice. I wondered if he was Fae. He didn't look it; or at least he didn't look like my preconceived notion of what a Fae would look like. Obviously, I didn't know much.

The "warm, cozy" place Lachlan took me to turned out to be a basement under what smelled like a bakery—I tried to catch a glimpse of my surroundings, but Lachlan herded me inside before I could. The basement was divided into two rooms, one of which looked suspiciously like a guard house, and one of which looked suspiciously like a cell, with a door that looked about six inches thick and featured a heavy wooden bar.

I balked. "Oh, no," I said, backing up. "I am *not* going in there."

Lachlan closed the door behind him. I shoved the hood down so I could glare up at him. He wasn't intimidated—shocking, but true.

"It's for your own protection," he said with a shrug that looked almost sheepish.

"You have *got* to be kidding me!"

"I'm afraid your aunt considers you a flight risk. You would not be safe unprotected in Avalon, so she's decided to make certain you stay put."

I shook my head stubbornly, calculating my chances of getting around Lachlan and out the door. They were not good.

He sighed. "Please, Dana. I've no wish to be a bully, but you must go in." He shifted from foot to foot, looking remarkably uncomfortable. "This is not how I would have chosen to handle the situation, but Grace is your blood relation, and I am not. I have to respect her decision."

I snorted. "That makes one of us."

Lachlan looked . . . distraught. To my surprise, I found myself feeling sorry for him. Guess it sucked being caught in the middle.

The reality was I didn't have much of a choice. Even if I somehow got past Lachlan, what was I going to do? Go running out into the streets of Avalon by myself when there was a possibility Aunt Grace was telling the truth and I was in danger?

With a heavy sigh—and one last longing look at the front door—I stomped across the room to my cell. Lachlan closed the door behind me, and I heard a heavy thunk that could only be the wooden bar sliding into place.

chapter four

The cell turned out to be not as depressing as I'd thought. If it weren't for the barred door—and the fact that it was a basement with no windows—I could almost have convinced myself I was in a quaint little B&B. The bed was small but looked soft and inviting. The bathroom featured a claw-foot tub, and the gas fireplace added instant warmth. Best of all, my suitcase and backpack lay tucked in one corner. How they got there was anyone's guess, but I'd put my money on magic of some kind. I couldn't see Grace carrying my bags for me, even if she could have beat us here.

Pleasant as the room was, I couldn't forget the sound of the bar thunking into place. This truly was a cell, and even if the jailor seemed kinda nice, the warden, Aunt Grace, was something else entirely.

I paced the cell for about half an hour, trying to come up with an escape plan. Of course, I didn't know where I could go even if I miraculously got out of this room. A search of my suitcase and backpack showed that my passport, my credit card, and all my cash were missing. If I wanted out, I was going to have to recover them. Or find an accomplice.

My plans—if you could call them that—were interrupted by the sound of the bar sliding up. Seconds later, Lachlan stepped into the room. In one massive hand, he held a tray on which sat a teapot and cups. When he pushed the door closed and lowered his hand, I saw a plate adorned with a selection of scones. My stomach made an embarrassing rumble, which Lachlan was good enough to ignore.

He set the tray down on a small table with two chairs. Lachlan pulled one of the chairs out for me like a gentleman. I was too hungry to pass up the opportunity, so I scarfed down two of the warm, delicious scones in record time. Lachlan hovered while I ate, and every time I sneaked a glance at him, he was smiling with what looked like pride.

"Did you make these?" I asked.

He nodded and jerked his thumb toward the ceiling. "That's my bakery upstairs."

"They're delicious," I told him, though I'm sure he'd gotten that message already.

The food temporarily made me feel better, but my mood sank again when Lachlan picked up the tray to leave. Soon, I would be alone in my cell again.

Lachlan gave me a sympathetic smile. "Your aunt Grace means well," he told me. "I know she's been less than diplomatic—"

I couldn't help my snort of laughter. Yeah, that was one way to describe it. Lachlan looked hurt by my laughter. I guess he really liked Aunt Grace, since he did his best to defend her.

"She has been under a great deal of stress lately," he explained, "and your arrival has—" He frowned and didn't finish his sentence.

"My arrival has what?"

"Let's just say you're one more complication in an already complicated life."

"Why?" I asked, throwing up my hands in frustration. "I was just coming here for a visit to meet my father! Why is everyone making such a big deal out of it?" Okay, I'd had the illusion that I was actually coming to *live* with my father, but after less than a day here, I'd pretty much given up on that idea.

Lachlan stared at his feet, the corners of his mouth tight with displeasure. "It's not my place to explain it to you."

But I got the feeling he really wanted to. "Please, Lachlan," I said, trying to sound desperate and pathetic. Okay, not that that was hard to pull off, but I wasn't trying to *hide* it. "Please tell me what's going on."

For half a second, I thought he was going to cave. But then the line of his mouth firmed up and he shook his head. "I'm sorry. It's not my place."

Please let my father come for me tomorrow, I prayed.

"You should get some sleep," Lachlan said, rising and picking up the tray.

On cue, a massive yawn welled up from my chest. He smiled at me. "I'll be right on the other side of the door," he told me. "If you need anything, just holler."

I swallowed my next yawn as Lachlan left and barred the door behind him.

chapter five

Maybe I was just being contrary, but the fact that Lachlan had suggested I go to sleep made me want to stay awake. Not the easiest thing to do when battling jet lag, a full stomach, and a cheery fire. If I didn't keep myself busy, I was going to lose my battle against sleep, so I dug my laptop out of my backpack. I thought maybe I could shoot a quick e-mail out to Mom, letting her know what a mess I was in. Maybe she'd sober up enough to come riding to my rescue. But—surprise, surprise—my prison cell didn't come equipped with Wi-Fi. I had a couple of dirty books I'd downloaded from the Internet—since I pay the bills in the family, my mom never notices the charges—but reading dirty books while locked in a cell just seemed . . . wrong.

For the first time since I'd snuck out of the house to catch my flight, I felt a twinge of guilt. Could Mom hold herself together enough to pay her own bills without me there? I imagined her sitting, alone and sloshed, in our house with no water or electricity. Then I shook my head at myself. She'd been leaning on me more and more as the years went by, but whether she acted like it or not, she *was* an adult, and she could take care of her own damn self!

At around seven, Lachlan brought in another tray. My stomach rumbled. Those scones had worn off at least an hour ago. This time, the tray held an enormous panini sandwich, dripping with melted cheese and mayo, along with a small garden salad. I guessed this came from his bakery as well.

When he took the tray away, he once again suggested I should get some sleep. At that point, I was practically asleep on my feet, but I was still too stubborn to do as I was told. Just to prove that I *wasn't* taking his advice, I started warming up my voice with a series of vocalises. Then I practiced the songs I'd been working on with my voice teacher before I'd run for what I thought was greener grass. I suspected Lachlan was listening, even through the six-inch-thick door, so I mentally urged myself to perform for him. Maybe his heart would melt at the beauty of my voice and he'd set me free.

Yeah, and I thought I saw a pig flying just last week.

I lost myself in the music for a while, the songs flowing out of me one after the other. While I sang, I almost forgot that my father was in jail and my aunt Grace was keeping me locked up "for my own good." I closed my eyes and allowed the music to transport me to another world.

Eventually, I noticed a burning sensation on my chest. For reasons I couldn't explain, the cameo had grown very warm, almost like I'd been holding it near the fire. I took it off and examined it, trying to figure out why it was hot, but it cooled off so fast I wondered if I'd been imagining things.

Once I stopped singing, it hit me again how achingly tired I was. My eyelids weighed ten tons each. Figuring I'd more than proved my point to Lachlan, I decided that now was the time to let the exhaustion take over.

I couldn't see changing into my PJs under these circumstances, so I settled for taking off my shoes and socks and exchanging my jeans for a pair of loose, beat-up workout pants. Then I climbed into the small but relatively comfortable bed. It was dark out, and I'd turned off the overhead light, but there was too much of a chill in the air to turn the fireplace off. I fell asleep staring into the silent, flickering flames.

It was still dark when I woke up, completely disoriented. For the first few moments, I couldn't figure out where I was, but it didn't take much time for the memory to rush back. My head felt thick and heavy, and everything around me felt unreal. I glanced at my watch and saw that it was two A.M. I flopped over onto my other side, sure I'd be asleep again in seconds, but then I heard the sound of footsteps outside my door.

Belatedly, I realized that I'd heard some kind of thud, and that's what had awakened me. I'd thought that it was some remnant of a dream, but as I heard the grating sound of the bar being raised, I decided it hadn't been a dream after all.

I quickly sat up, scrambling to disentangle myself from the covers. Perhaps I'd heard more than I remembered, or perhaps it was just a premonition, but I felt certain the person opening my door wasn't Lachlan. Seconds later, I was proven right when a man pulled open the door and stepped into my cell.

I stopped struggling with the covers, unable to keep myself from staring. Standing in the doorway to my cell was probably the most gorgeous guy I'd ever seen. He was tall—though he'd probably look like a midget next to Lachlan—and slender, with really long blond hair that draped his shoulders like a cape. It was too dark in the flickering firelight to tell what color his eyes were, except that they were very light—and had the distinctive upward tilt of the Fae. He'd probably have been too perfect to be truly gorgeous if it weren't for the slight unevenness of his nose, which looked like it had been broken at least once.

He looked younger than most of the Fae I'd seen, though he was older than me. I wondered if he had a baby face, or whether he was really a Fae teenager. I supposed there was such a thing, even though Fae adults became effectively ageless.

He broke into a crooked smile, and I realized that I was staring at him like I was some twelve-year-old meeting the Jonas Brothers. I mentally shook myself by the scruff of the neck and managed to get the covers out of the way. My bare feet didn't much like the cold stone floor, but I wasn't about to take my eyes off the Fae long enough to put my shoes and socks on.

"Who are you?" I asked when he just stood there grinning.

"My name is Ethan, and I'm here to rescue you."

O-kay. Maybe I was dreaming after all. The fog in my head thickened as I tried to figure out which of my million questions I should ask first.

Ethan was still grinning. Guess he was really enjoying my witty dialogue. "Unless you find your present accommodations to your liking and wish to stay."

"Just grab her and let's go," said a girl's sharp voice from the other room. I couldn't see her with Ethan blocking the doorway. I wondered where Lachlan was.

Ethan cast an annoyed glance over his shoulder. "I'm trying to show some courtesy," he said. "You have heard of courtesy, haven't you?"

The girl called him a couple of names I won't repeat, and I felt a surge of disappointment. Despite the less-than-friendly exchange, there was a familiarity to their dialogue that suggested they were pretty chummy. Then I rolled my eyes at myself. Why on earth would I care?

Ethan turned his attention back to me. "We really should get going. We haven't got much time."

I managed to tear my eyes away from him to pull on my socks, thinking furiously the whole time. Was there any reason I should go with this guy? (Other than that he was a hottie, that is.) I had no idea who he was or why he wanted to rescue me—if he really *was* trying to rescue me—and Aunt Grace had warned me I was in great danger. Of course, I trusted Aunt Grace about as far as I could throw Lachlan.

I bit my lip, stalling by retying my shoelaces. I'd thought to myself earlier that if I wanted to escape, I'd need an accomplice. Had fate finally taken pity on me and sent me exactly what I needed? Or were Ethan and his girlfriend the *real* bad guys? Just because he was gorgeous didn't mean he wasn't rotten to the core. Then again, if they were the bad guys, I wasn't going to have much choice in the matter. There were two of them, and only one of me. Maybe I should try screaming?

Ethan took a step closer. "You'll want to come along with us quietly," he told me, and there was a hint of warning in his voice. "If we had more time, I could gently persuade you that you can trust us, but that will have to wait until we get you out of here."

I glared up at him. Somehow, he didn't look quite so hot anymore. I jumped when the girl entered the room and shoved Ethan aside. She was also Fae, and she looked even younger than Ethan, maybe even my age. If she'd had that distinctive bump on her nose, she'd be the female version of Ethan, with the same long blond hair, slim build, and light-colored eyes.

"Hey!" Ethan protested as he stumbled, but the girl ignored him, muttering something under her breath as she advanced on me.

I decided now would be a good time to scream after all, but when I opened my mouth, nothing came out. Either I'd just come down with the world's most sudden case of laryngitis, or the girl had just cast a spell on me. I decided that put her and Ethan firmly in the "bad guy" column. I tried to dodge past her, but she grabbed my arm. She was willowy thin like a supermodel, but she certainly wasn't weak. My struggles made the cameo slide under the collar of my shirt. It was hot again, and I would have tried to move it away from my skin if I hadn't had more important things to do, like shaking off the Fae girl's grip. Her fingers dug into my arm bruisingly hard, and she tugged me toward the door.

Ethan kept out of her way, but he was still giving me that cocky grin like he found all this really entertaining. He made an elaborate mock bow.

"Dana Stuart," he said formally, "I'd like to introduce you to my sister, Kimber. Also known as the Bitch from Hell." He laughed as he said it, so that it came out sounding halfway affectionate, but Kimber gave him the finger with her free hand.

The gesture just seemed wrong. Very un-Fae-like. Where was the icy reserve my mother had told me about?

I tried to dig in my heels, but Kimber was way stronger than she looked, and I couldn't fight her any better than I could have fought Lachlan. It was all I could do to keep my feet under me as she yanked me over the threshold into the guard room, Ethan close on my heels.

I still had no voice, but a silent gasp escaped me when I saw Lachlan. He was lying facedown on the floor. A bright splash of blood spattered the floor near his head. Kimber ignored my shock, dragging me toward the exit.

"He'll be all right," Ethan assured me. "It would take an army to do him any lasting harm."

As if to prove Ethan's point, Lachlan groaned softly. Ethan's eyes widened, and he pushed on my back while Kimber continued to pull my arm.

"We'd best get moving," he said. "I doubt Lachlan will be happy with me when he wakes."

I was half-pushed, half-pulled up the stairs and into the street. My voice still wasn't working, and though I struggled as hard as I could, there was no escaping, and the street was deserted. A covered, horse-drawn wagon waited at the curb. Kimber pulled up the tarp with one hand, revealing the straw-covered wagon bed. Then she shifted her grip to my waist and, ignoring my flailing arms, picked me up and flung me into the straw.

She started to climb in after me, but Ethan stopped her with a hand on her arm.

"You drive," he said. "I'll keep our passenger company." He waggled his brows, and Kimber rolled her eyes. She didn't argue, though.

My heart galloped, and I was so scared I was shaking. I didn't want to be alone and helpless in the back of this wagon with a man who was strong enough to knock Lachlan unconscious. Especially not when he'd done that little brow-waggle thing. I feared I knew exactly what he was planning to do to me while his sister drove the wagon.

Ethan climbed onto the wagon and dropped the tarp back over the back, blocking out all the light. Oh, God, now I was alone with him *in the dark*. I scrambled as far away from him as I could, until my back hit something solid. Then I started fishing through the straw with both hands, hoping against hope to find a weapon.

"You've no need to be frightened," Ethan said, and to my immense relief his voice came from near the back of the wagon. "We're relatively harmless, Kimber and me."

"Tell that to Lachlan," I found myself saying, amazed at how calm I sounded. Then I realized it meant my voice had come back, and before Ethan could silence me again, I screamed as loud and long as I possibly could.

Eventually, I had to stop or I was going to pass out.

"That's an impressive set of lungs," Ethan said, not sounding the least bit annoyed by my attempt to get help. "My ears may never recover." I could hear the laugh in his voice, and it took a little of the edge off my fear. That sounded more like playful teasing than menacing kidnapper talk. I still wasn't convinced he was "harmless," and I wasn't exactly feeling playful, but it didn't sound like he was about to attack me.

"The wagon is spelled to be soundproof," he continued. "I borrowed it from a friend of mine who swears it's much more comfortable than the backseat of a car, if you know what I mean."

Eww. Yes, I knew what he meant. And I hoped the straw had been changed since the last time Ethan's friend had gotten lucky.

My shoulders slumped in defeat, and I suddenly felt overwhelmingly tired again. Tears burned my eyes. I hadn't trusted Grace, but I'd at least *hoped* she was telling me the truth and she would bring my father to me when he was out of jail. I had no clue what Ethan and Kimber wanted from me. I tried to breathe slowly and deeply to calm myself.

"As I was saying, you have no need to be frightened," Ethan said, as if my little scream-fest had never happened. "I'd never have taken Lachlan in a fair fight. I came at him from behind and hit him before he even knew I was there. For which some-day I'm sure he will reward me handsomely."

"Who are you, and where are you taking me?"

"We're taking you somewhere where you will be safe from Grace Stuart."

I snorted. "Yeah, and *she* was locking me up to keep me safe from hordes of enemies who were out for my blood. I didn't believe her, and I don't believe you, either." I crossed my arms over my chest, though Ethan wouldn't be able to see the defiant gesture in this dark. Or maybe he could—for all I knew, Fae could see in the dark.

"I can't blame you for that. I apologize for our methods, but if we'd taken the time to explain everything, Lachlan would have woken up long before we were through."

I noticed he'd totally ignored the "who are you" part of my question. I decided to try a different tack. "Let's pretend I be-lieve you. Why are you 'helping' me? How do you know who I am? How did you know where to find me?"

"One question at a time!" Ethan said, and again it sounded like he was teasing me.

I ground my teeth, wishing it weren't so dark so I could see if my glare was having any effect on him. This whole kidnapping thing might seem like a big joke to him, but after everything that had happened to me since my plane had landed, I wasn't in much of a laughing mood. I rubbed my tired eyes. I couldn't focus my thoughts enough to choose one question to ask. Thankfully, Ethan took pity on me and chose one himself.

"Your father and your aunt are both hoping to be appointed Consul when the current Consul's term has ended. Whichever one has you in their power could stand a much greater chance of being appointed."

"What?" I cried. "Why?"

"That I'll have to explain a little later. But I will explain, I promise. Anyway, in answer to your question of why Kimber and I are helping you, we would prefer not to see Grace Stuart as Consul. She's one of the top contenders, and having you under her control could cement her victory. It's well past time for Avalon to enter the twenty-first century, and she's as old-school as they come. Your father isn't exactly progressive, either, but he's better than Grace. I don't know what she told you to explain why she locked you up, but there's a good chance you would never have been heard from again if we hadn't gotten you out of there."

"Are you saying she was planning to kill me?" I squeaked. I might not have liked or trusted Aunt Grace, but the idea that she might kill me had never entered my mind. It seemed so far-fetched as to be ridiculous. But then, so did a lot of stuff that had happened so far.

"She probably wouldn't kill you," he admitted. "Unless that was the only way to keep you from your father."

The wagon came to a stop, and Ethan used that as an excuse not to elaborate. "I'll answer as many questions as you like, once we get you to safety," he said. "But until then, I need you to be quiet." He mumbled something under his breath.

I knew without having to test it out that my voice had just taken another vacation.

chapter six

I sure was glad there were no mirrors around when I climbed out of the back of that wagon. Aside from the fact that my clothes were all wrinkled from being slept in, and my hair was badly in need of a brush, I was also covered in little bits and pieces of straw. Ethan, though he'd been sitting in the same wagon, must have been wearing some kind of straw-repellant, because he looked as perfect as he had when he'd climbed in. He decided to rub it in by reaching out and plucking a piece of straw from my hair. When I glared at him, he just winked at me and reached for my hair again. I batted his hand away, but then couldn't resist running my hands through my hair, trying to smooth it down and remove any remaining straw.

I looked around and discovered that I was in a gated flag-stone courtyard, surrounded by low brick townhouses. The townhouses looked much less exotic than most of the other buildings I'd seen so far in Avalon, though the stone courtyard did add a bit of atmosphere.

A figure dressed all in black detached itself from a pool of shadow and approached. I couldn't see him very clearly, because he wasn't looking my way, but any brief hope that he might help me died when Kimber mutely handed him the horse's reins. I guessed this was the wagon's owner, Ethan's horny friend, and I was really glad when he gave Ethan a brief nod, then led the horse and wagon away instead of sticking around.

"Student housing," Ethan explained, indicating the buildings around us with a wave of his hand. "The university is just down the road. That's my flat," he said, pointing at one second story window, "and that's Kimber's." He pointed at a window directly across from it. I took another glance at Kimber, but she still didn't look old enough to have her own "flat." Of course for all I knew she was some kind of weird Fae that stopped aging at sixteen and she was actually older than my mom. Then Ethan grinned again. If Fae got laugh lines, he would be wrinkled up before he was thirty. "But that's not where we're going."

Kimber had come up behind me while he talked. She didn't touch me, but I knew she was ready to grab me if I gave her half an excuse. Ethan pushed up the sleeves of his long-sleeved T-shirt and adjusted his stance like he was about to lift something heavy. Only there was nothing there to lift.

Behind me, Kimber snorted. "Stop being a show-off and get on with it."

Get on with what? I wondered.

Ethan took a deep breath, then held his hands out in front of him at about chest level, palms down. Something made a scraping sound, like rock sliding against rock. Ethan took another breath, then slowly raised his hands a few inches.

My jaw dropped open when a set of flagstones lifted from the floor of the courtyard. Ethan moved his hands to the side, and the flagstones moved with him, revealing a ladder that disappeared into a dark pit. He set the flagstones down, then blew out his breath in a big whoosh. He was sweating and out of breath, but he smiled.

"I'm getting better at that," he said, talking right over me at Kimber.

"I'm so impressed I can hardly stand it," she responded.

Ethan looked deflated by her tone, but he fired back anyway. "I'd like to see *you* do it."

From Kimber's silence, I gathered she couldn't. Ethan smirked at her, then lowered himself onto the ladder and began to climb down into the darkness. I shuddered and tried to back away from the pit, but of course Kimber was there, driving me toward the ladder. My voice was still useless, so I couldn't even protest.

"It's your choice whether to use the ladder or not to get down," Kimber said, and another shudder shook me. I had no doubt she'd shove me right in if I didn't force myself onto that ladder.

My hands were shaking as I lowered my legs over the rim and got my feet on the ladder. I wasn't usually afraid of the dark, and I'd never noticed any claustrophobia before, but the thought of climbing down into that unknown darkness had me near panic. The only thing I wanted to do less than climb down was *fall* down with Kimber's help, so I concentrated on taking one step at a time, hoping my now sweaty hands wouldn't lose their grip on the metal rungs.

Below me, I heard the echoing murmur of Ethan's voice, and a torch flared to life. I looked down to see him standing at the mouth of a tunnel about ten feet down. He beckoned for me to keep moving, and I just barely managed to unfreeze enough to take another step.

"Don't worry," he said. "I'll catch you if you fall."

Somehow that wasn't as reassuring as I think he meant it to be. I kept descending anyway, anxious to feel solid ground beneath my feet. I hadn't gotten all the way down when Ethan reached up and put his hands on my waist, steadying me. Surprised, I squeaked and stumbled down the last few steps, landing much closer to him than I'd expected. I realized the squeak meant my voice was back, and it occurred to me that now might be a good time to try another scream. Ethan smiled down at me. His hands were still on my waist, and I hesitated for a moment, struck speechless by his touch. By the time I'd recovered, the flagstones had moved back into place and blocked the opening above.

Kimber jumped when she was less than halfway down, landing silently and gracefully beside me. Ethan moved away, grabbing the torch off the wall.

"This way," he said, leading us into the tunnel.

It was chilly down here below ground, and I had to clench my teeth to keep them from chattering. The mouth of the tunnel was lined with cement, but after a few feet, the walls, floor, and ceiling were all solid rock. I realized with a start that we were actually *inside* the mountain.

Other tunnels branched off from the main one, disappearing into the darkness, but Ethan kept going straight. I could definitely work up a big bout of claustrophobia if I thought about how much weight was pressing down on the roof of this tunnel. I forced myself not to think about it, but it wasn't easy.

Eventually, Ethan led us down one of the side tunnels, and we weren't more than a few yards in when I heard the echo of distant voices. Neither Ethan nor Kimber seemed alarmed by the sound, and though it was hard to tell in the echoing tunnel,

I was pretty sure we were moving toward the voices. When I saw the golden-orange glow of firelight in the distance, I knew I was right.

Finally, we reached an archway, braced with heavy wooden beams. I followed Ethan through that archway, and then came to a stop, gaping at the sight that met my eyes.

The tunnels we'd been traveling through were clearly man-made, but now we were in what had to be a natural cave. Stalactites jutted from the ceiling like dragon teeth, and the chairs and sofas that were scattered around the floor were surrounded by stalagmites. Along one wall of the cave, an underground stream, clear and surprisingly deep, flowed.

The only light came from torches that dotted the walls and the sides of the largest stalagmites, but it was enough to illuminate the whole cave. There were about a dozen people in the cave, sitting in little clusters of chairs and sofas. They all stopped talking when Ethan and Kimber and I walked in, and I felt every pair of eyes staring at me. I'd never much liked being the center of attention, and I liked it even less now, when I was all rumpled and wrinkled and standing next to someone as gorgeous as Ethan. I told myself I wasn't intimidated and stared back.

I'd say about half of the people in that room were Fae, and half certainly looked like humans. A couple of them held some of those el-cheapo clear plastic cups I associated with keg parties. (Not that I'd ever been to a keg party. I didn't run with the crowd that went to them. Actually, I didn't run with a crowd at all, but that's beside the point.)

Belatedly, I saw the big metal keg that sat in the center of the cave. Ethan had said the apartments we'd seen before we descended were student housing. Looking from face to curious face, I estimated there were maybe one or two who were legally old enough to drink. At least in the States. I had no idea what the drinking age was in Avalon.

I gave Ethan what I hoped was an imperious look. "You went to all this trouble just to bring me to a kegger?"

His lip twitched into yet another grin. "Not exactly. Welcome to the most literal Student Underground on the planet." The people nearest to us laughed at his stupid pun. "I'll introduce you around later, but first I owe you some explanations."

Pretty soon, our grand entrance apparently lost its entertainment value, and everyone went back to talking amongst themselves—or drinking themselves stupid. Kimber brushed by me and joined a couple of obviously Fae guys on one of the couches. She looked completely different once she plopped down between them, her ice-queen face thawing into a friendly smile, the stiff posture relaxing into something that looked almost human. One of the guys slung his arm around her shoulders, and she seemed to have no objection.

"She's really not so bad," Ethan leaned over and whispered. "I just bring out the worst in her."

I figured a diplomatic silence was my best option. Ethan's eyes twinkled, like he knew he hadn't come close to convincing me. There was enough light now for me to see those eyes were a striking shade of blue, almost teal. They were not the eyes of a human being, despite the fact that he acted nothing like the stereotypical Fae. (Kimber, on the other hand . . .)

The other humans in the cave had dressed for the chilly temperature below ground, but my short-sleeved T-shirt left me shivering. The cold appeared not to bother the Fae. Ethan guided me to an unoccupied love seat. There was a knitted afghan draped over the back. Ethan handed it to me, and I gratefully wrapped it around my shoulders. Then he gestured for me to sit beside him. It was closer than I was totally comfortable with, but I sat anyway, huddling into the warmth of the afghan.

Ethan propped his elbow on the back of the couch, turning to face me. For once, he wasn't grinning or otherwise looking amused.

"How much do you know about Avalon politics?" he asked.

"Umm . . . pretty much nothing." I winced, hating to show my ignorance. I'd been thinking of living here. Surely I should have read up on more than where the best restaurants and shopping were.

The grin was back. "Don't feel bad about it. Very few people who don't live in Avalon or at least spend a lot of time here know very much. And what they think they know is usually wrong.

"You do know that in the past, humans and Fae have fought quite bitterly over Avalon."

I nodded. Avalon was the most coveted, most fought-over piece of land in the world, beating out even Jerusalem. But there'd been peace in Avalon for over a hundred years, ever since it declared its independence both from Great Britain *and* from Faerie. It was now its own sovereign state, even though it was surrounded by England. Kind of like Vatican City.

"Avalon is ruled by what we call the Council," Ethan continued. "There are a dozen general members of the Council: six humans and six Fae. The humans are democratically elected, and the Fae are *not* so democratically elected." He went on before I had a chance to ask him what that meant. "There is a thirteenth member of the Council, the member who has the power to break any ties when the Council votes. That member is the Consul, and he or she is appointed by the Council.

"Every ten years, the Consulship must change hands between Fae and human so that neither race can have the majority for too long. The current human Consul must be replaced by a Fae in a little more than a year." His expression turned sardonic. "You chose perhaps the worst possible time to decide to pay your father a visit, as the candidates are now crawling out of the woodwork."

"Okay, fascinating as this civics lesson is, what I really want to know is what *I* have to do with all of this," I said.

"Maybe nothing," he said, and I think I did the look-like-a-moron jaw drop again. "We'll have to wait until the sun's up to find out for sure. I can't explain that part yet. There's a, er, test we're going to give you when it's daylight. That will tell us if you will play a role in reality, or just in your family's most ambitious dreams."

I stuttered, trying to ask some kind of intelligent question while my mind reeled in confusion.

"I know I'm being vague," Ethan said. "But I don't want to influence you and invalidate tomorrow's test."

"What kind of test?" I finally managed to ask, my voice sounding strangled.

He touched my arm reassuringly. "Nothing to be frightened of, I assure you."

I'd be the judge of that! "And after I take this test, will I be free to go?"

He frowned, the expression almost like a pout. "You're free to go *now*, if that's what you really want. Would you have somewhere safe to go?"

From the way he asked, I guessed he already knew I didn't.

"Do you know if my father's really in jail?" I asked instead of answering.

Ethan nodded. "When someone of his stature is arrested, it's big news. From what I hear, though, it's little more than a formality—though his enemies are doing their best to slow down the wheels of justice."

I swallowed hard. If my dad didn't get out of jail ASAP, I was seriously screwed. More screwed than I already was, that is.

Ethan reached over and took my hand, stroking the back of it with his thumb. The contact sent a little zing through me. "Don't worry," he said. "You'll be safe with Kimber and me."

I cocked an eyebrow at him skeptically, though my heart was going pitter-pat at the feel of his hand on mine. No, it wasn't any big deal, but it was new to *me*. Dating was part of everyday life for most girls my age, but between keeping up with my schoolwork and running the household when Mom was too drunk to bother, I didn't exactly have a lot of free time. The one and only date I'd ever agreed to go on ended in disaster when my mom got drunk and fell down the stairs. I had to take her to the emergency room when I was supposed to be meeting my date, and I was too chicken to reschedule.

"You look exhausted," Ethan said gently. "Would you like to lie down and get some rest? Kimber and I are kind of the co-leaders of the Underground, so we should stay until the party's over. Or I could get you a beer and you can join us if you'd like."

The "party" seemed to consist of people sitting around drinking and talking. Not exactly tons of excitement when my body kept wanting to drag me back down into sleep. "I think maybe I'll just close my eyes for a minute," I said, fighting a yawn.

Ethan let go of my hand and slid off of the love seat onto the floor, making room for me. When I lay down, I noticed the spot where he'd been sitting was deliciously warm. I snuggled into that warmth, painfully aware that Ethan was sitting close enough to touch. His hair was so shiny it seemed to glow in the torchlight. I found myself fascinated, mesmerized by the play of light as sleep crept up and seized me.

chapter seven

So far, each time I'd woken up in Avalon, something majorly sucked. This time was no exception.

A piercing scream brought me from dead asleep to wide-awake panic in one second flat. A couple more voices joined in, the screams bouncing and pinging off the stone walls and ceiling. Some of the torches had gone out, leaving parts of the cave hidden by shadows.

Ethan sprang to his feet in front of me, and to my shock, a long, thin knife appeared in his hand. "To me!" he bellowed, loud enough to be heard over the sounds of terror, and soon a handful of the students came charging out from between the stalagmites toward him.

Two human boys were supporting a third, whose shirt was shredded, his chest bleeding from what looked like claw marks. Behind them, Kimber and the Fae boy she'd been so chummy with were backing toward us instead of running, each menacing the surrounding darkness with knives that looked just like Ethan's.

I clutched the afghan tightly under my chin, totally mystified as to what was going on, knowing only that it was bad. *Really* bad, judging by the wide-eyed terror on the human boys' faces.

"Don't move!" Ethan ordered me without turning to look, and he stepped forward to put himself between us humans and . . . whatever was out there.

Realizing the wounded boy was about to collapse, I sprang off the love seat. His friends gave me appreciative nods as they laid him down. The wounds on his chest looked nasty, and there was enough blood to make me feel light-headed. I had the sensation that I'd stepped into the middle of a nightmare. This just *couldn't* be happening. My life was aggravating in the extreme, but it wasn't *dangerous*. There had to be some perfectly reasonable explanation for the screaming, the bleeding, and the weapons.

The sense of unreality kept me from being as scared as I should have been. One of the boys tore his sweatshirt off over his head and stuck it over the wound, applying pressure. The wounded boy groaned in pain.

To my shock, the other boy had drawn a gun, though he pointed it at the floor as his eyes darted back and forth, searching for a target.

What kind of students *were* these?

I stopped worrying about the gun when an awful shrieking sound, like fingernails on a blackboard, only ten times worse, split the air. With all the echoes, I couldn't tell where it came from, but the three Fae seemed to have a good idea. They stood side by side, knives at the ready as they faced one particularly dark pool of shadow.

Then the shadow moved, stepping into the glow of the torch-

light. I clapped my hand over my mouth to keep from screaming, because whatever it was, it wasn't human. Not even close.

It looked like it was made of sticks and straw, with a vaguely
humanoid shape and huge black eyes. The sticks that made up
its fingers were sharpened at the end, and several of them glis-
tened with blood. My stomach almost revolted when I noticed
another sharpened appendage, this one jutting out from between the creature's legs. There was blood on *that*, too.

It opened its mouth, and another of those awful screeches
made me cover my ears. Two more creatures just like it emerged
from behind a couple of stalagmites.

The Fae put some space between one another, each facing off
against one of the creatures. The human boy was trying to line
up a shot, but the Fae were in the way.

"Will bullets hurt them?" he asked suddenly.

Ethan, slowly and carefully advancing on the creature he'd
targeted, shouted a quick no over his shoulder.

"Shit!" the human boy said, and I couldn't help agreeing
with him. He put the gun away, then chivalrously pushed me
behind him.

The creatures shrieked again, then all three of them sprang
in unison. I swallowed a scream of my own.

"Jason!" a voice behind me cried in terror.

The gunman—Jason, apparently—whirled around, and I did
the same. Another one of the creatures had snuck up behind us
and was perched on the back of the couch. Those eyes were as
expressionless as ink blots, and yet I still felt its gaze almost like
a physical touch as it stared at me. The boy on the couch froze
in terror, and if the creature had wanted him, he'd have been
history. But it had eyes only for me. It shrieked again, then
leapt off the back of the couch toward me.

Instinctively, I ducked and dove forward, sending myself under the creature's leap. Unfortunately, Jason was right behind me, so when I ducked, the creature slammed into his chest. He went down hard.

I did scream then. I couldn't help it.

Jason's friend surged forward and grabbed the creature, pulling it away. Already, a set of claw marks marred Jason's face. The creature whirled on Jason's friend, twiggy arm striking out in a backhanded blow that sent him flying. The creature crowed in triumph and seemed to grow bigger as I watched. Fixing its gaze on Jason, it started forward. I scrambled to my feet, looking around frantically for something I could do to help.

What I did next was pure instinct. I was unarmed, and even if I'd had one of those Fae knives, I'd be more likely to hurt myself than hurt these creatures. But I couldn't just stand there uselessly, hoping some big strapping man would come save the day, not when the creature was advancing on the obviously wounded Jason.

I was more terrified than I'd ever been in my life. I grabbed the afghan that was still wrapped around my shoulders and flipped it like it was a sheet I was trying to drape over a bed just right. It came to rest directly over the creature's head, and I let go.

My hope had been that blocking its vision would slow the creature down at least a little, but my plan worked better than expected. The creature tried to pull the afghan off its head, but the yarn kept getting caught on all the little sticks and twigs that jutted out of its body. Shrieking in outrage, the creature began shredding the afghan with its claws.

The distraction gave Ethan just enough time to come running. His knife flashed again and again as he plunged it through the afghan and into the creature below. Black icky stuff dripped from the blade, and the creature's shrieks turned to sounds of pain. But Ethan didn't stop stabbing it until the shrieks subsided and the creature collapsed to the floor and stopped moving. I blinked, and suddenly the creature's body lost its shape and became nothing more than a pile of sticks and straw and gross black sludge.

The sudden absence of screaming and shrieking made me feel like I'd lost my hearing—except I could hear my frantic breaths as my mind tried to absorb everything that had just happened.

Ignoring me for the moment, Ethan bent to check on Jason while Kimber and her friend tended to the other two boys. Jason's eyes were squinched shut in pain, and he clutched what looked like a handkerchief to his bloody face. Ethan had torn his shirt open and was now probing gently at his ribs.

"Broken," I heard him mutter under his breath when Jason flinched under his light touch. "It's going to get worse before it gets better," he warned, then put both his hands on Jason's chest.

I saw the flash of fear in Jason's eyes. I didn't know him, wouldn't even have known his name if the other boy hadn't called to him, but I guess taking care of my mother for all those years had given me a nursemaid instinct. I knelt on Jason's other side and took hold of his hand. He squeezed gratefully.

Ethan was mumbling again, and I felt the little hairs on my arms stand at attention. Ethan was obviously doing some sort of magic, and though that wasn't unusual in Avalon, it still felt surreal to me. Then Jason screamed, his back arching as his hand nearly crushed mine.

It lasted only a few seconds, and then Jason's whole body sagged and he breathed a huge sigh of relief. He closed his eyes, and I figured he'd just passed out.

"What *were* those things?" I asked Ethan as I began shaking in delayed reaction.

I could see the muscles clenching in his jaw as he ground his teeth. "Spriggans," he said, then spit as if the word tasted bad.

That didn't exactly clear things up for me. "What's a Spriggan?"

He sat back on his heels and pushed his hair away from his face. "Creatures from Faerie. Creatures that are not allowed to set foot in Avalon."

"Unseelie creatures," Jason said, and I saw that he hadn't passed out after all. He was also eyeing Ethan strangely.

We've already established that I was woefully ignorant of the workings of Avalon and Faerie, but I did know at least a little something about the Seelie and Unseelie Courts. All of Faerie was divided between the two Courts, which were sometimes at war, and sometimes at an uneasy peace. The Seelie Fae were the "good" Fae, although when speaking of Fae, "good" is a relative term. The Unseelie Court was home to all the bad guys—goblins and monsters and things that go bump in the night. And, apparently, Spriggans.

Ethan frowned down at Jason. "They are no kin to me, so stop looking at me like that." He helped Jason sit up.

"Sorry," Jason said, avoiding Ethan's eyes.

Ethan patted his shoulder. "No harm done, and I can't blame you after what just happened. It's creatures like Spriggans that give the Unseelie Court a bad name."

It took me a moment to make sense of this exchange, but when I did, my eyes widened to what I felt sure were comic proportions.

"You're Unseelie?" It was somewhere between a question and a gasp of horror.

"I am," Ethan confirmed. "As are approximately half the Fae who reside in Avalon. And no, we are no more uniformly evil than humans are uniformly good."

Jason looked only halfway convinced. But then, he was still in obvious pain. I frowned at Ethan, not at all sure how to take this little bit of news. He'd seemed perfectly at home wielding that knife and stabbing the life out of those nasty creatures, and it was hard not to wonder—yet again—if he was one of the good guys or one of the bad guys.

"I thought since Avalon seceded from Faerie, the Fae here weren't supposed to be affiliated with the Courts," I said. "They're only supposed to matter in Faerie."

Ethan laughed dryly. "That's true in theory. Reality is somewhat different. You'll notice many houses and businesses in Avalon displaying either white or red roses. White roses mean the house or business is Seelie; red roses mean it's Unseelie." His eyes fixed on my chest. I looked down and noticed that the cameo lay outside my shirt. The cameo with the white rose on it.

Had Dad's thoughtful gift had some invisible strings attached? He'd never mentioned that wearing the white rose declared me to be a Seelie girl. It seemed to me he should have told me, and I couldn't help wondering why he hadn't.

Ethan met my eyes, and I suspected he knew what I was thinking. "Neither Kimber nor I wear the red rose," he said. "As far as we're concerned, it's an outdated custom that desperately needs to be abandoned. I've never even set foot in Faerie, so why should I declare allegiance to the Unseelie Court?"

I wasn't too sure how I felt about the cameo anymore. I couldn't quite bear to take it off—right now, it was the only link I had to my dad. But I did tuck it back under the neck of my shirt where it didn't show.

chapter eight

I shivered once more in the cold of the cave. There was no way I was using that afghan again, so I just tucked my hands under my arms and bit my lip. I'd worried that more students had been hurt, but apparently I'd slept a couple of hours and most of them had gone home before the attack. Kimber and the unwounded human boy, whose name was Brent, grabbed one of the other couches and dragged it closer to where the rest of us sat huddled in our safety-in-numbers group. Jason sank into it gratefully, though the movement made him grimace in pain.

"I thought you healed him," I said, giving Ethan a puzzled look.

His expression was grim, and I noticed dark circles under his eyes. They seemed to have popped up very recently, since I didn't think they'd been there before the attack.

"I've healed the ribs themselves. The soft tissue around them is probably still bruised as all hell." He patted his friend on the shoulder. "Sorry, mate. I'm not too good at this yet."

Jason gave me a sardonic look. "He's being modest."

"There's a new one," Kimber muttered, but no one cracked a smile.

"Ethan's a magical prodigy," Jason continued. "Most healers have to train for years to be able to mend bone, and they have to train so hard they can barely manage any other magic."

Kimber sniffed disdainfully. "And if Ethan hadn't wasted his energy showing off earlier, he might have been able to heal the flesh wounds, too."

"Enough, Kimber!" Ethan snapped, springing to his feet. "How was I supposed to know—"

"Um, guys?" I asked tentatively, partially to head off the argument, partially because I was really worried. "Do you think there are more of them? I mean, what if they come back?" I shivered again, and this time it wasn't from cold. I looked at the piles of guck that used to be monsters and wondered if any of this could possibly be real.

"I doubt it," Ethan said, but he didn't sound too sure. "If there were more of them, they'd have all attacked together." Pointedly turning his back on Kimber, Ethan turned to the last of the human boys, the first one who'd been injured.

The wound had looked really bad when I'd first seen it, but when Ethan carefully peeled the sweatshirt away, it looked like it had stopped bleeding. Three angry red lines slashed across the boy's chest, but the cuts weren't as deep as I'd originally thought. Ethan did another healing spell, but apparently he was really low on juice. The wounds closed, but just barely. It would take very little to rip them open again. When Ethan finished the spell, he swayed on his feet, and for a moment, I thought he was going to pass out. Instead, he lowered himself to the cave floor and sat with his head propped against the end of the couch and his eyes closed.

I glanced up at Kimber, who was still giving her brother a sour look. "Can you finish up the healing?" I asked, and I could tell right away that it hadn't been a good question to ask.

Her expression turned even more sour. "No." She crossed her arms over her chest and looked away.

O-kay. Guess that was kind of a touchy issue. I looked at the other Fae, the one who might or might not be Kimber's boyfriend. He shrugged.

"I can't do enough to make a real difference," he said. "Even if I do a bit of patchwork, we'll still have to take them to the hospital."

"So are we going to have to talk to the police about this?" I asked. Maybe the police would help me, get me out of this mess.

No one met my gaze, and I had the feeling my question had made them all uncomfortable. Then again, I'd seen a startling number of weapons make an appearance when the Spriggans attacked. Perhaps the Student Underground had too much to hide to risk talking to the police.

"That won't be necessary," Ethan said. "Spriggans aren't under police jurisdiction. We'd have to talk to the border patrol, and I'm sure you'll agree that's not a good idea at the moment."

I wasn't as sure about that as Ethan assumed, but I wasn't up to making an issue out of it, either. "Then can we get out of here? Please?"

No one had any objection to that idea. Ethan helped Jason to his feet, and Kimber helped the other boy. Everyone seemed capable of walking, though it was impossible to miss the strain on the human boys' faces.

When we left the cave, I was pretty sure we weren't headed back the way we had come, but my sense of direction sucks. I'm the kind of person who can get lost in a closet. Turned out I was right for once, though. Ethan didn't think he had the strength to lift the flagstones again, so instead he took us to a different entrance to the underground tunnels. Conveniently, this one was located in the basement of the Fae boy's house. I still hadn't gotten his name, nor that of the second wounded human, but this didn't really feel like a good opportunity for introductions.

We split up from there, the humans and Kimber's friend heading to the emergency room and leaving me with Ethan and Kimber. The three of us trudged back to the apartment complex. There was hardly anyone on the streets this late at night. I wondered if monster attacks were commonplace in Avalon. Surely in all her efforts to make me never want to set foot in the place, my mom would have mentioned attacks by nightmarish Fae creatures in the streets of Avalon. But there had to be a reason that the human boy had had a gun and the Fae had all been armed with knives.

Remind me why I'd thought coming here would be a good idea?

When we got back to the courtyard, Ethan took hold of my arm, like he was trying to prop me up, though I'd been walking just fine.

"You look exhausted," he said.

"So do you."

He smiled crookedly, but the expression was strained. "Some sleep will do us both good."

He started steering me toward one of the buildings, but Kimber cleared her throat loudly. Ethan turned to glare at her.

"What do you take me for?" he growled at her.

After all that had happened, I was a little slow on the uptake, so at first I didn't understand what they were talking about. Kimber put her fists on her hips and glared right back. I sensed that there were layers of meaning behind those glares, but for the life of me, I couldn't figure out what they were.

With a grunt of disgust, Ethan let go of my arm and gave me a nudge toward Kimber.

"Fine!" he snapped, and without another word or glance at me, he turned away and stomped toward his building.

And that's when I finally got it. He'd been planning to take me up to his apartment. Just me and him. My face heated with a blush. I kept my head down so Kimber wouldn't see.

"Come on," she said with a wave of her hand, and I followed her while trying to come to terms with my own naïveté.

If Kimber hadn't objected, I'd have followed Ethan up to his apartment without thinking about the implications. I mean, yeah, he was a really hot, too-old-for-me Fae guy, and even though it kind of felt like he'd been flirting with me all night, the idea that he might have interest in a not-overly-attractive halfbreed teenager was kind of silly. But still, he was a *guy*, and I wasn't a kid anymore.

Kimber's apartment didn't look like what I pictured as student housing. Not that the apartment itself was all that special, but the interior was something else. If you hid away a few of the telltale modern conveniences—like the phone and the TV—I swear the room could have been lifted straight from some nineteenth century manor house. It was like a set from a Jane Austen movie. And I'd bet everything I owned—which, granted, wasn't much at the moment—that the furniture was all genuinely antique, not reproductions.

The place was beautiful but strangely cold. Kind of like Kimber herself. Everything was in shades of pale blues and greens, and there was nothing that looked out of place. The magazines on her coffee table were neatly stacked. The remotes for her TV and DVD player and stereo were arranged side by side with what looked like the exact same amount of space between them. I wondered if she'd needed a ruler to do that, or if she'd just eyeballed it.

"I only have one bedroom," she said as I stood in the middle of the room wondering what I was supposed to do now. "The sofa isn't great for sleeping, but it's much more comfortable than the floor." She grinned at me, suddenly looking much more like Ethan. "I'd offer you my bed, but I'm not that altruistic."

She seemed to have thawed since we'd entered the apartment. Her shoulders were more relaxed, and her smile looked open and easy. Either she suffered from multiple personality disorder, or Ethan made her uptight. I was betting on the latter.

"How are you holding up?" she asked with sudden sympathy. "I can't imagine what you must be going through."

"I'm pretty freaked out," I admitted. "But other than that, I'm basically okay."

She nodded in what looked like approval, then disappeared into her bedroom, emerging shortly afterward with the promised pillow and blanket.

I eyed the sofa doubtfully. It looked about as cushy as a park bench—like it was meant to be looked at, not sat on.

"I'm sorry I don't have anything more comfortable," Kimber said, seeing the direction of my gaze.

"It's fine," I told her, not wanting to sound ungrateful. "It's better than being locked in a cell, even if that bed was nicer." I could have done without the Spriggan attack, and it would have been nice if Ethan and Kimber hadn't made my rescue feel so much like a kidnapping, but I was glad not to be spending the night under Aunt Grace's thumb.

"Thanks for getting me out of there."

She frowned and looked away. "That was mostly Ethan's doing. I was just along for the ride."

Call me crazy, but I got the feeling she was just a touch bitter about it. "You helped, too," I told her.

She dismissed my claim with a self-deprecating grunt.

"You did!" I insisted. "Those Spriggans might have killed us if you hadn't been there."

Her face brightened. "I *did* kill one of the Spriggans," she said, sounding excited by the thought. "And I didn't even need magic to do it." Her smile was positively brilliant, and there was a happy twinkle in her eyes.

"If you start jumping up and down and clapping with glee, I'm outta here," I muttered, and got the laugh I'd been going for. Kimber the Ice Queen had left the building.

"I feel quite the warrior princess," she said. "And that was quick thinking on your part, too, tangling the Spriggan in your blanket."

The praise made me blush. "Umm, that was really more luck than anything."

"Nonsense! We both did quite nicely under fire. We can be warrior princesses together."

I smiled at the image. "As long as I don't have to wear a chain-mail bikini, I'm fine with that."

"It's a deal," she said, holding out her hand for me to shake. "Now, I don't know about you, but it's time for *this* princess to get some sleep. Is there anything else you need before I abandon you?"

The list of things I needed would take an hour to recite, but I put on my bravest smile. "Nope, I'm good."

"All right then. See you in the morning."

Giving the couch a baleful look, I pried off my shoes and arranged the pillow and blanket as best I could. Then I climbed into my makeshift bed and tried not to think. I fell asleep before I could decide if the couch rated as torturously uncomfortable, or merely miserable.

The next time I woke up, there was no crisis, which made for a nice change. My neck and back were stiff and sore, and my head didn't feel much clearer than it had when I'd first touched ground in London, but at least no one was kidnapping me and no monsters were attacking me.

Stretching in a vain attempt to work some of the kinks out, I stood up and headed toward the kitchen where various noises indicated Kimber was up.

I rounded the corner in time to see her pour some Cheerios into a bowl, and had to swallow a laugh. Who knew a Fae ice princess would eat something as mundane as Cheerios for breakfast?

I must have made some noise despite my effort to be quiet. Kimber turned and gave me a grumpy, first-thing-in-the-morning look.

"Want some?" she asked, shaking the cereal box.

My stomach growled its approval, and I nodded. I couldn't help watching her out of the corner of my eye as I poured my cereal and doused it with milk and sugar. She moved with the uncanny grace of the Fae, but she looked far more human this morning than she had last night.

She was still naturally beautiful enough to make me feel like Ugly Betty by comparison, but her hair was tied up in a messy knot at the top of her head, and she was wearing faded flannel pajamas that looked like they were meant for a guy. I surreptitiously checked her feet for bunny slippers, but she wasn't quite *that* human.

It was when I glanced at the clock over the stove that I nearly choked on my mouthful of cereal. It was almost noon. I couldn't believe I'd slept that long.

"Ethan'll be here around one," Kimber told me. "Then we'll take you out to conduct our . . . test."

I swallowed hard. Ethan had said it wasn't anything to be afraid of. But then again, he'd said I'd be safe in the cave last night, so he wasn't what I'd call a reliable source. I stirred my Cheerios around in my bowl, my appetite gone.

Kimber pulled a sponge from the cabinet under the sink and used it to wash her bowl. I wasn't surprised to find that she wasn't the sort to leave dirty dishes lying around. She shot me a glance.

"It's really no big deal, you know. The test."

I nodded and tried to smile. But if I wasn't going to trust Ethan's word for it, I saw no reason why I should trust his sister's.

Kimber pursed her lips. "You're just going to look at something and tell us what you see. Real simple. Okay?"

I can't say I was convinced, but I dropped the subject anyway. "Can I ask you a question?"

Her lips twitched in an almost-smile. "Apparently so."

Har-dee-har-har. "Do people in Avalon always carry knives and guns around?" I remembered the shock of seeing Jason draw a gun and wondered for the umpteenth time what I'd gotten myself into.

Kimber thought about that question for a moment before she answered. I wondered what she'd decided to leave out.

"It's not what I would call common practice," she said. "But we are the Student Underground, and Avalon politics can get cutthroat. Literally. If we didn't have Ethan, we might not scare anyone enough for them to bother us. But Jason wasn't lying when he said Ethan is a prodigy. He can do amazing things now, and it's scary to think what he'll be like when he's older and has more experience." She made a sour-lemon face—inferiority complex, anyone?—before she continued.

"He'll be a force to be reckoned with someday, and some people might prefer to reckon with him now while they still can. So he's single-handedly made our Underground into a threat, and the rest of us are at risk by association. And that's why we make a habit of always being armed."

"Aren't there, like, gun laws or something?"

She laughed. "We radicals like to think of laws as more of 'guidelines.' Besides, I'd rather risk someone going all technical on me about carrying a concealed weapon than be unarmed when attacked by Spriggans."

She was being real chatty this morning, despite her obviously edited answers. I figured as long as she kept answering my questions, I'd keep asking them. "So are there a lot of Spriggan attacks in Avalon?"

I'd stopped eating my cereal, even though there were some milk-sodden O's left in the bottom of the bowl. Kimber took the bowl from my hand and washed it while she talked.

"Not usually. Only the humanoid Fae are allowed into Avalon, though it's a lot harder to keep Fae creatures out than it is to keep humans out. The border on the Fae side doesn't have the kind of immigration system that you humans do." A frown furrowed her forehead. "But the Spriggans would only take orders from Unseelie Fae. I can't imagine why any of the Unseelie power players would want to attack our Student Underground. We're known to favor an Unseelie candidate."

"Maybe they were after *me*," I suggested. After all, everyone kept telling me I was in mortal danger. "Aunt Grace was attacked yesterday, and she said she thought her attackers were after me."

Kimber raised an eyebrow at me. "She was attacked, you say?" There was no missing the skepticism in her voice.

"That's what she said. And she had this big bruise on her face."

Kimber snorted. "I bet you she was faking it. Even *I* have enough magic to heal a bruise. My guess is she was trying to scare you into doing what she wanted."

"I wouldn't put it past her," I mumbled. "But even if that was all a big, fat lie, the Spriggans could have been after me, right?"

Kimber shook her head. "They couldn't have known where you were or that you were with us. No, they were after Ethan, and the rest of us were just in the way."

Does it make me a bad person that I was glad they were after Ethan instead of me?

I could have easily kept asking her questions till the sun went down, but Kimber had apparently had enough.

"I can lend you something to wear if you want to throw your clothes in the wash," she said, striding out of the kitchen, which now looked as neat and pristine as if no one had eaten there for a week.

"It would have been nice if you and Ethan had grabbed my bags when you kidnapped me," I grumbled. At five foot six, I wasn't exactly a midget, but Kimber was much taller. I didn't think I'd fit into her clothes real well.

She looked me up and down with an appraising eye. "I have some capris that should be just about right on you."

Kimber was wrong. The capris didn't look right on me—they looked like capris that were too long. But at least they weren't the same clothes I'd slept in. With the pants, Kimber lent me a long-sleeved T-shirt. Good thing it had elastic cuffs; otherwise the sleeves would have swallowed my hands whole.

It was a gray and gloomy day when Kimber and I headed out to the courtyard to meet up with Ethan. Occasional splats of rain dripped from the clouds, but neither of the Fae seemed to think a raincoat or umbrella was necessary. I shivered in the damp chill and pulled the long sleeves over my hands after all.

Ethan must have noticed me shivering, because he stepped up beside me and threw an arm around my shoulders, pulling me close to his side.

I froze. I know it's not really a big deal to have a guy put his arm around you, but still . . . Ethan wasn't just any guy. He was a guy who'd make the most gorgeous human in history look ordinary. Plus he was Fae. Plus he was older than me.

Kimber seemed bothered by the gesture, her shoulders stiffening as she glared at Ethan. It was like she was a whole different person when Ethan was around. Even her body language was different, more tense and wary. I liked the Ethan-free Kimber better.

Ethan nudged me out of my frozen-rabbit impersonation by starting to walk. With his arm so firmly around me, I had no choice but to move with him. I swallowed hard and stared at the rain-slicked cobblestones at my feet.

Ethan's body was warm against mine, and I actually stopped shivering. Okay, maybe having his arm around me felt pretty good, even if my heart *was* jackhammering and my nerves made me about as graceful as a three-legged elephant.

"Better?" Ethan asked, rubbing his hand up and down my arm and creating even more heat. Especially in my face, which must have been red as a matador's cape.

I like to think of myself as being unusually mature for my age, and in a lot of ways, I'm sure it's true. How many sixteen-year-olds are responsible for paying the bills and balancing the checkbook, after all? But I had about as much experience with guys as your average preteen, and it was showing. My tongue seemed glued to the roof of my mouth, and I was hyperaware of how he was touching me. I didn't dare look at him and was glad my hair was at least partially shielding my face.

"Knock it off, Ethan," Kimber said, but there was a hint of resignation in her voice.

"Knock *what* off?" he asked. "All I'm doing is keeping her warm, since you didn't bother giving her anything thicker than a T-shirt."

Kimber grumbled something I didn't quite catch, but it didn't sound complimentary. I wondered if she even *owned* anything thicker than a T-shirt, since it sure seemed that the Fae didn't mind the cold at all. And the warmth that radiated from Ethan's body was considerable, making me wonder what their normal body temperature was.

Maybe he *was* just trying to keep me warm. But I still couldn't relax, and it was a minor miracle that the two of us didn't hit the dirt in a pile of tangled limbs as our sides bumped in haphazard rhythm.

Walking got easier when we reached the main road. I was not a big fan of the cobblestone streets. Sure, they were nice to look at, but they were a twisted ankle waiting to happen. I bet high heels weren't a real popular fashion choice in Avalon.

There wasn't much on the far side of the road, just a strip of well-manicured grass and a super-strong-looking guardrail right at the edge of the cliff. Just the thought of being in a car accident on this road was enough to make my stomach shrivel. Maybe riding horses through the city wasn't as weird as I'd first thought.

There wasn't a whole lot of traffic, so the three of us had no trouble getting across the road, even with my uncoordinated gait. I couldn't quite figure out where we were going, though. I looked up and down the strip of grass, and there was nothing of any interest as far as the eye could see.

Well, except if I looked out over the rail into the distance, but I didn't feel much like doing that. It seemed I was more afraid of heights than I'd thought.

"Where are we going?" I asked, pleased to find that I actually was still capable of speech.

"Right here," Ethan said, and we came to a stop.

"Here" didn't appear to be any different from anything else along the strip of grass. I frowned, but I didn't feel like asking any more questions. If Ethan wanted me to take this stupid test of his, then it was up to him to explain what I was supposed to do.

There was a noticeable stretch of silence before he spoke again, and I think he was annoyed that I managed to outwait him. Score one for me!

"Look out into the distance, and tell us what you see."

At least he wasn't asking me to look *down*. Slowly, I raised my head, having no idea what to expect. I braced myself for something scary.

But all I saw was a heavy blanket of mist that made it impossible to see very far past the moat.

"Am I supposed to see anything unusual?" I asked, but I was beginning to feel a flutter of relief. If I didn't see anything unusual, that meant I wasn't what they thought I was. Which meant I wasn't important to anyone's political ambitions, which meant I still had hope of moving in with my dad and having a close-to-normal life. Maybe the nightmare would soon be over.

I swayed, suddenly dizzy, and I was glad Ethan still had his arm around me. My stomach lurched, and I burped up the taste of Cheerios. Eww.

"I don't think I do well with heights," I said, quickly shifting my gaze back to the grass at my feet.

"Just give it another minute," Ethan said.

"No thanks. Not unless you want me to barf on your shoes."

He moved around behind me, and suddenly his hand was on my chin, forcing my head up. I felt the warmth of his breath against my skin as he spoke into my ear.

"One more minute," he urged.

My first reaction was to close my eyes in protest. But he didn't let go of me, and when I tried to jerk away, his other arm wrapped around me and held me still.

"Just look," he said. "Please."

It was the "please" that changed my mind. He sounded almost desperate, and I realized that whatever I saw—or didn't see—meant a lot to him. I could deal with a minute or two of queasiness.

Besides, Ethan probably knew some kind of spell that would force me to open my eyes and look. I didn't want to go there.

With a sigh of resignation, I slowly opened my eyes, braced for the dizziness and nausea. It was there waiting for me, and I held my breath, hoping I wouldn't be sick. The warmth of Ethan's arms around me helped steady me, and I gazed out into the distance.

I still couldn't see anything but the mist. Except . . . There was something weird about the mist. I stared at it hard, trying to figure out what it was. Through the mist, I could see patches of the English countryside beyond the moat . . . only, there was a glimmer of something . . . else. A faint image that overlay the countryside, like a photo that had been double-exposed. I tried to focus on that elusive image, and suddenly, it came clear.

Just beyond the moat stretched a deep green forest. Not a pasture or building in sight, except as a faint afterimage.

"Whoa!" I said with a gasp, my heart leaping in my chest as my throat tightened in near-panic. I tried to back away, but Ethan was still holding me.

"What do you see?" he asked.

I shook my head, still staring out into the mist, trying not to believe what was right before my eyes. I blinked, and the forest was still there. Oh, crap. I shifted my focus to the afterimage of English countryside, and as I stared at it, it solidified once more, the forest fading into the background, but not disappearing.

"What the hell . . . ?" I mumbled. I was getting dizzier by the moment, and I felt sure that I was going to fall down, into the mist that shifted continually before my eyes.

"Let her go," Kimber said, and I felt her hand on my arm. "We already know what she sees."

"I want to hear her say it!" Ethan insisted. He was still holding my chin up, his face right next to mine. I'd have freaked out about him being so close if I weren't feeling so awful.

"Look at her face, you wanker!" Kimber said, her voice sharp as needles. "She's about to faint."

Surprisingly, fainting sounded like a really good idea. If I fainted, I'd be unconscious, so I wouldn't have to see the impossible anymore, nor would I have to feel so dizzy and sick. Then maybe when I woke up, all of this would go away and I'd find it was all just a bad dream. The mist started to turn dark around the edges.

chapter nine

For the record: fainting sucks. I'd always thought of fainting as just losing consciousness for a few seconds. I didn't realize it involved nausea, dizziness, shivers, and clammy skin.

I came to, sitting on the grassy shoulder, my back resting against something hard and warm as Kimber repeatedly smacked my cheeks. I blinked, but she didn't stop immediately. My cheeks were stinging and my eyes watering from the blows, and I've already described how wonderful I didn't feel.

"Stop that!" I snapped. I ducked my head and tried to block her arm with mine, but her reflexes were faster than mine and she got in one more "gentle" pat.

"Are you back in the land of the living?" she asked.

I glared at her. The wall at my back shook, and with a start, I realized I was leaning against Ethan, and he was laughing. With a snarl, I pulled away from him and sprang to my feet.

Way too fast. Can you say "head rush"? I swayed and flailed my arms for balance. Wouldn't you know it, Ethan was there again, his hands on my shoulders, steadying me.

"Take it easy," he said. "Unless you enjoyed fainting so much you'd like to do it again."

"No thanks," I mumbled, and I let him support my weight while the world stopped spinning.

The little splats of rain had turned more aggressive and almost qualified as a steady drizzle. And the seat of my pants was soaked through. God, please let that be because the ground was wet. I'd had enough humiliation for one day, thank you very much.

"Let's get you inside and out of the rain," Ethan said. "And I bet you could use a hot cup of tea."

I tried not to make a face at the thought. "I could really go for a cup of coffee right now," I said, but neither Ethan nor Kimber seemed that interested in what I wanted.

Once again, Ethan put his arm around my shoulders, only this time Kimber didn't bother to argue. I was trying hard not to think about what I'd seen and what it might mean, and even harder not to think about the fact that I'd actually fainted, so I wasn't as focused on the warmth of Ethan's body next to mine. When I snapped out of my temporary daze, it was to find that my arm had somehow found its way around his waist, and that I was now matching his stride. No more awkward hip bumps.

When we got back to the courtyard, all three of us went up to Kimber's apartment. Kimber gave me some dry clothes, and I ducked into the bathroom to change. It occurred to me that my life might have been much easier if I'd lied and said I saw nothing unusual when I'd looked out into the distance. I was a pretty good liar—Mom gave me plenty of occasions to practice—but I doubt I'd have been able to pretend nothing was wrong in the face of the dizziness and nausea.

I looked at my face in the bathroom mirror once I'd finished changing, and I hardly recognized myself. My eyes were a little too wide, my face too pale. I leaned forward and inspected the roots of my hair, half-expecting to see it had turned white, but it still looked normal.

I splashed hot water on my face, and that brought some color back to my cheeks. Then I took a deep breath and went to join Ethan and Kimber in the living room. At this point, I was beginning to suspect I didn't *want* an explanation for what I'd seen, but I supposed I was going to get it anyway.

Ethan and Kimber were sitting on the sofa I'd used as a bed last night, their heads bent together, their voices no louder than a whisper. Ethan was looking earnest, and Kimber was scowling at him. I wondered if she ever smiled when Ethan was around.

They both noticed me at the same time, Kimber interrupting herself mid-sentence while Ethan sat up straight and flashed me one of his dazzling smiles. The smile warmed me like I was standing in a ray of sunshine, and I found myself smiling back in spite of everything.

There was a prissy china tea set on the coffee table, and Kimber made a racket fussing with the pot and then pouring three cups. I knew she wasn't even remotely clumsy, so the noise was probably meant to annoy Ethan. It seemed to work. He stopped smiling at me and rolled his eyes at her.

I took a deep breath, not realizing that I'd stopped breathing entirely while his eyes had been on me. My heart did some weird fluttery thing in my chest. I could get used to Ethan looking at me like that, smiling at me and bathing me in warmth.

I shook my head at myself. *Out of your league, Dana,* my inner voice said. It was nice to have a hottie like him treating me like a woman instead of a girl, but I didn't dare let myself think of it as anything other than habitual flirting on his part. I'm not ugly—how could I be with Fae blood running through my veins?—but I'm not anything special, either. Certainly not pretty enough to attract the attention of someone like Ethan. He was hot even for a Fae, and he could have his pick of women prettier, more worldly, and more sophisticated than me. I'm a big believer in not getting my hopes up.

I felt shy and vaguely silly as I took a seat on an antique straight-backed chair perpendicular to the sofa. I picked up the cup of tea Kimber had put in front of the chair—beside her, not Ethan, of course—even though I didn't really feel in the mood for tea. Especially not when I saw the little specks peppering the bottom of the cup. Apparently, they didn't use tea bags in Avalon. Sigh.

I raised the cup to my lips and took a halfhearted sip. Then I lowered the cup back into the saucer and found myself staring at the tea leaves, wondering what a gypsy would read in them. I had a feeling it would be nothing good.

"So are you guys going to tell me what's going on now?" I asked, still looking at the tea. Almost like if I didn't look at the Fae, they wouldn't speak to me and tell me what my shifting vision had meant to them.

"You're a very special girl, Dana Stuart," Ethan said.

Against my will, I found myself looking up at him, getting trapped by his gaze. I may be naive, but I'd seen enough movies and TV to recognize the R-rated look in those striking teal eyes of his. My throat tightened, and I wasn't sure whether I felt hot or cold. It took all I had not to squirm.

"My name's Hathaway," I said weakly. My parents had never married, and I'd carried my mom's name my entire life. I didn't feel inclined to change that now.

His lips quirked, but his eyes still had that dark, hungry gleam in them. "Stuart or Hathaway, you're special."

Kimber cleared her throat loudly. Ethan pouted at her.

"You are such a buzz kill," he grumbled. She started to say something, but he cut her off, his attention back on me. "You know your father is one of the elite, one of the most powerful Fae in Avalon."

Now I *did* squirm. I wished my mom had told me the truth all these years so I'd have known what I was getting into when I came to Avalon. But she'd told me so many contradicting stories that it had been impossible to determine what was truth and what was fiction. Unfortunately, I could no longer deny that my father's exalted status among the Fae was one of those truths.

"The Fae are not a spectacularly fertile people," Ethan said. "We don't have children with each other all that often, and we have children with humans even more rarely." He grinned. "Kimber is kind of a freak of nature, because she was born less than two years after me."

Kimber smacked his arm. Hard. "Most people consider me a miracle baby, not a 'freak,'" she said. But the look in her eyes suggested this wasn't the first time she'd heard the word *freak* used to describe her. I instantly liked her better, understanding that her prickliness was a defensive behavior.

"Usually," Ethan continued, "a child of mixed blood will inherit primarily its mother's . . . traits, for lack of a better word."

"Maybe *heritage* is a better description," Kimber suggested, having apparently shrugged off her hurt.

Ethan rolled that word around his mind for a moment, then nodded. "Yeah, I guess it is. So a child born of a Fae mother is much more Fae than human, and a child born of a human mother is much more human than Fae."

"Which is why a child born of a Fae mother can't pass from Avalon to the mortal world, and vice versa," Kimber said.

Ethan nodded. "Exactly. But the most powerful Fae also have the most dominant genes. So when someone like Seamus Stuart has a child with a human woman, that child will be more Fae than the average half-blood. When the circumstances are just right, that child can be a *literal* half-blood, truly half human and half Fae. And instead of being affiliated solely with her mother's realm, that child is affiliated with *both* realms."

"They're called Faeriewalkers," Kimber said, "because they can pass freely from Avalon into Faerie, or into the mortal world, whichever they choose."

"Which makes them powerful enough," Ethan continued, and it was almost like the two of them had rehearsed this conversation, each memorizing their lines so they could trade off to maximum effect. "But what makes the Faeriewalkers even *more* powerful is that they can carry technology into Faerie."

"And magic into the mortal world," Kimber added.

I sat there gaping like an idiot, and I felt almost as dizzy as when . . . I shied away from the memory of looking over that guardrail into the misty distance.

I swallowed hard and finally found my voice. "Holy shit!" I said. I'm not usually much of a cusser, but if ever there were an occasion to start cussing, this would be it. This was way, way worse than I'd thought even in my wildest dreams. And here I'd come to Avalon in hopes of having a *more* normal life.

"So when I looked out into the distance . . ." I started, my voice sounding weird and scratchy.

Ethan nodded. "You were seeing what Faeriewalkers call the Glimmerglass—the window that looks out into the mortal world and Faerie at the same time. I've heard it's . . . disorienting."

I managed a nervous laugh as I wiped my clammy palms on my pants legs. "That's one way to describe it." I remembered the dizziness and nausea, the memory so strong my stomach lurched even now. "How many of us are there?" I asked, because there was no point in arguing I wasn't a Faeriewalker. I wished I could convince myself I'd been hallucinating earlier, but I knew what I'd seen.

I felt, rather than saw, the look Ethan and Kimber exchanged. By some silent arrangement, it was Ethan who answered.

"The last one before you died about seventy-five years ago."

I nodded sagely. And then I leapt to my feet, knocking over my chair, and barely made it to the bathroom in time to puke up my Cheerios.

chapter ten

I locked myself in the bathroom and stayed there for the better part of an hour. Kimber and Ethan each made one attempt to get me to come out, but they gave up when I didn't answer. I'm sure they could have forced the door open if they'd wanted to, but luckily for me, they left me alone.

I'd always despised my mom for her drinking, but I swear, if there'd been any alcohol handy, I'd have tried some in hopes that it would make everything go away. I sat on the closed toilet, my knees drawn up to my chest, my arms wrapped around my legs, wondering if there was any way I could get myself out of this mess. Aunt Grace had said that even if I left Avalon, I'd be a target now that people knew about me. And since Grace had my passport, it wasn't like I was getting out of Avalon anyway.

Tears stung my eyes. Why couldn't my mother just be a normal mom? Why couldn't she just go to some stupid twelve-step program and dry out? She'd never even *tried*. If she'd only tried to stop drinking, maybe I never would have gotten so fed up I had to run away, and none of this would have happened.

I didn't need her to be perfect, I just needed her to be sober. Was that too much to ask?

I sniffled, then dashed the tears from my eyes. If there was one thing I'd learned in my life, it was that tears didn't get me anywhere. I was the one who always had to keep my head while my mom had hysterics over the crisis-du-jour. I'd gotten very good at setting my own feelings aside to be dealt with later, so that's what I did now. It was harder than usual, but eventually I managed to pull myself back together.

Ethan was gone when I finally ventured out of my cave. Kimber was clattering around in the kitchen again, and I headed toward the sound. I smelled something cooking. At first, I thought it smelled like rice, but I realized that wasn't right. My stomach, having thoroughly emptied itself of its meager contents, thought whatever it was smelled pretty good.

When I entered the kitchen, Kimber was mashing something the color of paste and the consistency of vomit through a strainer. Suddenly, it didn't smell quite so good anymore. Thick, off-white liquid dripped through the strainer into a small pot sitting on the stove. When she'd forced every bit of liquid she could out of the strainer, she dumped the contents into the trash.

"Almost ready," she said, not looking at me, her whole concentration fixed on her task. Steam wafted into her face, and I saw that a fine sheen of sweat coated her skin. Whatever she was doing, it was hot work.

"I'm afraid to ask," I said, "but *what's* almost ready?"

She poured a good-sized dollop of honey into the pot and stirred it around. Then she turned on the stove, and low blue flames caressed the bottom of the pot.

"Your hot posset," she said, reaching into the cabinet over

the sink and pulling down a bottle of something that had the distinctive amber color of alcohol.

"What's a posset?" I asked as I watched her pour a generous dose of—I squinted at the label—whiskey into the pot.

"It's what you give someone if they have a cold. Or if they have a headache. Or if they've had a bad day. Or if they can't sleep. Or if—"

"Okay, got it. Cure-all remedy. But I'm too young to drink."

She laughed, wiping the sweat from her brow with her forearm. "Legally, I am, too, but that's not going to stop me. I had my first posset when I was five. You're older than five, aren't you?"

I sniffed the air, trying to identify the smell, but all I could recognize was the whiskey. "But what *is* it? What's in it, other than enough booze to make me wear a lampshade on my head?"

She shrugged and stirred the posset, which was steaming merrily. "Milk. Oatmeal. Honey. A bit of nutmeg. And the fine Irish whiskey, of course."

Oh, gross! Oatmeal? Who puts oatmeal in a *drink*? I wondered how I was going to get out of drinking it without being completely rude.

Kimber turned off the stove and got out a couple of mugs, filling each one to the brim with the thick, milky liquid. I'm sure I was making a face, but that didn't seem to discourage Kimber. She thrust one of the mugs at me, and I took it almost by reflex. Then I just stood there staring at it, wondering if I was going to have to make another run for the bathroom.

"I promise it's not poisonous," Kimber said as she blew on her posset, then took a delicate sip. "And there's almost no situation a good, hot posset can't make better."

I hesitated a moment longer. Then I thought about being attacked by Spriggans last night, about looking through the Glimmerglass this afternoon, and finding out that I was the one and only Faeriewalker currently in existence, and I decided that drinking the posset couldn't possibly be such a big deal after all.

I took a tentative sip, and, of course, instantly burned my tongue. And the sip continued to burn as it slid down my throat and spread into my chest and stomach. I pounded my chest with my fist.

"Smooth," I said in an exaggerated croak.

Kimber grinned, the expression making her look more like Ethan than ever. "Have some more. It'll grow on you."

"What, like mold?" I asked, but I took another sip anyway. The whiskey and honey tastes were both very strong, so I was able to halfway forget I was drinking milk with oatmeal in it. And, though I would never admit it out loud, the stuff was definitely warm and soothing, with a decadent, creamy texture that told me not to even *think* about how many calories were in it.

We drank in companionable silence for a while, Kimber cleaning up the kitchen so it was once again pristine in its never-touched perfection, me just leaning against the counter. The posset burned less and less with each sip, and I tried to tell myself that the alcohol was steaming off. I'd never had more than a sip or two of anything alcoholic before, but I doubted it was the warm milk that was making my limbs feel all loose and warm.

"You really drank this when you were five?" I asked. Did my words slur a little bit, or was that my imagination?

"I'm sure the ones my mother made me were considerably weaker. And I think she used wine instead of whiskey. But yeah." She smiled again. Gee, the posset seemed to be having a nice effect on her, too. "You can see why it's a cure-all, huh?"

My head felt woozy when I nodded, but it wasn't too bad. The posset had calmed the last of my nerve-induced nausea, and I was now positively famished. Luckily, Kimber had anticipated the return of my appetite, and before I had a chance to ask her for food, she produced a plate of sliced fruit and finger sandwiches from the refrigerator.

Still standing in the kitchen, we took turns picking goodies off the plate. I particularly liked the little cucumber sandwiches and the fresh strawberries, and I probably could have eaten the whole plate myself. Then again, that posset had been filling.

"Can I ask you something?" I asked as Kimber popped a couple of raspberries into her mouth. She gave me a droll look, and I remembered her dumb joke the last time I'd asked her that. I didn't wait for her answer this time.

I examined the strawberry in my hand with great concentration. "Is Ethan really flirting with me, or is that just how he is with anything female?" Kimber's reactions suggested that it really was flirting, but I couldn't fathom why he'd bother.

Kimber didn't answer immediately, so I stole a cautious glance up at her face. Her lips were pursed, and there was an unhappy look in her eyes that I didn't understand. So much for the positive effects of the posset.

"It's no big deal if he is," I assured her. "I can handle it." I said that with all the confidence of someone who has to fend off horny boys right and left, but of course I was lying. I'd forgotten to breathe when he'd looked at me with those hungry eyes of his, and my skin still felt the phantom warmth of his side against mine.

Kimber shook her head and looked me straight in the eye. "No, you can't handle it," she told me bluntly. "He's charmed lots of more experienced girls than you out of their knickers."

I gave a pseudo-offended sniff. "For all you know, I'm the school slut."

She laughed. "Yes, and that's why you blush every time he looks at you."

Busted. I decided to try a different tack. "Okay, so he's really flirting with me. Why? I didn't think guys his age were interested in high school girls." Especially not half-human high school girls who weren't all that pretty.

Kimber got that tight look around her eyes again, and she thought a long time before answering. "Ethan likes to think of himself as a big manly-man, but he's only eighteen. I know you're younger than that, but he'd still consider you to be fair game. Besides, you're not a typical high school girl. You're a Faeriewalker. You have the potential to be . . . very powerful. And Ethan's very fond of power."

I looked quickly away from her face, not wanting her to see my expression, whatever exactly it was. I don't know what I'd hoped she'd tell me. Maybe I'd hoped she'd stroke my ego a bit, tell me I was so clever and witty that Ethan couldn't help but fall at my feet and worship me. Of course, I'd have known she was lying. I wasn't all that clever and witty in normal life, and around Ethan I acted like I had an IQ of about seventy.

But to think he was flirting with me because I was powerful, or could be in the future . . .

My opinion of him lowered considerably, although I suspected when I saw him again my common sense might go right back out the window. I mean, just because he was attracted to power in general didn't mean that was why he was attracted to *me*, right? The fact that I might be powerful could be just a co-incidence. Besides, he hadn't known for sure about me until this afternoon.

I shook my head at myself. None of this mattered anyway. As long as I was with Kimber, Ethan wasn't going to do more than give me the occasional smoldering glance. And maybe after dealing with Ethan for a bit, I'd be more ready when a boy who was actually in my league was interested. Best to act like a gib-bering idiot around a guy who was unattainable than around one I actually had a shot at.

"I'm sure Ethan really likes you," Kimber said gently. I guessed she'd figured out that telling me Ethan was attracted to my power didn't give me warm fuzzies. "He wouldn't be flirting quite so much if he didn't. It's just . . ." She shook her head. "It's just that there's always more than meets the eye with him."

"You and he don't get along so well, huh?" I asked tenta-tively. It wasn't really any of my business, but even a moron could see they had issues.

Kimber's face closed off and she looked away. "Let's not talk about Ethan anymore, okay?"

Kimber's cell phone chirped, and I was strung so tight I jumped and let out a little screech. Kimber banished her glum look, suppressing a smile.

Kimber grabbed the phone from the counter and read a text message. Her eyes widened, and she said something in a lan-guage I was completely unfamiliar with. I felt sure it was a cuss word, though.

Kimber slammed the phone down, then grabbed my arm and started hauling me across the kitchen.

"Hey!" I protested, stumbling along after her.

"Shh!" she hissed. "That was Ethan. Your aunt just stormed his flat, and you can bet she'll come here next."

I swallowed my next protest and allowed Kimber to drag me into her room. I balked when she opened her closet door and tried to shove me in. The rest of her apartment may have been obsessively neat, but the closet was a nightmare of clothes, shoes, boxes, and assorted other junk all crammed in willy-nilly. It looked like I'd need a crowbar to get in.

"You have to hide!" Kimber insisted. "Quick. Or would you prefer to spend more quality time with Grace and Lachlan?"

I wasn't sure I bought the theory that Aunt Grace wanted to make me disappear, permanently. But I had no desire to be locked up again, and while I wouldn't go so far as to say I *hated* Aunt Grace, I thoroughly disliked her.

I shoved my way into the crowded closet, Kimber pushing and pulling to get me past various obstacles. I ended up wedged in a corner between a stack of shoe boxes piled from floor to ceiling and a big, billowy, froufrou dress trimmed with feathers that tickled my cheeks.

The doorbell rang. Kimber hastily stuffed everything she'd moved back into the closet. I was buried deeply enough that I couldn't even see the door, but it sounded like getting it to close was something of a struggle.

And then the closet door clicked shut, and I was alone in the dark. I sighed and shut my eyes, trying to forget that I was hiding in a dark, claustrophobic closet while my wicked aunt Grace was way too close for comfort. Every time I breathed, the feathers on Kimber's ridiculous dress fluttered against my skin, the tickle growing more annoying with each breath. I tried putting my hand between them and my cheek, but it turned out my hand was just as ticklish.

I couldn't hear anything. I hoped that meant Aunt Grace wasn't actually searching the apartment for me. If she wasn't searching, then maybe I could get out of this closet before I lost my mind. Assuming I hadn't lost it already. If she *was* searching for me, it occurred to me that she might be able to do some kind of magic to find me. Note to self: ask Kimber for more details about how magic works if and when you have a chance.

It's hard to keep track of time when you can't see or hear, but it felt like I was in that closet forever. It grew stuffy almost immediately, and sweat trickled down the small of my back and between my pitiful excuse for breasts. I was seriously tempted to tear the feathers off of Kimber's dress, but I was afraid someone might hear me and I'd give myself away.

Just as I was beginning to wonder if Kimber had left me here long after Grace had left just for a practical joke, I heard voices approaching. My breath caught in my throat and my heart started to hammer when I recognized one of those voices as Aunt Grace's.

I let my breath out slowly and quietly. My heart hammered against my chest, and sweat beaded on my forehead.

"Would you like to look under the bed?" I heard Kimber ask, and she sounded drily amused. "Or how about in the closet? Though I'd open that door carefully if I were you. Things have a tendency to fall out. I don't think she'd fit in one of my drawers, but you're welcome to check there too if you'd like."

Was Kimber nuts? Why was she actually *suggesting* Aunt Grace search the closet?

I clapped a hand over my mouth to keep from gasping when

I heard the closet door swing open. No matter how much I told myself I didn't think my aunt would kill me, there was no denying I was terrified. I pressed myself harder into the corner, but just as we'd had to move a lot of junk to get me in here, Aunt Grace would have to move a lot of junk before she'd be able to see me. I held my breath as I heard hangers clanking together and shoes hitting the floor. Kimber laughed as if she didn't have a care in the world, and I wished I could reach her to smack her.

The closet door slammed shut, and I could hear the fury in Aunt Grace's voice.

"Fine!" she snarled. "You or your brother have hidden her somewhere else. Don't think I won't find her! And you and whoever else was involved in her abduction will spend the next twenty years behind bars."

Kimber said something in answer. I didn't catch it, but I guess Aunt Grace did, because the next thing I heard was a loud slap, followed by Kimber's gasp. I clenched my fists and bit my tongue to keep from shouting a protest. I'd disliked—and feared—Aunt Grace since the moment I'd met her, and it seemed my instincts had been spot on. I started groping blindly in search of a weapon. If Grace hit Kimber again, I was fully prepared to charge out of the closet and come to her defense. (Yes, I knew that would be dumb, but I would have felt like a coward if I'd hidden in the closet while Kimber got hurt.) Luckily, there were no further sounds of violence before the angry stomp of Grace's footsteps told me she was leaving.

chapter eleven

I was not in the most cheerful of moods when Kimber came back to dig me out of the closet. My nerves were shot, I was sweating like a pig, and I was so mad I wanted to punch her beautiful, delicate face. (Never mind that I'd been ready to charge to her rescue moments ago.)

"What the hell were you thinking?" I asked as I practically fell out of the closet, tripping over a tennis racket on the way out. Who knew the Fae played tennis? How terribly . . . ordinary.

Kimber grabbed my shoulders before I did a face-plant, but I jerked away from her. Unfortunately, I then stepped on a shoe. My ankle gave way, and I landed on my butt. And I'd thought I was in a bad mood *before* I got out of the closet!

I sat on the floor, peeling strands of hair away from my sticky, sweaty face. I glared first at the strappy red sandal with the ridiculously high heel that had toppled me, then at Kimber, who looked like she was about to bust a blood vessel trying not to laugh. I wasn't finding it anywhere near so funny.

I scrambled to my feet with as much dignity as I could

muster—which was about zero—and wished I were a few inches taller so I didn't have to look up at Kimber.

"'Why don't you look in the closet?'" I said, doing a terrible impression of Kimber's accent. "Were you *trying* to get me caught?"

She rolled her eyes—she seemed to do that a lot—and gave me a condescending smile. "If I'd acted like I had something to hide, Grace would have torn the place apart searching for you. This way, she wasn't expecting to find anything, so she didn't look very hard."

I hated to admit that Kimber's logic made sense. So I didn't. "I practically had heart failure when she opened that door. At least you could have warned me what you were planning to do."

"Sorry," she said, but she didn't sound terribly repentant.

Ignoring me, she started shoving stuff back into the closet. I could have helped her, I suppose, but I wasn't feeling all that helpful.

"Are you all right?" I asked grudgingly.

Kimber rubbed her reddened cheek. "I'm fine," she said with a rueful smile. "I should know better than to mouth off to someone like her.

"I guess we're going to have to find you somewhere else to stay," she continued, still cramming things into any available space. "Grace could come by for another surprise inspection, and I don't want to assume we'll get lucky twice."

"I've already got a place to stay," I said. "With my *father*."

Kimber frowned at me. "You mean you *will* have a place to stay, when he gets out of jail. I checked on his status while you were hiding in the bathroom. He's scheduled to come up before the Council tomorrow. But at least for today, he's still locked up."

I stifled a curse. My heart sank as I began to realize how

thoroughly my life sucked right now. I was on my own, without a penny to my name or even a change of clothes, in a country so foreign there should be a new word for it, and with nowhere to go. I wanted to go home. Who would have thought it would come to this within two days of my setting foot in Avalon?

"I have to get out of Avalon," I said, talking more to myself than to Kimber. Grace had said I wouldn't be safe even outside of Avalon, but I wasn't so sure. My mom and I had gotten really good at relocating over the years, and because she was always trying to make sure my dad couldn't find us, we'd learned how to move without leaving a trail. Sure, I wanted to meet my dad and all, but not if it meant staying here and dodging Aunt Grace and Spriggans and who knew what other nightmares might come out of the woodwork.

"It sounds good in theory," Kimber said, closing the closet door and turning to me with a look of sympathy on her face. "But your aunt Grace is captain of the border patrol, and you know she'll have the Gates on high alert looking for you. Even if you *could* get through immigration without a passport."

"But I'm an American citizen," I whined. "They can't keep me here against my will." Maybe I could put in a call to the U.S. Embassy in London and they could get me out of here.

Kimber put her hands on my shoulders, giving them a firm squeeze. "You're a Faeriewalker. The government of Avalon won't give a damn if keeping you here against your will causes some kind of international incident. You'd be considered worth the fallout."

Great. Just great. I was trapped in Avalon, my aunt was hunting me, my dad was in jail, and the only people who seemed to be on my side were a pair of Fae teenagers I barely knew.

Kimber gave my shoulders another squeeze before she let go. "It'll be all right. Between Ethan and me, I'm sure we can keep you safe until your father is free."

"Thanks," I said, my throat tightening. She and Ethan were by far the best thing that had happened to me since I'd set foot in Avalon. If it weren't for them, I'd still be locked up in Aunt Grace's cell—or worse. "I'm really glad you guys came for me last night."

Kimber smiled at me, but there was something strangely sad about the expression. "We'll have to lay low during the day, but tonight when it's dark, we'll get you out of here to somewhere safer."

"Safer like the cave last night?" I mumbled, but though I was sure Kimber heard me, she didn't respond.

"Grace probably has someone watching my apartment and Ethan's, so you have to stay inside and stay away from windows."

Sounded like a fun day. "If I'm going to skulk around in the shadows waiting for nightfall," I said, "then I want to spend some time getting a crash course in magic. What it can do, how it works, stuff like that. I'm just about clueless."

She didn't look happy about the idea. "Ethan's the magic expert in the family," she said.

I shrugged. "I'm not asking you to *show* me magic. I'm asking you to *tell* me about it. You can do that, can't you?"

She sighed. "Fine. But I could use another hot posset first."

I could get used to drinking hot possets, I decided as I took a sip from my steaming mug. My mom had tried making me warm milk a couple of times when I was a kid and couldn't sleep, but it had been totally gag-worthy. This was sooo much better.

At my insistence, Kimber had used a lot less whiskey this time, though she'd poured some extra into her own mug.

"Do your parents know you put whiskey in your posset?" I asked.

Kimber sniffed in what looked like disdain. "They wouldn't care if they did."

She made sure to stay between me and the living room window as we retreated into her bedroom, where the heavy curtains would guarantee no one saw me. She sat on the edge of her bed, and I sat on a comfy chair tucked into a corner under a floor lamp. On the table by the chair sat a textbook that looked like it weighed about eight tons, and a dog-eared, yellowed paperback. I was nosy enough to peek at the titles. The textbook was *Calculus of a Single Variable: Early Transcendental Functions*, and the paperback was . . . *The Secret Garden* by Frances Hodgson Burnett, which I remembered reading when I was about eight. I blinked and looked back and forth between the two books and Kimber. Her cheeks turned a delicate shade of pink.

"Sometimes I need a break from ponderous academic reading," she said with a shrug.

"So you're a math major?" I asked, because I couldn't imagine anyone having a textbook like that if they weren't really, really into math. She didn't look like any math geek I'd ever met. Hell, Ethan had said she was two years younger than him, and Kimber had said Ethan was eighteen—which made Kimber way too young for college, unless she was some kind of a prodigy.

"I haven't declared a major yet," she said. "But I'm leaning toward engineering."

A Fae engineer. It just sounded . . . wrong. And how many jobs were there for engineers in Avalon? It wasn't like engineering would be a useful skill in Faerie, so if she wanted to make use of her degree, she'd have to do it here. Of course, considering the quality of her clothes and furniture, she might be one of those annoying people who don't have to work for a living.

"And in case you're wondering," Kimber continued, "Ethan will be a freshman in the fall, and I'll be a sophomore. He may have gotten the magic in the family, but *I* got the brains."

The look on her face said she wasn't happy about that, which surprised me. Considering her obvious rivalry with her brother, you'd think she'd be thrilled to be ahead of him in school.

"That must drive Ethan nuts," I said, and yes, I was fishing.

Kimber took a sip of her posset before answering. "Actually, he couldn't care less. He's got the magic, and that's what counts."

I felt a surge of indignation on Kimber's account. "You don't think being incredibly smart counts for something?"

She smiled wryly. "To humans, maybe. To the Fae, not so much." She tilted her head to one side. "In human terms, it would be like Ethan was a superstar football player, and I was the brainiac younger sister. Who gets all the glory in that situation?"

I saw her point, but still . . . "That sucks."

She laughed, but it wasn't a happy sound. "Tell me about it." She sobered quickly. "Actually, Ethan has a lot in common with a human superstar athlete. He's got an ego the size of Mount Everest, and he's used to girls falling at his feet in admiration."

The look in her eyes was a warning, but I pretended not to notice. I would come to my own conclusions about Ethan, thank you very much. It's not that I didn't believe what she was telling me—it's just that I couldn't help hoping I meant more to Ethan than a notch on his bedpost.

I didn't think talking about Ethan was a good way to further what I was beginning to think was a budding friendship, so I changed the subject.

I cleared my throat. "So, about magic . . ." Not very subtle, but I wasn't sure subtlety would work.

Kimber stared at me long and hard before she finally allowed our previous subject to drop. She shook her head at me in a last sign of disapproval, then asked, "What would you like to know about it?"

I took another sip of my posset as I tried to figure out what to ask first. "What can it do?" I asked, then decided that was probably the stupidest, vaguest question ever. But Kimber didn't find it as stupid as I did.

"In theory, magic can do just about anything, if the caster is skilled enough." Her eyes glazed over as she searched for what she wanted to say. "Magic is an elemental force, native to Faerie. It's not quite sentient, but it's close."

I shivered, because the idea of sentient magic was just, well, creepy.

"When you cast a spell, you draw the magic into your body—kind of like when you draw a deep breath before you dive into a pool. Then you release the magic you've drawn in, and—if you're any good at it—it does what you want it to do.

"We vary in how much magic we can draw to ourselves—the more magic we can draw, the more dramatic a spell we can cast. At least in theory. In reality, drawing the magic is the easy part. Getting it to do what you want . . ." She shrugged. "That's a lot harder."

"So what is it that makes Ethan a magical prodigy?" I asked.

I knew I was combining two of Kimber's least favorite subjects—Ethan, and his superior magical abilities—but I wanted to understand about magic, and this seemed like a necessary step.

On cue, the corners of Kimber's mouth tugged downward. "First, he can draw a lot of magic. Second, he has incredible endurance. Drawing and directing the magic is exhausting. And third, he's scary-good at getting the magic to do what he wants.

"There are some spells that almost all of us can do. Things like locking doors, or lighting candles. They're so common, they're easy. It's like teaching your dog to sit—just about anyone can manage that, but it would take someone with more skill to teach the dog a trick. If you have more skill with the magic, you can make it do things ordinary people can't."

"Like make me lose my voice?" I asked.

Kimber grinned. "Actually, that's a very common spell, usually used against unruly children. No, something harder would be major healing spells, or illusions. Many of us could manage to do them with a lot of work and practice. Just like many humans could theoretically do brain surgery, but few are willing to put in the massive effort required to learn how to do it.

"What makes Ethan scary-good is that he can make the magic do lots of different, unrelated things. Most people have to really specialize. Sorry to use yet another analogy, but this is really hard to explain to a human. Let's say a certain kind of magic—like healing magic—understands a specific language, like French. If you learn to speak French, then you can get the magic to do what you want. But the more complicated the spell, the more French you have to know to be able to do it. And maybe illusion magic speaks Mandarin, and attack magic speaks Swahili. You'd have to know three completely unrelated languages in order to communicate with them all. So that's why most people have to specialize. Ethan, on the other hand, can pick up a new 'language' at the drop of a hat."

And it gave Kimber a serious inferiority complex on top of the normal sibling rivalry. I couldn't blame her, especially when Ethan seemed to enjoy lording his abilities over her.

"So is it some special language of magic you guys speak when you cast spells?" I asked.

She shook her head. "The words don't matter. The language thing was just an analogy. People who are really good at magic can even use gestures instead of words. You just have to teach the magic that when you say 'abracadabra,' it means you want it to lock the door."

I nodded sagely, still not sure I really got it, but figuring any further explanation would just make my head hurt. I decided it was high time I asked the question that was eating at me more and more as Kimber explained things. "Can Aunt Grace use magic to find me?"

"If she could, she'd have done it already. Locating spells are hard—finding someone or something that isn't there is kind of an abstract concept and hard to communicate—so it's one of those categories you really have to specialize in to be any good at."

Well that was a relief, at least. "Does Aunt Grace have a specialty?"

Kimber looked kinda grim. "Yeah."

"Well, what is it?" I prompted.

Kimber sighed. "Attack magic."

And that blew my temporary relief right out of the water.

. . .

By the time Kimber had finished her extra-strength posset, she was distinctly mellow. I wouldn't go so far as to say I was mellow myself, but I was a lot more relaxed than I'd been since I'd first set foot in Avalon. I'd never had a real close friend before. Sure, there'd been girls at my various schools who I'd sit with at lunch, or hang with for a while after school. But whenever I started to get close to someone, Mom would insist it was time for us to move again, and I'd be forced to start over at square one at my new school. After a while, getting too close was just more trouble than it was worth.

I was relaxed enough that I decided to ask a question that had been bugging me since I'd first caught sight of Kimber's apartment. Was it only last night? I felt like I'd been here for years.

"How come your parents let you have your own apartment?" My mom wasn't the most nurturing mother on the planet, but I had a feeling even *she* would balk at letting a sixteen-year-old live by herself.

Kimber looked down and away, and I knew I'd asked a sensitive question.

"Sorry," I said, wishing I could suck my words back. "I'll stop being so nosy."

Kimber looked up and forced a smile. "It's all right. You just hit a nerve, that's all."

I made to apologize again, but she cut me off with a gesture. "No, I mean it, it's okay." She let out a heavy sigh and seemed to brace herself before she began.

"My mom's been out of the picture since I was ten," she said, fidgeting with the ends of her hair while she talked. "She decided she wanted to go back to Faerie, but my dad was born in Avalon and wouldn't leave. They agreed that Ethan and I would stay with Dad, and it's been the three of us ever since.

"I'm sure my dad loves me in his own way, but he doesn't really try to hide that Ethan's his favorite. Well, Ethan wanted to move into student housing as soon as he graduated high school, and because whatever Ethan wants, Ethan gets, Dad let him.

"Dad and I had a big fight a while later, and I told him I wanted to move out. I told him that since I was in college like Ethan, I should have my own apartment like Ethan." Her eyes shimmered with tears, and her voice softened until it was little more than a whisper. "He said okay."

I winced in sympathy. "Your dad must have been pretty dense not to get that he was supposed to say no."

She laughed and blinked away the tears. "My dad is many things, but dense isn't one of them. He knew what I wanted—he just didn't care." She took a deep breath and straightened her spine. "But it's not that big a difference anyway. He's a total workaholic, so he's never home. I don't really see him any less now than I did when I lived at home."

Maybe my mom wasn't so bad after all. All her embarrassing, neglectful, and downright stupid behavior was caused by alcohol. I knew that somewhere, buried beneath the booze-brain, was a loving mother. Kimber didn't even have that.

"I think your dad really *is* dense," I told Kimber. "He's got to be if he doesn't realize how lucky he is to have you."

Her cheeks pinkened. "Thanks. But you don't have to try to make me feel better. I've . . . come to terms with it."

Yeah, right, I thought but didn't say.

"Do you mind if I ask *you* something?" Kimber said.

"After all the questions I've lobbed your way, it's gotta be your turn."

"Why did you run away from home?"

I grimaced. Why did it have to be *that* question? "Geez, does *everyone* know I ran away?" I asked, trying to deflect the question. I'd never told anyone that my mom was a drunk—in fact, I'd gone to great lengths to avoid having anyone find out—and I wasn't about to change that now.

One corner of Kimber's mouth tipped up. "The fact that you've never shown any interest in calling home for help was kind of a giveaway, but I didn't know for sure until now."

"Oh." I looked away from her too-knowing stare. "I don't want to talk about it, okay?"

"Sure," Kimber agreed, but I could tell my closing the conversational door in her face hurt her feelings. She forced a smile. "I feel an attack of the munchies coming on."

She hopped to her feet, and without thinking about it, I reached out and grabbed her arm to stop her from fleeing the room. After the way she'd just opened her heart to me, it would be completely bitchy of me to shut her out. I was going to have to bite the bullet and talk about my least favorite subject in the world.

"Sit down," I told her, giving her arm a little yank. "I'm sorry. It's just . . ."

I let go of her arm, and Kimber sank back down onto the bed. "You don't have to talk about it if you don't want to," she said gently. "You've known me for less than twenty-four hours. I shouldn't expect you to treat me like your BFF."

"It's okay—it's been an intense twenty-four hours."

She laughed faintly. "That it has."

I blew out a deep breath. My heart was pounding almost as hard as when I'd been hiding in the closet, and my shoulder muscles were so tight they hurt. But I knew I was overreacting. Kimber might look like the bitchy, popular cheerleader-type who could sneer at me if she knew about my mom, but she didn't act like it. Besides, it wasn't like there was a school full of other kids she could spread the story to.

Bracing myself for shock, or pity, or disgust, I forced my shameful secret out through gritted teeth. "My mom's an alcoholic." There. I'd said it. Out loud.

Kimber just sat there, waiting for me to continue. "And?" she prompted, when I didn't say anything else.

I stared at her. "Does there have to be more?"

She blinked. "Well, no. I guess not. It's just that you gave it so much build-up I thought it was going to be some horrible, dark secret, like she had a boyfriend who abused you or something."

Of all the reactions I'd been expecting, this wasn't one of them. "So you don't think my mom being a drunk is a big deal?"

She shrugged. "Sure, it's a big deal to you—you had to live with her. It's just . . . I don't know. It's not a stop-the-presses, red-alert, danger-Will-Robinson kind of thing."

"Danger Will Robinson?"

"You know, *Lost in Space.*"

I made a zooming-over-my-head motion.

Kimber made a mock-horror face. "It's a classic! But anyway, the point is, in the grand scheme of shocking news, an alcoholic mom just isn't that high up there."

It's funny, but I'd been worried that she'd look down on me when she knew—and I was glad she didn't. But it was such an anticlimax compared to what I'd been expecting that I swear I was almost disappointed. I mean, here I'd gone and told her this terrible secret, the one I'd never told anyone in my life . . . and she was all like, "Yawn."

"The kids at my last school thought it was pretty shocking," I protested. "They made my life a living hell when they found out."

She waved that off. "Yeah, but they were kids."

"Uh, newsflash: *we're* kids."

"But we're not normal kids," she said, and the words hit me like a kick in the gut. "I'm a sixteen-year-old college sophomore who lives on her own, and you're a Faeriewalker. Normal doesn't apply to us."

The truth of her words was hard to deny, although I'd been denying it for a very long time. I'd always tried to be as normal as possible under the circumstances, and I'd always known I'd fallen short. I just hadn't wanted to admit it.

"Hey, at least we can be not normal together now," Kimber said, and I couldn't help smiling.

"Who needs normal?" I responded. "Normal's *boring*."

And, at least for that moment, I actually meant it.

Kimber and I both leapt to our feet when we heard the distinctive sound of the front door opening and closing, then of footsteps coming from the direction of the kitchen.

"It's just me," Ethan called before we had a chance to get too worried.

He appeared in the bedroom doorway a moment later, a cocky grin on his face. My heart did a little ka-thump at the sight of him.

"You look terribly proud of yourself," Kimber said, using the sour tone I'd once thought was the only one she had.

His grin broadened. "I am rather brilliant, if I do say so myself."

"Which you do on a regular basis."

He was undaunted by the ribbing. "After I saw Grace this

afternoon, I knew someone would be keeping a close eye on the two of us," he said.

"Wow, brilliant deduction."

Ethan made a mock pouty-face. "You're ruining the story." I could tell by the look on her face how heartbroken Kimber was about that, but she resisted the urge to come out with another quip.

"I figured being constantly watched would rather cramp our style. So I managed to ditch my tail, and then came straight here." He looked at Kimber expectantly, but she shook her head.

"I'm not in the mood to play your straight man."

He turned the same expectant look on me, and my heart did another one of those ka-thumps. I couldn't *not* give him what he wanted, not when he was looking at me like that.

"How did you ditch your tail?" I asked, and hoped I didn't sound breathless.

His chest swelled with obvious pride. "I've finally got my invisibility spell working."

"This would be the spell you've used to make yourself invisible but that doesn't work on your clothes?" Kimber asked with a raise of her brows. She grinned at me. "He thought he was so clever, trying to sneak up on me, but the moving shirt, pants, and shoes kind of gave him away."

Ethan wasn't daunted. "The same! Only I've gotten it to work for the clothes now, too."

"How would you know? You can see yourself even when you're invisible." She glanced at me once more. "That's why he thought he could sneak up on me even though his clothes weren't invisible."

Ethan gave her a haughty look. "The fact that I doubled back and walked right past the bloke who was following me without him even looking up was kind of a dead giveaway."

"Okay. You managed to ditch the bloke, and the first thing you do is show up here, where you know someone is watching me. How is that helping?"

He gave her an exasperated look. "No one knows I'm here. If you leave the flat, our friends will follow you. Once you're out of sight, Dana and I will make a run for it." There was a twinkle in his eye that said this was all great fun to him. I wondered if he was forgetting all about that inconvenient little Spriggan attack last night.

Kimber didn't like the plan. I don't think she liked acting as a decoy, and I'm *sure* she didn't like leaving me alone with Ethan. But it seemed unlikely we'd find a better way to sneak me out without being seen, so she reluctantly agreed.

She gave me a significant look before she left, and I nodded to let her know I got the message not to let Ethan take advantage of our situation. I figured we'd be too busy running for our lives for him to make a move anyway.

What I hadn't taken into account was that once we made our great escape and the pressure was off, I would *still* be alone with him.

chapter twelve

Ethan and I waited in Kimber's apartment until she'd been gone about five minutes. My every nerve was aware of him, but he paid almost no attention to me, his eyes fixed on the slight gap between the drapes that covered Kimber's window. I sat on the edge of Kimber's bed, my hands clasped in my lap, my heart beating just a bit too fast. I wasn't even sure if my nerves were because of Ethan, or because of our escape attempt.

"Let's go," Ethan said briskly when he felt sure Kimber had successfully lured her watcher away.

I followed him through the apartment toward the front door, having to almost run to keep up. "Where are we going?" I finally found the guts to ask.

He held the door for me so I could step out first, then closed it and made a subtle hand motion. I heard the lock click shut.

"You'll have to trust me on this," Ethan said, taking my hand and leading me down the stairs to the courtyard.

The feel of his hand on mine was enough to strike me speechless, and I barely heard what he said. Of course, he was just holding my hand because he was leading me. It wasn't an intimate gesture, and it was wishful thinking for me to read anything into it. At least, that's what I told myself.

His words didn't register until we stopped right by the section of flagstones that covered the opening into the tunnels.

"Oh, hell no!" I said, and tried to yank my hand out of his.

Of course, he didn't let go. "We're not going back to the cave," he assured me. He mumbled something under his breath, and the flagstones moved aside.

I glanced up at the windows all around us. There were lights on in many of them, since it wasn't the dead of night like it was the last time we'd gone into the tunnels. "How many people do you suppose are watching us right now?" I asked, giving my hand another experimental tug, but he held on.

"It doesn't matter. The tunnels are something of an open secret. They're also vast, so if someone tells Grace we've gone into the tunnels, it won't be enough to go on."

"What about the Spriggans?" I asked.

"We took care of the problem last night," he assured me. "They may not have as much trouble sneaking into Avalon as humans do, but I seriously doubt someone would send them in two nights in a row. Now come on! Unless you want us still to be standing here arguing when Kimber and her tail come back."

To say I didn't like it was an understatement, but I had to admit I was feeling awfully vulnerable standing out here in the open. Gritting my teeth, I nodded, and Ethan finally let go of my hand so I could climb down the ladder.

The flagstones had sealed off the opening above us by the time my feet hit the floor of the tunnel. It was pitch dark, except for the thin beam coming from the flashlight Ethan held in one hand. I moved out of the way, and Ethan jumped from about halfway down the ladder, landing lightly. A human probably would have at least sprained an ankle trying a maneuver like that.

I had a sudden flash to today's magic lesson with Kimber, and it didn't add up with what I'd just seen.

"Last night, you didn't say any kind of spell to open the hatch," I said. "Why did you have to tonight?"

"I'm still working on doing nonverbal spells," he said. "It's a lot harder, and it takes a lot out of me." He looked uncommonly serious. "That's why I couldn't do a better job of healing last night. If I'd just opened the hatch the easy way . . ." He shrugged, not finishing his sentence.

I think I was supposed to say something to let him off the hook, but I remembered how he'd rubbed Kimber's face in it when he was showboating last night, and I figured he deserved to stew a bit. No matter how hot he was.

When I didn't say anything, there was an awkward silence, but Ethan broke the awkwardness soon enough by leading the way into the heart of the mountain once more.

Yesterday, we'd gone straight for a long way before we'd veered off toward the cave. Today, we took a side tunnel almost immediately, then took another, and another, until I was so thoroughly turned around I didn't have a clue where I was. I couldn't help wondering if that was by design. Was Ethan trying to make sure I couldn't get out of here without help?

So far, the only sign I'd seen that the tunnels weren't completely deserted had been the Underground's cave, but Ethan's and my path tonight led to a very different part of the tunnel system. We rounded a corner, and suddenly the tunnel widened significantly and was illuminated by electric lights. A broad stairway led up to what I presumed was the surface, and a steady stream of people went up and down that stairway. Their voices echoed in the enclosed space, but I could hear the muffled sound of loud music over those voices, and I could feel the beat vibrating the floor under my feet.

"There's a great nightclub down there," Ethan said, pointing to another stairway leading down. A neon sign over the stairway declared This Way to THE DEEP, with a flashing arrow. "I'll have to take you there someday when things settle down."

I wasn't sure what to say about that. It sounded almost like he was asking me on a date. I frowned. Actually, there wasn't really any *asking* going on.

Before I finished over-analyzing that one simple sentence, Ethan guided me down yet another branch of the tunnel, and we were back into dark, creepy, claustrophobic territory. I tried my best to keep track of our route after that so I could make my way back to the stairway to the surface if necessary.

We walked for about fifteen more minutes, only making two turns—few enough that even *I* might have a chance of navigating my way out.

Eventually, we came to a stop in the middle of a tunnel that looked like every other deserted tunnel I'd seen so far. I looked in both directions, but couldn't see anything special about this spot.

Then Ethan muttered something. If I didn't know better, I would have sworn he said "Open sesame," but that must just have been the unsettling echoes.

A door-shaped opening appeared in the wall out of nowhere. I blinked.

"It's an illusion spell," Ethan said, a hint of pride in his voice. "No one traveling down this tunnel would have any idea the doorway was here."

He gestured me in with a dramatic sweep of his arm, and I gingerly stepped through the space where moments ago there had been a wall. I half expected the wall to reappear when I was partway through, but it didn't.

The room behind the illusionary wall didn't exactly make me jump for joy. It was about the size of Kimber's bedroom, and the only furniture was a pair of cots, a card table, and a pair of folding chairs, unless you counted the large steamer trunk in the corner as furniture. Other than the meager furniture, there was a kerosene lamp on the table and a couple of ceramic pots, one under each bed.

"Tell me those aren't chamber pots!" I said as Ethan lit the lamp.

He gave me a sheepish smile over his shoulder. "This is only temporary," he promised. "As you've seen, there are places underground that have electricity and running water, but those aren't as well hidden."

"What *is* this place?" I asked.

Ethan finished lighting the lamp and turned off his flashlight. "One of the things the Underground does is try to help people who have certain, er, political problems. Sometimes, they need a place to hide out awhile. It's not luxurious, but no one—and nothing—is going to find you here."

My eyes started to sting, and I bit my lip hard to keep it from quivering. This little hideout could have doubled for a dungeon in some old historical movie. The bleakness of the space hammered home the bleakness of my situation. I'd always coped with stress by putting off my reactions until after the crisis was over, but since I'd set foot in Avalon, there'd been one crisis after another, and my control was seriously slipping.

Ethan crossed the distance between us in one long stride, and before I had any idea what he was going to do, he had wrapped his arms around me and pulled me into a hug.

"Don't cry," he murmured into my hair. "It's just until your father gets out of jail. It won't be more than a night or two, tops. And I'm not going to abandon you down here. We're in this together."

I thought about what it would be like if Ethan left me alone here, and that was enough to break through my resistance to crying. As much as I didn't like to admit it, it felt good to have him hold me. Tears slid down my cheeks, and I clung to Ethan almost desperately. He scooped me up into his arms, then set me down on one of the cots, practically on his lap. He was still holding me, one hand cupping the side of my head so that my face was pressed up against his chest, the other rubbing up and down my back.

His caresses were distracting enough that I slowly forgot my distress at my surroundings. The air in the tunnels was chilly, but Ethan's body was warm and cozy. And he smelled yummy. He was wearing some kind of cologne. Subtle, but with a spicy, earthy scent. I inhaled deeply, partly to help dispel the tears, partly because I wanted another sniff of his scent.

He pulled me all the way onto his lap, and I didn't think this was a "please don't cry" hug anymore. I swallowed hard, my pulse racing as I wondered what was going to happen next. Should I just be sitting here with my face buried in his chest? Should I raise my head so he could kiss me?

Or should I already be halfway across the room telling him to keep his hands to himself?

I've never been an indecisive person before in my life, but Ethan had my brain cells so scrambled that I couldn't do anything but sit there, the wheels of my mind spinning uselessly. His chin rubbed back and forth across the top of my head, his hands kneading the muscles of my back. Under different cir-

cumstances, I might have thought he was trying to be soothing, but with my head against his chest like that, I could hear
the acceleration of his heartbeat. I practically held my breath in
anticipation, my pulse ratcheting up to match his. I pressed
closer to his warmth.

I guess I was pretty tense, because Ethan chuckled softly,
the sound making my insides go squishy.

"Relax, Dana," he said. "I don't bite. And I promise not to
ravish you."

The heat in my cheeks was practically enough to burn through
his shirt. Bad enough that I was so nervous, but even worse
that he *knew* it. And he was laughing at me.

Okay, he was laughing at me while he still had his arms
around me, but still . . .

I forced myself to release the breath I was holding. "I, um . . .
I'm only sixteen," I said. "This is kinda new to me." And I
wasn't sure how much an eighteen-year-old guy would expect
out of me. I mean, he was basically an adult, and I was . . . not.

"No worries," he assured me. "Sixteen isn't that far in my
past. I remember what it's like."

I sincerely doubted he'd been anything like me when he was
sixteen. He had too much easy confidence for me ever to believe
he'd been shy around girls. But it was nice of him to try to
make me feel better.

"I take it you don't have a boyfriend?" he asked.

I was afraid to speak because I might say something stupid, so
I just shook my head. He put a finger under my chin and tilted
my head up toward him. My breath caught in my throat, and a
pleasant shiver trailed down my spine. His eyes, usually so light
in color, were made dark by his enlarged pupils, and he was
looking at me like I was a piece of candy he was just dying to eat.

He lowered his head and pressed his lips against mine.

My brain went into complete overload. Ethan's lips were warm and moist as they caressed mine, and he tasted oddly of cherries. I tried to mirror his movements, but I felt completely awkward, sure I wasn't doing this right.

His tongue brushed against the seam of my lips until I opened my mouth. He deepened our kiss, and I practically drowned in the taste and the feel and the smell of him. But hot as he was, as attracted as I was to him, I wasn't sure I wanted to be going down this road. I was alone with him in a secluded cave, and I was kissing him, and I felt how much he was enjoying himself, and I didn't know him well enough to be sure he'd stop when I wanted him to.

Ethan broke off the kiss and gently stroked some hair away from my face. I was so confused and embarrassed I didn't want to meet his gaze, but I found I couldn't look away. He smiled at me.

"You need to stop thinking so much," he said in a hypnotic murmur as he leaned in for another kiss.

I don't know where I found the courage to speak, but I did. "My mom decided not to think too much when she was with my dad, and that didn't turn out so well."

Ethan chuckled and pulled back. "I beg to differ," he said, his hand tracing the contours of my face, then brushing lightly down the column of my neck. "I think it turned out very well indeed."

It was a good line, and I felt myself flush with pleasure. A part of me was jumping up and down and screaming "don't be such a baby!" It was, after all, just a kiss.

But I couldn't help remembering Kimber's warnings. Ethan was a player, and no matter how hot he was, I didn't want to be his toy.

"I don't think this is a good idea," I said, and I tried to slide off his lap.

I wasn't completely shocked when his hold on me tightened. "You don't have to be afraid of me," he said.

It was another good line. Striking at my vanity, daring me to prove I wasn't afraid. But it was much too obviously a line, and I wasn't about to fall for it.

"Let go of me." I said it calmly, though there was a hint of panic in my core. If he wanted to press the issue, I'd be in no position to stop him. So I guess technically, yeah, I was a bit afraid of him.

I was all tensed up for battle, so I was pleasantly surprised when Ethan slid me off his lap and put some distance between us. He didn't even look annoyed with me.

"Better?" he asked, with one of his lopsided grins.

I doubted he was used to being turned down by anyone, but it sure seemed like he was taking it in stride. Which made me feel guilty for being so suspicious. If he were really playing me, surely he wouldn't have let me go so easily.

I let out a frustrated huff. Maybe he was right that I should stop thinking so much. But I didn't know how to turn it off. I clasped my hands in my lap and stared at them, wondering what was wrong with me. When a guy like Ethan kissed me, I should turn into a puddle of goo, not analyze it half to death. Maybe I was frigid.

"Don't look so miserable," Ethan said. "You're allowed to say no."

I risked a glance at him, and still saw no sign of annoyance or frustration on his face.

Then—totally against my will, I swear—my eyes darted downward, and I could see that, while he wasn't acting angry or anything, he was still real eager for my no to change to a yes. Naturally, I looked away quickly, but my face heated with yet another blush.

In one of her sober moments, when my mom had insisted we have "the talk" despite the fact that I'd known about the birds and the bees practically forever, she'd warned me that boys like to claim they are in dire pain when they are that excited and you don't put out. Since I was sure Ethan had noticed the direction of my gaze, and he'd have to be blind not to see how hard I was blushing, I thought now would be the perfect time for him to start laying on a guilt trip. But he didn't.

Ethan laughed, but it was a warm, friendly sound with no hint of mockery in it. "It won't kill me," he said. "And remember, I promised I wasn't going to take advantage of you. I keep my promises. All I wanted was to kiss you."

"Really?" I asked, and I'm sure I sounded as incredulous as I felt. I glanced at him through my eyelashes.

"Why would you find that so hard to believe?"

"Well, uh. You're . . . uh, older than me. And, uh . . ." Oh God, please kill me now. I didn't want to be having this conversation, and I surely didn't want to be making such a fool of myself. But my brain hadn't recovered from its earlier shutdown, and I couldn't seem to get a coherent sentence out of my mouth.

Ethan put me out of my misery by saying what I'd been too prudish to say. "Just because I'm not a virgin doesn't mean kissing has become only a means to an end. Believe it or not, I actually find it's nice all by itself." He gave me one of those sexy, quirky grins of his, and it made my insides flutter.

"So all you want is a kiss?" I asked. A little voice in my head said I was heading for one of those slippery slopes. I told the little voice to shut up.

"Well, maybe more than *one*. But basically, yeah."

Still, I hesitated.

"Look," he said, "if I try to push you to do something you don't want, you'll balk, and then you'll never trust me again. I'm not going to risk that."

My shoulders sagged a bit. It got real tiring, being on the defensive all the time, always keeping my eyes open for potential threats. I'd had to do it for as long as I could remember, because there was no way I could trust my mom to protect us. I was sick of it, and part of the reason I'd come to Avalon was to try to get away from that constant, ponderous weight of responsibility. So to hell with Kimber's warnings, and to hell with my own misgivings!

I raised my chin and made myself look straight into Ethan's eyes as if I had all the courage in the world. "All right."

I didn't sit on Ethan's lap this time, just sidled up beside him and offered up my mouth. When his lips touched mine, I felt a jolt, kind of like an electric shock that ran all through my body, from the tips of my toes to the ends of my hair, and suddenly it was surprisingly easy to stop thinking and just feel.

He teased me with gentle kisses, and I gasped with pleasure. He didn't have to urge me to open my mouth this time, and his tongue darted in for a taste. Another jolt of that delicious electricity flowed through me, and I wrapped my arms around his neck, delighting in the taste and feel of him. My limbs felt all tingly, and it was like a layer of fog shrouded my head.

I breathed in Ethan's scent, relished the warmth of his body, devoured his cherry-tasting kisses, and my common sense didn't have a thing to say about it. Somehow, I ended up lying down on the cot, my head on the pillow while Ethan bent over me, his chest against mine. In a distant corner of my mind,

I noticed his weight was pressing the cameo into my skin, and that it was once again strangely warm. Then he started stroking up and down my side over my shirt, and I stopped thinking at all. He was keeping his distance from anything . . . sensitive, but my body was fully aware of the possibilities. If my mouth hadn't been otherwise occupied, I might have asked him to break his word.

His tongue began to slide in and out of my mouth in a suggestive rhythm that actually made me groan. My every nerve ending tingled, and warmth gathered in my center, and it felt so, so good. . . .

Like I said, I wasn't really *thinking*, and my head was foggy at best, but I guess on some subconscious level, my guard never goes down completely. The tingling, the warmth, the foggy head . . . they all reminded me of something. They reminded me of how I'd felt when I'd drunk Kimber's extra-strong posset.

The realization was like a splash of cold water, and the fog dissipated like it had never been there. There was most definitely something wrong with this picture. I couldn't have gone from the bundle of raw nerves I'd been a few moments ago to this relaxed, comfortable, sensual woman I was now. Not without some outside help, that is. I pushed on Ethan's chest, and was relieved that he actually stopped. My breath came short, and my pulse was still rocketing, but I knew for sure Ethan had done something. Other than kiss me, that is.

"What did you do to me?" I demanded, struggling to sit up.

Ethan didn't even try to pretend he didn't know what I meant. "Take it easy," he said. "It was just a little spell to help you relax."

I was on my feet moments later, staring at Ethan in absolute horror. "You mean you have some kind of a roofie spell?" I cried. Humiliation heated my face, made me want to curl up in a ball and die. Could I *be* any more naive? Why hadn't I listened to Kimber?

He frowned, like he was actually surprised by my reaction. "No. Nothing like that." He stood up and took a step toward me.

I didn't think then. I just reacted with all the hurt and fury and, yes, fear in my body. When he reached for me, I jerked my knee up, and I got him just where it hurt most. He doubled over, clutching his privates. Shaking with delayed reaction, I grabbed the kerosene lamp and dashed out into the tunnel, hoping against hope that my sense of direction for once wouldn't fail me.

chapter thirteen

Tears flowed down my cheeks as I ran, trying to keep count of the tunnels as I passed so I'd turn down the right one, while also trying to put as much distance as possible between me and that horrible room before Ethan recovered. I didn't even bother dashing the tears away, just kept running until my lungs begged for oxygen and the muscles in my legs burned. I made the two turns that should then put me on a path straight to civilization, but I saw no sign of the nightclub and the stairway to the surface, nor did I hear the distant echo of voices. I kept running, hoping I'd just misjudged the distance, but there was still nothing. I tried doubling back to see if I'd made a wrong turn, but I'd lost track of how far I'd come and only ended up getting myself more confused.

Panic flickered at the edges of my mind as I realized I was now officially lost. I kept running, trying to retrace my steps, trying to keep moving so I wouldn't have to face the panic that continued to build in my brain.

Eventually, I had to stop, exhaustion winning out over horror. I collapsed to the tunnel floor and sucked in great gulps of air, so winded that for a moment I thought I was going to throw up.

That nightclub was down here somewhere, and it couldn't be all that far away, I told myself. Plus, Ethan had mentioned there were other populated areas down here. Even if I couldn't find the nightclub, I should eventually be able to find some sign of civilization. Just because I was lost didn't mean I was going to die, no matter how . . . alarming it was.

With a groan, I forced myself to my feet. I was so tired and wrung out I didn't know how I could face the seemingly impossible task of getting myself out of here. But it wasn't like I had much of a choice. I glanced at the lantern and shuddered to realize the kerosene wouldn't last forever.

I trudged for what seemed like miles, trying to keep going in a straight line on the assumption that if I kept going straight, eventually I'd get to the other side of the mountain and there'd be an exit. But whenever I started to feel like I was making progress, the tunnel would dead end, or take a sudden, sharp turn. For all I knew, I was going in circles.

My feet and legs ached, and the kerosene was looking dangerously low, and I was so scared I could barely function. I stopped in the middle of a corridor that looked just like all the others, and I sat with my back against the wall, giving myself a minute or two of precious rest before I hurled myself back out into the darkness again.

I drew my knees up to my chest and let my head rest against them. I figured crying would be a reasonable thing to do right about now, but my eyes remained dry. I'd hit a kind of emotional overload, and I felt numb and listless.

"Can you forgive me enough to let me get you out of here?" Ethan asked, and at first I assumed I'd inadvertently drifted off to sleep.

I lifted my head, and there he was, about ten feet away from me, sitting with his back to the wall just like I was. He had a flashlight in his hand, and he barely resembled the cocky, cheerful Fae I'd come to know. His shoulders were slumped, his head bowed, the expression on his face bleak.

Obviously, I had to be dreaming, one of those wishful-thinking dreams. Though I had to admit, it felt awfully real. "This *has* to be a dream," I mumbled out loud. "There's no way you could have found me."

"Not if I'd lost you in the first place," he said, fidgeting with the flashlight, turning it round and round in his hands. "I run fast, and you were carrying a light, so I was able to catch up with you before you got too far away. I figured you needed time to cool off, so I kept my distance until now."

You mean you kept your distance until you were sure I knew I couldn't get out of here by myself, I thought but didn't say. I decided this wasn't a dream after all, but I had approximately zero desire to talk to Ethan right now, so I just stared at him coldly.

The cold stare might have been more effective if he were actually looking at me, but he was still fascinated with that flashlight.

"The spell didn't take away your free will, Dana," he said to the flashlight. "If it had, then you wouldn't have been able to snap out of it. It was just a simple calming spell. It's not like it made you do something you hadn't already agreed to."

"Okay," I said, forgetting my plan not to speak to him, "so

instead of it being like a roofie, it's kind of like getting your date drunk in hopes that you'll get lucky."

His head snapped up, and he looked at me for the first time. "It's not that either!" he said, and there was some heat in his words. That seemed to embarrass him, and he looked away again. His voice softened. "I just thought you'd enjoy it more if you weren't so nervous. I get that it was a stupid thing to do. But there wasn't any malice in it, and I had no intention of taking advantage of you. I'm sorry I was an idiot."

My breath whooshed out on a sigh. He looked so dejected it was hard to doubt that he meant what he said. But I wasn't even close to ready to forgive him yet. "You remember how you said if you tried anything, I'd never trust you again? Well, as far as I'm concerned, you tried something. And I don't trust you."

He actually flinched, and I almost felt bad about it. Almost.

"Understood," he said. "But I presume you'll accept my help getting out of here even so."

"And go where?"

"Wherever you want."

I chewed that one over for a bit. I sure as hell didn't want to go back to that nasty little room in the tunnels, but I didn't want to find myself stuck with Aunt Grace, either. Not until I'd had time to consider my options, at least. I had no money or ID, so I still needed help, even though at this point I'd have preferred not to have to depend on anyone. Ethan had just forcibly reminded me that the only person I could ever truly depend on was myself.

"Could you put me up at a hotel incognito?" I asked. It wasn't what you'd call a long-term solution—I *really* hoped I'd finally be able to get to my dad tomorrow—but it was better than hiding underground or sleeping on Kimber's sofa while wondering when Aunt Grace would pop in for a surprise inspection.

I could tell Ethan didn't like the suggestion one bit, but he answered me mildly enough. "You'd be a lot safer in a less public place."

"If you think I'm staying in that little rat hole of a room, you're nuts. So unless you're going to keep me there against my will, it's a hotel or nothing."

He heaved a dramatic sigh. "All right, then. I know a place that's a bit out of the way. It's less secure than I'd like, but . . ." He shrugged.

With a groan of pain, I forced myself to my feet. "Lead the way."

The inn Ethan took me to was tiny, a bed and breakfast rather than an actual hotel. It was built straight into the side of the mountain, and made rather a pretty picture with ivy clinging to its walls and window boxes bursting with flowers—but no roses of any color, which told me the inn was probably human-run. I was sick of the Fae in general, so I was glad.

Ethan made me wait outside while he got a room. He didn't think it would be a good idea to have me come face-to-face with the innkeeper, and I supposed he had a point. I was a little young to be renting a room in a B&B, and I was American to boot. That would make me just a bit conspicuous.

It was getting close to midnight, and the streets of Avalon were quiet. There were no pedestrians, and only occasionally did a car pass by. Obviously, the nightlife in Avalon was uninspiring.

While I waited for Ethan to tell me it was okay to come in, I crossed the street and once more stood at the guardrail, looking out into the distance past Avalon. It was much harder to see the shifts in the dark, but the way the lights in the distance winked on and off depending on where I focused my gaze, proved they hadn't miraculously gone away—or been an illusion cast by Ethan.

I turned away when the view started to make me dizzy again. Ethan was just coming out the front door of the inn, and I saw the momentary alarm on his face when I wasn't standing exactly where he'd last put me. Then his eyes found me, and he let out a sigh of relief.

He darted across the street to join me, not trying to get too close. He was very aware that he'd taken up permanent residence in my dog house, and though he deserved it, I couldn't help missing the easy humor and flirting. I think his smiles and jokes had helped me keep the worst of my fear at bay, and I wished I could have that back.

Ethan leaned against the railing, looking out into Faerie, and I leaned my back against it, looking at the inn.

"I had to wake the innkeeper up to get a room," Ethan said. "We should give him a quarter hour to get back to bed before we go in."

I snorted. "What makes you think we're going in together?"

"Because I'm not putting you in that room until I've checked it out myself and made absolutely sure it's safe. And I've got the key."

I arched an eyebrow at him. "You think maybe Aunt Grace is hiding under one of the beds?"

It was pretty dark, so I couldn't be sure, but I thought he actually blushed at that.

"Guess I'm being paranoid," he said. But I couldn't help wondering if he'd had hopes for what would happen if we were alone in a cozy bedroom together.

I held out my hand. "Give me the key."

He put something in my hand, but it wasn't the key, it was a cell phone. "I programmed my home number into it. And Kimber's home and cell are both there, too. If you have any trouble whatsoever, or if something makes you nervous, give one of us a call. Preferably me, since I can spell myself invisible and get here without leading anyone else to you. But I'll understand if I'm not your first choice after . . ." He shrugged.

"Thanks," I said, tucking the cell phone into my pants pocket. "Now give me the key."

There was no missing how reluctant he was, but he handed the key over anyway. "It's room 201, right at the head of the stairs. Please don't leave the room until you've heard from Kimber or me. If your dad is still in jail, we'll try to find a better place for you to stay. This inn is pretty out of the way, but I had to secure the room with my credit card. If someone gets hold of credit card records—which doesn't seem like much of a stretch for Grace—then my putting a hotel room on it will be like a big, blinking billboard shouting 'Dana is here!' "

Oh, goodie. One more thing to worry about. But tonight, I was too exhausted to waste energy on any more worrying.

I gave Ethan a brief nod in place of a good-bye, then crossed the street and went into the inn without a backward glance.

I slept like the dead that night. Which was a good thing, because if I hadn't, I'd have been obsessing, but not about the right thing.

I figured I had every right to obsess about my situation,

about my fears for the future, about whom I should trust. But when I woke up the next morning, what was the first thing I found myself thinking about? Ethan's kiss. Has anyone seen my sense of proportion anywhere? Because I'd obviously lost it.

I tried not to think about it as I did the pre-coffee shuffle-walk to the bathroom. Then I tried not to think of it as I showered and brushed my teeth. I tried once again when I was getting dressed—still wearing Kimber's castoffs, because, of course, I had nothing to my name.

Obviously, trying not to think about it, to wonder how much of my enjoyment had come from me and how much from the spell, to wonder whether I'd overreacted, wasn't going to work when my mind had nothing else to focus on. So I decided to focus my thoughts elsewhere.

I dug Ethan's cell phone out of my pocket, then stared at it for a long, indecisive moment before dialing my mother's number. Yeah, it was oh-dark-thirty back in the States, but I didn't think she'd mind. I also didn't think she'd be able to help me—it's hard to get a heck of a lot accomplished when your brain is sloshing around in a pool of alcohol. But it would be nice to hear a familiar voice, even if she did spend the entire call screaming at me, which I fully expected.

Foolishly optimistic of me to think I'd get an answer. She was probably pretty upset about me running away like that, and I knew what my mom did when she was upset. I wondered how long this bender was going to last.

I hung up without leaving a message. What would be the point?

I glanced at the clock. It was a little after nine, and I had no idea when I'd be hearing from Ethan and Kimber. Kimber had told me my dad was coming up before the Council sometime today. It was too early to hope he'd be home by now, even if the Council saw him first thing.

I reached under the neck of my shirt and ran my fingers over the cameo. In all the ... excitement last night, I'd forgotten about how it had heated up once again. It felt cool and normal now. Maybe it was like a mood ring. I tried to think of all the times I'd felt the strange heat, and a pattern started to emerge: every time it had heated up, someone near me was using magic. I hadn't noticed it *every* time magic was used, but then it was only in contact with my skin when I tucked it under the collar of my shirt.

I frowned. The very first time I'd noticed the cameo getting hot was when I'd been singing in the cell beneath Lachlan's bakery. Maybe there had been magic at work then and I just hadn't known about it. Or maybe I was just making up a pattern where one didn't exist. After all, I couldn't specifically remember whether the cameo had been over or under my shirt all those times I hadn't felt the heat when magic was used.

Even though I'd just decided it was too early even to hope my dad was out of jail, I picked up the phone again and dialed his number. After all, it didn't hurt to try.

He answered on the third ring. "Hello?"

I was so surprised that for a moment I couldn't answer. Had I really just gotten that lucky? Or had the story about him being in jail been a big fat lie? "Hi, Dad," I said when I found my voice.

"Dana!" His cry was so loud I had to hold the phone away from my ear. "Where are you? I've been worried sick about you!"

I swallowed hard, wishing I could quiet the alarm bells that were clanging in my head.

"Aunt Grace locked me up in a dungeon," I said. It was a

slight exaggeration. The room she'd locked me in had been quite comfortable, but still . . .

Dad sighed heavily. "Dana, honey, I'm so sorry. I should have known she'd pull something like that, but I sometimes have a blind spot where she's concerned. She wouldn't have hurt you, though. That I'm sure of. And I would have found you before long and gotten you out of there."

"Well someone else got me out of there first, and I have to admit I'm feeling gun-shy."

"I can't imagine how you wouldn't after what you've been through. Tell me where you are, and I'll come get you immediately."

I yearned to just blurt out my location, to let my dad come get me and take care of me, make all the bad stuff go away. But, biological connection or not, he was a stranger to me, and I wanted some answers before I ran headlong into his arms. "Aunt Grace told me you were in jail." I tried not to make it sound like some kind of accusation.

"I'm afraid that's true," he admitted. "I suspect Grace engineered it, to make sure she could get to you before I could."

A lump formed in my throat, because instinct—or cynicism—told me I wasn't going to like the answer to my next question. "When did you get out?"

"Just yesterday," he said, and despite having anticipated the answer, my knees gave out and I sat heavily on the edge of the bed. "I've been searching for you since the moment I was free," Dad continued. "Grace said Lachlan was attacked and you were kidnapped. I knew bringing you here would cause some drama, but never anything like this. I'm so sorry."

Yesterday, I had told Kimber a secret I'd never told anyone

before. I'd actually allowed myself to *trust* her. And the whole time, she'd been lying to me, just pretending to be my friend so she could keep me away from my father. The knowledge made me ache from head to toe. All my habitual caution, and I'd fallen for her act hook, line, and sinker.

"Yeah, that's pretty much what happened," I said, my voice raspy with the tears I refused to shed.

"Are you all right?" he asked, sounding exactly how a concerned dad was supposed to sound. Was his concern an act, too? Would anyone in all of Avalon tell me the truth about anything?

"I'm fine," I lied.

Dad hesitated. Any idiot would be able to tell from my voice that I was anything but fine, but I wasn't ready to talk about it now. Maybe I never would be. Thankfully, he let it pass.

"Let me come get you," he said. "We can talk more in person."

"I'm at the Stone's Throw Inn," I said. "Room 201."

"I'll be there in fifteen minutes at the most."

"Okay." I closed Ethan's phone without saying good-bye, leaving it on the nightstand.

chapter fourteen

The fifteen minutes I spent waiting for my dad to arrive provided me with ample time to wonder how my meeting him was going to shake out. Everyone I'd met in Avalon so far had lied to me, and in a way, my dad was one of them. After all, he'd sent me the cameo without telling me wearing it would be like saying I root for Team Seelie. And I'd always wondered why he'd sent for me as he did without once asking if my mom was okay with it. I'd been willing to overlook that little detail because I'd wanted what he was offering so badly, but now I thought I should have asked more questions.

I thought I'd hear my dad's footsteps on the wooden stairs before he arrived at my door, but I didn't. His sudden knock made me jump and gasp, and at first I didn't answer him, my feet practically frozen to the floor.

"Dana?" he asked. "Are you all right, honey?"

I let out the breath I hadn't realized I was holding and wiped my suddenly sweaty palms on my pants. Then I unlocked the door and swung it open wide, getting my first glimpse of my father.

The Fae, once they've reached adulthood, at least, are age-less. Intellectually, I knew that. But it didn't lessen the shock of opening the door to a man I knew was my father and seeing someone who could have passed for twenty-five.

He had a typical Fae build, tall and slender, but he exuded a sense of wiry strength. His hair was very blond, cropped short around his aristocratic face. His eyes were the same cold blue as Grace's—and mine, for that matter—but there was a kind of . . . weight to them that made him look older. Despite the youthful appearance of his face, his eyes were not those of a young man.

"Dana," he said, his voice sounding almost awed as he looked me up and down. I felt like I was being inspected, but since I was doing the same to him, I could hardly complain.

For a moment, I thought he was going to hug me, and I tensed. I'm not a real touchy-feely person in the best of times, which these weren't.

I was more relieved than I could say when he reached out his hand for me to shake instead. Ah, the famed Fae reserve. I'd almost forgotten about it, since Ethan didn't fit the mold.

I shied away from thoughts of Ethan.

"Hi, Dad," I said, feeling inexplicably weird calling him that. It hadn't felt so weird on the phone.

"My poor child," he said softly, giving my hand a firm squeeze. "I can't imagine what you've been through these last few days."

I shuddered. No, he probably couldn't.

"Let's get you home," he continued. "I've collected your suit-case and your laptop from Grace." He smiled. "I suspect you'll be more comfortable in your own clothes."

"Before we go," I said, "I'd like to ask you something."

He nodded gravely. "All right."

"Why were you so eager for me to come to Avalon?"

He blinked in surprise. "I discover I have a daughter whom I've never met, and it's a *surprise* that I would want to meet you?" he asked incredulously.

"But you never even asked about my mom. You never thought it was funny that you only ever talked to *me* about the plans. There's more to it than just wanting to meet me." My throat tightened, but I think I managed to keep the pain of that declaration out of my voice.

Dad sighed. "Dana, I knew what it meant that your mother disappeared from my life without telling me she was pregnant. I knew it meant she wanted to keep you away from me. From the first time you and I talked, I knew you were going behind her back, and she would have stopped you if she'd known."

It sounded plausible, I had to admit. But if there was one thing I knew for sure now, it was that all my mom's warnings about my difficult place in Avalon politics were true. Maybe my dad really was eager to meet his long-lost daughter just for my own sake, but I didn't think so.

"So your wanting to meet me has nothing to do with you wanting to be Consul and me maybe being a Faeriewalker."

Ethan and Kimber had lied about a lot of things, but I could see right away from the look on his face that this wasn't one of them. This silence was even longer than the last. When he finally broke the silence, I could tell he was picking his words with great care.

"I understand that my position might make it hard for you to trust my motives. Yes, I would like to be Consul. But I wanted to meet you because you're my daughter, not because you were part of my political ambitions."

My throat tightened again. He was telling me exactly what I wanted to hear. I wanted it to be true so, so badly.

Dad pursed his lips. "I'm going to make an educated guess that it was the so-called Student Underground who kidnapped you. Am I right?"

I gave him a skeptical look. "Since I called from Ethan's cell phone, I'd say that guess was *very* educated."

He nodded. "Indeed. And how much did Ethan tell you about himself and his Underground?"

Oh, God. Please tell me I wasn't about to hear something else I'd rather not know!

"I'll take your silence to mean you don't know much," Dad said. "Ethan is the son of Alistair Leigh, who is the leading Unseelie candidate for Consul. Naturally, Ethan and his Underground support Alistair's candidacy, so whatever he may have told you about me could well be colored by his own political leanings."

Yep, that was something else I'd rather not have known.

So *that's* why Ethan was so interested in a not-particularly-attractive, half-blood high-school girl. Not because he'd fallen in love with me at first sight. Bad enough to think he'd wanted me as just another notch on his bedpost, but to think he'd tried to seduce me for cold-blooded political purposes was unbearable.

How I wished I'd held strong last night and not let him kiss me. My mouth tasted sour, and at that moment I pretty much hated him. He'd ruined my first kiss!

I remembered how hard Kimber had tried to convince me that Ethan wasn't good for me. She'd even told me he was attracted to my power. She'd tried her best to warn me without actually explaining what she was warning me about. Too bad she'd been busy stabbing me in the back while she'd been "helping" me.

I swallowed the lump in my throat, determined to deal with

my heartbreak later. I couldn't put my faith in Ethan or Kimber anymore; I'd never even considered putting my faith in Aunt Grace; and even if I'd wanted to put my faith in my mom, she wasn't answering the phone. There was a limit to how much faith I could put in *anyone*, but my father, the stranger, sounded like the best deal available.

"Can we get out of here now?" I asked, and my dad, with a look of sympathy in his eyes, agreed.

The Stone's Throw Inn was situated relatively low on the slopes of the mountain, and I was glad Dad had brought his car, a racy little red number that I guessed was an Italian sports car of some sort. You know: the kind that wouldn't be caught dead doing something so crass as putting the make and model where just anyone could see them. The bucket seats were so low I felt like my butt would hit the pavement if we went over a speed bump. Not that I'd seen any sign of speed bumps anywhere in Avalon, but you get the idea.

Dad laughed as he climbed in. "I know, it's a bit excessive for use in Avalon," he said, patting the dashboard like it was his pet dog. "I'd love to be able to drive out into the mortal world and see how fast it can really go."

The engine purred as he started the car and pulled out of his parking space onto the steep, curving road that would take us higher up the mountain.

"I think you'd get a handful of speeding tickets before you ever found out," I muttered, feeling the car's quiet power as it accelerated effortlessly despite the steepness of the road.

He laughed. "Most likely."

I didn't know what the speed limit was in Avalon—there

never seemed to be any signs—but I bet my dad was breaking it as he zipped up the road. I tried not to white-knuckle the door handle as we zoomed around the curves. In an ill-advised moment, I glanced out the side window. On this bright, clear day I could see for miles. Unfortunately, I was seeing miles and miles of deep green forest. Faerie.

I turned away without blinking. The too-fast car ride was hard enough on my stomach without adding the nausea-inducing view through the Glimmerglass. When I faced front again, I caught my dad's sideways glance, and I fully expected him to ask me what I saw. But he didn't, and I was relieved. I really didn't want to talk about the whole Faeriewalker thing right now.

Dad's house was nowhere near as quaint as Aunt Grace's. The entire bottom floor was a two-car garage—but in the space that would hold the second car, there was a horse stall instead. It was empty at the moment, the floor clear of straw, but a faint barn scent in the air told me the stall wasn't just for show. Did that mean Dad made frequent trips into Faerie?

We had to take a spiral staircase to get up to the second floor, where the actual living area began. Moving in and out of this place must be a nightmare. (Says the girl who's had to go through the torture of moving enough times to know.) Even carrying a suitcase up and down those stairs would be something of a challenge.

When we emerged from the staircase, we were in a spacious living room, with a tiny kitchen tucked into one corner. The entire wall facing the street was floor-to-ceiling windows. I tried to avoid seeing the view—you know, that whole seeing into two worlds thing—though I guessed it was spectacular.

Instead, I looked around the living room, trying to get a sense of the man who was my father from the look of his home.

The stereotype of the Fae is that they're old-fashioned (mostly because the vast majority of them are about a jillion years old). Grace's house and Kimber's apartment had both fit the stereotype with their antiques and conservative decor. Dad's place did not look like the kind of house a Fae should live in. Not with those big, modern windows, or the modern art on the wall, or the Danish modern furniture. I'd always hated Danish modern, but that was my mom's favorite, and I was beginning to guess why.

"The master suite is on the second floor," my dad said, "and there's a guest room and small library on the third floor." Apparently he didn't consider the garage a floor. "Would you like to change clothes and freshen up? Then maybe we can get to know each other better."

"That would be great," I said, trying to sound chipper, though now that I was here I felt nervous and awkward.

"Make yourself at home," Dad said, gesturing at a door that I'd thought was a coat closet but that turned out to be a stairway. I guess since the Fae weren't big on coats, they didn't need coat closets.

I stopped with my foot on the first step, turning to look at my dad over my shoulder. "You're not going to lock me in, are you?"

He looked shocked by the suggestion. "Of course not! You're my daughter, not my prisoner. And I am not your aunt Grace."

I sure hoped not. I nodded and started up the stairs, though I have to admit I was very tense as I climbed. When I made it to the third floor (or fourth floor, depending on your point of view), I saw that the guest room was about as inviting as the living room had been. Sparsely furnished, everything with that plain, stripped-down look of Danish modern, and instead of a cushy bed, there was a hard futon.

I felt better about the room when I saw my suitcase and backpack sitting neatly in the corner.

Never before had I been so glad to see my own clothing. I picked out my favorite pair of cargo pants and a heavyweight sweatshirt that might be enough to counter the chill of an Avalon early summer day. And I was more than ready to change into fresh underwear, since the ones I was wearing were still damp from being washed in the sink last night.

Feeling a bit paranoid, I didn't close the bedroom door, afraid that if I did, I'd be locked in despite Dad's promise. However, I did close the bathroom door most of the way as I hastily changed. I kept listening hard for the terrible click of a door closing, of a lock turning, but it didn't happen.

When I was finished changing, I brushed my hair and secured it in a ponytail, then dabbed on some clear lip gloss. A light dusting of blush on my cheeks, and I looked almost like myself again, except for the haunted expression in my eyes.

Oh, well. I had a right to look haunted.

Feeling much more comfortable in my own clothes, I headed back downstairs to face my dad once more.

He was sitting on the sofa, which faced an oversized plasma TV instead of the view, thank goodness. An ice bucket on legs stood off to the side, and there were a pair of champagne flutes on the coffee table. I must have looked as surprised as I felt, because Dad answered my question without me having to ask.

"It's not every day a man gets to meet his long-lost daughter," he said. "A celebration is in order, don't you think?"

"Um, I'm only sixteen." The excuse hadn't worked with Kimber and her posset, and it didn't work with Dad either.

"I guarantee we won't be arrested by the drinking-age police. Now come join me. We have a lot to talk about."

At this point, I didn't much want to talk about *anything*. I wanted to pretend for a while that this trip had gone exactly as planned, that I'd come straight here from the airport and this was the beginning of a better life.

I took a seat on the other end of the sofa as Dad went about opening the champagne. I was tensed and ready for the pop of the cork, but that didn't stop me from jumping anyway. The corners of Dad's eyes crinkled, but he didn't full-out laugh at me.

He poured us each a glass, then handed one to me. I looked at it doubtfully. The milk, honey, and nutmeg in Kimber's posset had toned down the taste of the whiskey, but this was pure champagne. I know a lot of other kids my age would be thrilled to get to drink something with alcohol in it. But those kids hadn't lived with my mom.

"Drink up, Daughter," Dad said.

It shows the state of mind I was in that I couldn't force myself to take a sip until after I'd seen him drink. Why I'd suspect my father of wanting to poison me was anyone's guess. Any day now, I was going to start worrying that "They" were watching my every move. I rolled my eyes at myself and took a tentative taste of the champagne.

The posset had been surprisingly tasty. The champagne . . . not so much. I couldn't help wrinkling my nose at the flavor, though I suppose it was rather rude.

"It's an acquired taste," my father told me.

I put the glass down on the coffee table. "It's not a taste I'm real anxious to acquire."

"And why is that?" he asked, with a tilt of his head.

I looked away from him and gave him a half shrug. "Well, you know my mom."

A beat of silence. "What about her?"

She'd been a lush since my earliest memory. It had never occurred to me that there might have been a time in her past when she hadn't been. I swallowed hard.

"Didn't she drink too much when you were dating her?"

"Ah," Dad said, and he put his own glass down. "I understand. She drank no more and no less than most women her age." He sighed. "But I'm not entirely surprised she developed a problem with alcohol. There is no place on earth quite like Avalon, and I imagine cutting oneself off from it entirely would be . . . difficult on someone who'd spent all her life here."

His words detonated like a bomb somewhere inside me.

My mom hadn't been an alcoholic when she lived in Avalon. She'd left Avalon not because she *wanted* to, but because she was determined to protect me from the hell that was Avalon politics. And leaving her home had been so hard on her, she'd started to drink too much.

Oh, God. All these years I'd spent despising her, blaming her . . . And it was *my* fault she was a drunk.

chapter fifteen

Either I was hiding what I felt better than I thought, or my dad wasn't very observant. He'd shattered my entire view of my mom with just a few casual words, and he didn't even notice.

"Well, if you don't want the champagne, how about some tea?" he asked.

I didn't want tea. I didn't want anything, except, maybe, not to have heard what I'd just heard. But I nodded anyway, and Dad headed off to the kitchen, giving me a few minutes to collect myself. It wasn't nearly enough time, but I'd been dealt enough shocks in the last few days that the pain turned to numbness pretty quickly. I didn't think the numbness would last forever, and the fallout when it wore off was probably going to be nasty, but for now, I was grateful for it.

The phone rang, the sound so mundane that it helped draw me out of my head and back into the real world. I heard my father answer from the kitchen.

"Yes, she's here," he said, and he sounded really amused. There was a silence, during which the tea kettle started to whistle. "Of course I did," my father said, and the kettle's whistle cut off abruptly. "What kind of a fool would I be if I didn't?" He paused for whoever was on the other end to say something, and then he laughed. The sound grated on my nerves for some reason I couldn't define. Maybe because there was a tinge of nastiness in it. Or maybe that was just my imagination. "I'll give her your warmest regards," my father said, "but I sincerely doubt she wishes to speak with you right now. It was good of you to call and check on her."

There was a beep of the phone turning off, and then some clattering around in the kitchen. Dad came back into the living room with a tea service on a tray. As a general rule, the people of Avalon weren't as British as I'd been expecting, but they did seem to love their tea.

He had already poured two cups, with their telltale little specks on the bottom that said he'd never dream of using a tea bag. I was feeling miserable enough that the tea was more appealing than usual. I plunked two lumps of sugar into my cup and stirred the contents around absently.

"Was that Ethan?" I asked, because when I added up the half of the conversation I'd heard, it only made sense if he'd been talking to Ethan.

"Yes," my father said. "He was calling to make sure you'd made it home all right." His smile turned sardonic. "And to find out whether I'd told you who he was, of course. Was I correct in assuming you didn't wish to speak to him?"

I nodded and finally stopped stirring my tea. The sugar had dissolved long ago. "Would you have let me talk to him if I'd wanted to?"

His eyebrows arched in surprise. "Of course. I'm not fond of him, and I'm even less fond of his father, but I won't dictate whom you may or may not speak to."

I cocked my head at him. So far, he wasn't seeming very dad-like. "There are plenty of fathers who wouldn't let their sixteen-year-old daughters talk to guys they don't approve of."

He put his teacup down and turned to face me fully, his expression grave. "You are not a child, and I will endeavor never to treat you as one," he told me.

I almost argued with him. At my age, I spent most of the time trying to convince people I *wasn't* just a kid, but right now, I wanted to be. I wanted to be taken care of, to have the responsibilities taken off my shoulders, to have someone else make all the tough decisions.

If that's what you really wanted, a little voice in my head whispered, *you could have stayed with Aunt Grace in the first place. Then you wouldn't have had to make any decisions at all.*

"Do you have any questions for me?" my dad asked. "Avalon tends to overwhelm the average tourist; I can't imagine what you must be thinking after everything that's happened."

I'd passed "overwhelmed" long ago. But despite all my turmoil, I did have some questions. First and foremost: "What's to stop Aunt Grace or Ethan from kidnapping me again?"

"My resources are considerable," he said. "You'll always be safe in this house. Neither Grace nor Ethan is strong enough to overcome the spells I've placed on it."

"What about Lachlan?"

Dad dismissed him with a wave of his hand. "Lachlan is a non-issue. He may be a physically impressive specimen, and I would not wish to face him in combat, but it would take something more sophisticated than brute force to breach my defenses." His voice held a hint of contempt that I didn't understand.

"But he is Fae, right? Even though he doesn't look it?"

Dad didn't actually wrinkle his nose, but his facial expression wasn't far from it. "He is a creature of Faerie, but he is of the lower orders. His sort is not customarily permitted in Avalon, but with Grace championing him . . ."

Apparently, Dad was a snob. Lachlan might have been my jailor, but he was still one of the nicest people I'd met in Avalon. I felt almost offended by Dad's attitude. I must have looked it, too, because he traded the nose-in-the-air expression for one of rueful amusement.

"We are a very class-conscious bunch, we Fae," he said. The amusement faded. "You must understand that although Avalon has officially seceded from Faerie, the Fae are still Fae. We recognize one another as Seelie or Unseelie, even though technically we don't owe allegiance to the Courts anymore. And in Faerie, the concept of all men being equal is so ridiculous as to be almost sacrilege. The Sidhe—what you think of when you think of Fae—are the aristocracy of Faerie. Lachlan is not Sidhe. I am."

I narrowed my eyes at him, still feeling defensive on Lachlan's behalf. "So what you're saying is that because you're Sidhe, you're better than him?"

I expected him to say something placating. Instead, he just looked me in the eye and said, "Yes."

I blinked in shock. There were a lot of people in this world who thought they were better than everyone else, but I couldn't ever remember hearing anyone actually *admit* they felt that way.

"Lachlan is a troll," my father continued. "He wears a human glamour—if he didn't, even Grace wouldn't have been able to bring him in legally—but that doesn't change what he is beneath."

I felt sick to my stomach. Dad wasn't just a snob—he was a bigot. I had wanted to like him, maybe even love him eventually, but I couldn't imagine liking a bigot.

Dad leaned toward me, and it was all I could do not to lean away in response.

"The Fae of Avalon play at being human," he told me, "but we're not. We will always be creatures of Faerie first, citizens of Avalon second. Some young bucks like Alistair Leigh think they can change that, but the Fae do not change. We will never be an egalitarian people, nor will we ever break free from the Courts.

"We belong to the Court of our parents, and we belong to that Court as long as we live. Anyone who says otherwise is either deluded or naive."

I had a feeling there was a subtle message in my father's words. *We belong to the Court of our parents.* In other words, even though I'm half human, I "belong" to the Seelie Court. Of course, he'd already given me that message when he'd sent me the cameo. I just hadn't been able to read it.

"That is the reason tensions always run so high when it is time for a Fae to take the position of Consul," my father continued. "Whether the Consul is Seelie or Unseelie matters little to Avalon's human citizens, but to the Fae . . ." He shuddered theatrically, then flashed me another rueful smile. "I'd like to hate your mother for spiriting you away, not even letting me know you exist." The smile faded, and he sighed. "But try as I might, I can't blame her."

I didn't know what to say to that, so I didn't say anything at all. I could blame my mom for a lot of things she'd done, but trying to keep me out of Avalon wasn't one of them. If I'd known the truth from the beginning, I never would have come.

I leaned forward to put my cup, still half-full, on the table. As if it had a will of its own, the cameo slid out from beneath my shirt. I was sure my dad noticed, though he didn't say anything. It would probably have been a good time to confront him about sending it to me without explaining the significance, but I just didn't want to deal with that bit of subtle deceit right now.

"I never did finish answering your question," my father said, and I was relieved he didn't force the issue of the cameo. "You are protected in the house because of the strength of my spells. Outside the house, you are vulnerable, so you must never leave the house alone."

My heart sank. Maybe Dad was going to keep me prisoner just like Aunt Grace.

"I will hire a . . . companion for you," he continued. "When you leave the house, you must be with me or with your companion."

"By 'companion,' you mean, like, a bodyguard?" That idea was just too weird for words.

"Something like that, yes. It's for your own safety."

Yeah, and it was supposedly for my own good that Grace had locked me up. However, I knew an argument I couldn't win when I heard it, so I didn't bother trying. At least I wouldn't be cooped up all day anymore. Maybe I'd even get to see some of the *nice* spots in Avalon instead of exploring dark, creepy tunnels in the heart of the mountain.

That idea perked me up a bit, and I managed a tentative smile for my dad. I wasn't too happy about the whole bigotry thing, but other than that, Dad seemed relatively nice. I had my own clothes, and an almost-comfortable room to call my own. And I would finally have a chance to play tourist, if only for a little while.

Things were looking up.

chapter sixteen

Dad took me out to lunch at a quaint sidewalk café in the heart of Avalon's shopping district. Avalon is one of the last hold-outs in the battle against chain stores and fast food restaurants. Most of the stores were mom-and-pop types, and the restaurants were unique. But even Avalon isn't immune to the changing times. Right across from the café where we ate lunch, there was a Starbucks, and a little ways down the street, there was a Gap.

The "companion" Dad had hired joined us just as we were finishing lunch. I was leaning back in my chair, doing a bit of people-watching, when a man caught my eye. He was striding toward us purposefully, and he looked like he'd just come from Central Casting after auditioning for the part of a secret service goon. Tall, muscular, unsmiling, wearing a dark suit and—get this—dark glasses. All he needed was one of those curly rubber thingamabobs hanging from his ear and he'd be perfect.

Dad smiled when Secret Service Man approached, standing up and holding out his hand. Secret Service Man didn't smile back, although he did shake hands and nod something that might have been a greeting.

"Perfect timing, Finn," Dad said. "We were just finishing up." In fact, the waitress chose that moment to dart by and return Dad's credit card. He signed the receipt without even looking. "I'd like you to meet my daughter, Dana."

Finn gave me the same formal nod he'd given my father. I had to struggle not to laugh. I wondered if there was a bodyguard stereotype he *didn't* fit. I mirrored the nod, and if Finn had a clue I was mocking him, it didn't show.

Dad sat back down, though Finn remained on his feet at high alert.

"I have some business to take care of this afternoon," Dad told me, and I realized I didn't even know what he did for a living. He went on before I had a chance to ask. "Finn will take good care of you while I'm gone and will escort you home when you're through." He opened up his wallet and pulled out a generous handful of euros. "I figured you might want to do some shopping while you're in the neighborhood. I believe you Americans call it 'retail therapy.'"

That made me chuckle. Yeah, some retail therapy might be just what the doctor ordered. Though I'd never been shopping with a big, hulking goon in dark sunglasses looming over my shoulder before. It ought to be . . . interesting.

I took the money Dad was handing me, then gasped when I saw it was five hundred euros. I guess when you're in the big leagues like my dad, you don't worry too much about having your pocket picked. I opened my mouth to protest that it was way too much money, but he interrupted me before I could.

"I've missed sixteen years worth of birthday and Christmas presents," he said. "I think I'm entitled to spoil you now that I finally have the chance."

I still didn't want to take his money. I mean, that was more cash than I'd ever seen in my life. Between the constant moving and the frequent drunken absences, my mom had never been too good at holding a job. We always had enough to keep a roof over our heads and food on our table, but rarely had any more.

I swallowed my protest and stuffed the handful of bills into the pocket on my leg, which I then made sure was tightly buttoned. "Thanks," I said. "That's very generous of you." My paranoia started jumping up and down and saying, "He's trying to buy your affections!" Ugh. I really hate being so suspicious.

We shared another warm father-daughter handshake before Dad went off to work and left me with Finn the goon, who so far hadn't given any indication that he could speak. That might make it easier for me to just pretend he wasn't there, that I was just off on a fun shopping jaunt all by myself.

Turned out that shopping with Goliath always looking over my shoulder wasn't as much fun as I'd expected. Not that I'd really believed I could pretend he wasn't there, but I hadn't realized how edgy the constant scrutiny would make me. Not to mention that he made the store staff nervous, hovering there looking intimidating.

"Any chance you could give me a little breathing room?" I asked him as we left a silversmith's store. I'd have loved to have taken more time looking at the jewelry, but Finn had made the shopkeeper so visibly nervous I decided the only decent thing to do was get out.

Finn shook his head.

I frowned up at him. "Do you talk?" Maybe that was on the blunt side, but I was getting tired of his strong, silent-type act.

One corner of his mouth twitched, like he was suppressing a smile. "Only when necessary," he answered. He had the deep, rumbling voice that went with his size. He was nowhere near as big as Lachlan, but he was still one of the biggest Fae I'd ever seen. At least, I was assuming he was Fae. A human bodyguard wouldn't have done me much good against Fae kidnappers and their magic.

"I find it necessary for you to explain why you have to stand this close all the time."

He lowered his glasses so I could see his striking, emerald-green eyes with their distinctive Fae tilt. Those eyes were like a secret weapon, so gorgeous I felt my own eyes widening in surprise. Then he cracked a smile, and my breath caught in my throat. He'd give Ethan a run for his money in the oh-my-God-you're-gorgeous arena.

"I have to be close enough to put myself between you and harm, if necessary," he said. The smile disappeared, and he pushed the glasses back into place, transforming himself once more from stud-muffin to Secret Service Man. Apparently, that was the end of our conversation.

To tell you the truth, I was kind of glad he'd put the glasses back up, or I might have tripped over my own feet staring. It's not like I'd never seen a good-looking guy before, but let's face it, the Fae take good-looking to a whole new level.

I kept wandering, but I hadn't bought anything yet. Then I saw one of the few chain stores that had a foothold in Avalon: Victoria's Secret. Cruel creature that I am, I couldn't resist going in, wondering how Finn would react.

Of course, he *didn't*. React, that is. He just followed me around as usual, the sunglasses firmly in place. Even with his eyes hidden and his I'm-a-scary-dude vibe, I caught one of the sales girls checking out the rear view. It made me smile.

I headed for the panties that were on sale—I could buy a bra, but it would be little more than window dressing on my pathetically flat chest. Hoping to make Finn squirm, I held up a pair of black thong panties, checking the price tag while I kept watch on him out of the corner of my eye. Still nothing. Guess he wasn't that easy to embarrass. I, on the other hand, was probably blushing like crazy. This plan had definitely backfired.

Not wanting Finn to know that I'd been browsing just to annoy him, I bought the thong, as well as some more practical underwear. You can never have too much underwear. Especially when you hate doing laundry. I then handed the bag to Finn for him to carry. He hesitated for a second, and I swear I could feel those laser-beam eyes on me even through the dark glasses. I blinked up at him innocently, enjoying the evidence that I'd cracked his composure. He regained it real fast, though, taking the bag from me without comment. I wished I had a camera, because he looked pretty funny carrying a Victoria's Secret bag while trying to maintain his dignified, bad-ass goon look.

My feet were starting to hurt, so despite a distinct lack of swag to show for my shopping efforts, I headed back to the Starbucks I'd seen. Of course, with my sense of direction, I took a couple of unintended detours along the way. When Finn figured out I was lost, he found his voice long enough to ask me where I wanted to go. Then he clammed up again as he led me to Starbucks.

I bought a venti mocha with plenty of whipped cream. I offered to get something for Finn, but he shook his head.

I had just picked up my drink and was scanning the small store for an open seat, when Finn suddenly stepped in front of me. I almost ended up pouring the entire contents of my cup down his back, since I'd taken the lid off to take a sip.

"Hey!" I protested, but he just stood there like a wall. I wasn't even sure he felt the hot coffee that soaked the back of his spiffy suit jacket.

"I have no ill intent," a voice said. *Ethan's* voice.

I felt a cold lump form in the pit of my stomach as I peeked around Finn's body to make sure my ears weren't deceiving me. But no, that was Ethan, standing just inside the doorway. My heart clamped down painfully in my chest.

Ethan held both hands up in a gesture of surrender. "I just want to talk to Dana for a moment," he said. He must have seen me, but he had eyes only for Finn at the moment. Can't say I blamed him. Not for that, at least.

The cameo suddenly felt hot against my chest, and I reached up to fidget with it. It wasn't so hot as to be uncomfortable, but it was definitely warmer than it should have been. My skin prickled like there was a current of static electricity running through me.

"Sir, I'd advise you to keep your distance," Finn said, and he sounded dead serious. A couple of the other customers had noticed the standoff and were now looking at us curiously. I hoped a fight wasn't about to break out.

Ethan looked away from Finn and caught my gaze. "I really need to talk to you about something," he said.

I folded my arms across my chest—careful not to spill any more precious drops of mocha—and glared. "I have nothing to say to you." I hoped I sounded angry, though looking at him again made my chest ache. I shouldn't have felt so betrayed, not when I'd known all along that he was too good to be true. But I did.

Ethan ran a hand through his hair. "I couldn't have screwed

things up any more if I'd tried," he said, "but you don't know everything yet. There's something else I have to tell you."

The prickling sensation hadn't gone away. Was lightning about to strike or something? I uncrossed my arms and rolled my shoulders, hoping to dispel the feeling.

"Go ahead and talk," I said in my flattest voice.

"In private," Ethan said.

"Not gonna happen," Finn countered.

Ethan looked exasperated—and even, maybe, a bit scared. "I don't mean private as in a room with a closed door. I mean private as in the two of us sit down at a table and you do your looming a few feet away. I'm no match for a Knight, and we both know it. She'll be in no danger."

Note to self: ask Dad later what a Knight is. Because I could hear the capital letter, and I knew it meant something more to these two than it meant to me.

Finn was silent a long time. Long enough for some of the observers to get bored and look away. I was beginning to think the cameo was going to burn me after all—and the prickly feeling was going to make me go crazy—when all of a sudden it stopped. The cameo cooled way faster than it should have, and the prickling was gone.

"It will be as my lady wishes," Finn said, and I was glad I hadn't taken a sip of my mocha or I would have choked on it.

My lady? Had we suddenly been transported back to the middle ages? But no, somehow I didn't think they had Starbucks back then.

Ethan turned a pleading look on me. "Dana, it's very important. Believe me, I wouldn't be risking a Knight's wrath if it weren't."

I sure didn't *want* to talk to him at the moment. In fact, I was pretty sure I never wanted to talk to him again. But I doubted I'd be able to sleep at night if I didn't hear whatever it was Ethan had to tell me.

"All right," I said.

Finn guided me to a couple of comfy seats in the corner. There was a human woman—probably a tourist, based on the I ♥ AVALON T-shirt she was wearing—in one of those chairs. Finn didn't even have to say a word to intimidate her into vacating the seat. I looked up at him.

"You're kind of a jerk, you know. She was there first."

Finn gave no indication that he'd even *heard* my rebuke, much less taken it to heart, but Ethan had a coughing fit that I suspected wasn't coughing at all.

I sat down in the chair that had been vacant all along and let Ethan take the tourist-lady's chair. Finn moved away to hover by the door, and I felt absurdly grateful for the distance.

I tried to be cool and expressionless as I sipped my mocha and focused my gaze just beyond Ethan's left shoulder instead of on his face.

"I'm sorry," he said, and it was so inadequate I immediately lost that cool and expressionless look I'd been going for. For a moment, I seriously considered giving him a hot mocha facial. He shook his head before I could tell him where to shove his apology.

"That's not what I wanted to talk to you about," he said. "I just wanted to say it, even though I know it doesn't make anything better, and even though you probably don't believe me."

"You're right; I don't." I took another sip of my mocha, and noticed my hand was shaking. I was keeping the pain tightly contained, but it wouldn't take much for it to burst out of my skin, and I refused to be responsible for what happened when it did.

Ethan took a deep breath, as though *he* were the one who was hurting. "Before I tell you what I need to tell you, I want you to know that I would never, ever have let any harm come to you."

Oh, crap. This didn't sound good at all. I decided maybe I'd better put my mocha down, because if my hand shook any harder I'd be wearing it. My hands clenched into fists, and I looked at Ethan with what I'm sure was an expression of pure dread. The fact that he looked just as bad as I felt did not bode well.

"It's about the Spriggan attack," he said. "I know Kimber told you they were after me, and she truly did believe that. She wasn't in on it."

"In on what?" I asked, my voice so faint I was surprised he could hear me.

Ethan let out a heavy sigh. "The Spriggan attack."

I swallowed on a dry throat. "Kimber wasn't in on the Spriggan attack. Meaning you *were*." Because there was no other way to interpret his words.

He grimaced. "Yes. Sort of. But it wasn't supposed to be like that."

I'll give Ethan one thing: he had the courage to look me in the eye when he told me just how much of a bastard he'd been.

"I was supposed to win you over to our side," Ethan said. "My father's side, that is. I wanted you to be grateful to me, and not just for getting you out of Grace's clutches."

"So you arranged for me to be attacked?" I asked, my voice an unflattering squeak. "You let those creatures hurt your friends? They could have been killed!" I leapt to my feet, but Ethan reached out to grab my arm.

"Let me finish," he said.

The cameo heated, and the nasty prickling started again. I saw Finn coming toward us. But if I let him interfere now, I might never hear the whole story. And no matter how much it hurt, I needed to know the whole story.

I sat down with a thud. Ethan let go of me, and I waved Finn off. Once more, the prickling stopped and the cameo cooled. It had to have something to do with magic, though why it was suddenly making me feel like an electric eel, I didn't know.

Ethan took another deep breath. "Yes, my father and I arranged for you to be attacked. That's how the Spriggans found us in the cave. But Dana, it was only supposed to be *one* Spriggan, and it was supposed to ignore everyone else and come straight to you. That's why I was sitting by your side the whole time, so the Spriggan would have to go through me. It would have scared you, but I'd have been way more than a match for one Spriggan. I would have gotten to play the dashing hero, and no one would have gotten hurt.

"I swear to you, Dana. Neither my father nor I would ever want any harm to come to you. We wanted to win you to our side, not *hurt* you. But obviously, something went wrong, and the Spriggans attacked in numbers. And whatever went wrong, it wasn't an accident."

"Huh?"

"My father and I would never have sent them to hurt you. But *someone* did. Someone found out what we were planning and upped the stakes, as it were."

I decided I needed more mocha despite my shaking hands. Actually, what I *really* needed was one of Kimber's possets, extra-strength. I barely tasted the mocha as I swallowed.

"So what you're trying to tell me, even though you haven't come right out and said so, is that you think someone's trying to kill me." He'd hinted darkly before that Aunt Grace might try to make me disappear, but as much as it frightened me, the threat had never seemed terribly real to me.

"Yes. And I have no idea who. I'm sure your father is keeping you well guarded." His eyes flicked toward Finn then back to me. "But he should be aware of what's at stake."

I shook my head. "Why did you tell me?" I asked. "You could have just told my dad." And if there was any mercy in the world, my dad *wouldn't* have told me, and I wouldn't have to deal with yet another blow.

Ethan looked down at his hands. "I didn't tell your father because I thought you deserved to hear it from me. And if you'd like to have your Knight beat the crap out of me, I won't complain." He glanced up at Finn again. "I think he'd enjoy it."

It made a nice fantasy. Too bad I wasn't ruthless enough to actually do it.

"Do you have any other bombshells to drop, or are we through here?" I asked.

Ethan looked miserable. I was spitefully glad. "I've said what I needed to say," he said.

I picked up my mocha and stood. The cup was still almost half-full, but I didn't want it anymore. Besides, it was now lukewarm. Which meant I didn't have to worry I was scalding him when I tossed the remains in Ethan's face.

I think Finn might have cracked a smile as he held the door open for me, but I wasn't sure.

chapter seventeen

My retail therapy hadn't worked as well as I'd hoped. All I had to show for my shopping spree was that single bag from Victoria's Secret, but although instinct told me my dad wouldn't be happy that I'd made such little use of his gift, I just couldn't see continuing after my chat with Ethan. Not that I'd been having that great a time to start with.

I thought sure Finn was going to ask me about my conversation with Ethan, especially after the whole mocha-in-the-face thing, but he didn't say a word. His social skills could use some work. Then again, I wasn't real anxious to talk about it, so the silence wasn't completely unwelcome.

Finn took me back to my dad's house. I thought he might drop me off there, seeing as Dad said the house was completely safe, but he came in with me.

"In case you want to go out again later," he said, which was a veritable speech from him.

It was a plausible explanation, but I couldn't help wondering if he did double duty as prison guard. So I pushed the issue.

"I'm exhausted," I said. "I don't see myself going out again today. At least not until Dad gets home."

He shrugged his sturdy shoulders. "I'll be here if you change your mind."

"Can't you just give me a phone number? I can call you if I want to go out, and you won't have to kill the rest of your afternoon just sitting around the house."

"That's my job," he said.

Yup. Definite jailor material here. "Is there anything I can say that will get you to leave?" I asked. "Because I'd really like some time to myself."

"I can wait in the garage if my presence disturbs you."

The garage which, conveniently, I'd have to pass through if I wanted to leave the house. Not that I *wanted* to leave the house by myself, not when there could be people out there wanting to kill me. I'm not the stupid airhead from three thousand bodyguard stories who thinks, "Gee, someone's trying to kill me. Let me ditch my bodyguards so I make a nice, juicy target." I just wanted to know I *could* leave if I wanted to.

I'd wanted a great many things since I'd come to Avalon. I hadn't gotten any of them yet.

I was feeling almost bitchy enough to make Finn hang out in the garage, but I knew I wasn't being fair. Like he said, he was just doing his job. It wasn't his fault I didn't like it.

"Fine!" I said in a huff. I grabbed my Victoria's Secret bag and made a grand exit, stomping up the stairs to my room. Childish, I know, but I figured I was entitled.

There was a phone in my room, so I made another attempt to call my mom. I didn't know what I was going to say to her, especially after finding out why she'd become an alcoholic, but everything that had happened to me in Avalon so far felt almost surreal. The idea of touching base with reality—even the depressing reality of my mom and her drinking—held a lot of appeal.

I got her answering machine again. I couldn't think of anything to say in a message, so I hung up.

If I didn't keep myself busy, I was sure I'd spend the rest of the afternoon brooding, so I plugged in my laptop and finally started reading one of the dirty books I'd downloaded, but I couldn't keep my mind on it. The moment something remotely sexy started to happen, I'd find myself remembering the feel of Ethan's lips on mine, the warmth of his body as he leaned over me. Which would immediately lead to the memory of how he'd lied to me and betrayed me.

My spiral into misery was interrupted by the sound of the doorbell. For half a second, I hoped it would be Ethan, coming to prostrate himself at my feet and beg forgiveness. But I was never going to forgive him, and even if it might have been satisfying to see him grovel, I couldn't take seeing him again.

Footsteps made the stairs creak, and moments later, Finn appeared in my doorway. He'd ditched his jacket and tie, as well as the sunglasses, and all I could think was . . . wow! If he walked around without his Secret Service Man disguise, he'd be a menace as every woman behind the wheel of a car would forget to look at the road. If it weren't for the Fae tilt to his eyes, I swear he'd be a leading candidate for the next James Bond.

"You have a visitor," he said, and I had to suppress a laugh, because his accent was just close enough to British to make me think, "Bond. James Bond."

"If it's Ethan, you can tell him to forget it," I said, the urge to laugh instantly disappearing.

Finn shook his head. "It's Kimber. But if you don't wish to speak to her, that's perfectly understandable, and I'd be happy to send her away."

Maybe sending her away would have been the right thing to do. She'd hurt me worse than Ethan had, if only because I'd let down my guard and trusted her, while I'd always remained wary around Ethan. It made my heart ache just to think about how she'd lied to me. And yet . . . Yesterday, when we'd sat in her room together, I'd had a tantalizing glimpse of what it would be like to have a real friend, a friend I didn't have to hide anything from, and I'd liked it. A lot.

I didn't know if I could find it in my heart to forgive her—assuming she actually *did* like me and wanted forgiveness—but I'd never know if I didn't talk to her. Besides, I'd given Ethan the chance to explain himself this afternoon. It was only fair that I give Kimber the same shot.

"I'll be down in a minute," I told Finn, and he nodded.

I took a couple of deep breaths as I listened to Finn's retreating footsteps. I gathered what I could of my courage and dignity, then headed down to the living room.

Kimber was sitting primly on the couch when I emerged from the stairway. I looked around for Finn, but he was nowhere to be found.

"He's downstairs," Kimber said, standing up and turning to face me.

I was glad not to have to play out this scene with an audience, though I hated the idea of Finn having to hang out in the garage. I walked closer to Kimber, my arms crossed over my chest, my chin jutting out. Kimber stared at her feet for a moment, then found the courage to meet my eyes.

"My father made me swear not to tell you anything," she

said, sounding miserable. "It didn't seem like we were doing anything so terribly wrong at first. We were just getting you away from Grace and being friendly. I told myself there was no harm in it. But then Ethan started flirting, and I realized there was more to the plan than just being 'friendly.' "

My throat ached. "Yeah, because why else would a guy like him give a girl like me a second glance?" I asked, and I almost winced at the bitterness in my voice. I reminded myself for the millionth time that I'd known from the start that Ethan's interest was too good to be true.

Kimber's eyes widened. "That's not what I meant!"

"Isn't it? Because I can't imagine how else you'd have been so sure it was all some part of this big conspiracy of yours."

Kimber sank down onto the couch, and she looked so hurt it was hard to remember the ice princess I'd first met. "That's not it at all," she said, and I could have sworn she was fighting tears. "It's just that I'm a cynic, and it was too . . . convenient that he 'just happened' to fall for you under the circumstances."

I let out a heavy sigh. "From one cynic to another, tell me why I should believe anything you say?"

She looked up at me, and there was a shimmer of tears in those lovely eyes of hers. "I can't think of one good reason why you'd believe me," she said with a sniffle. "But I wish you would anyway. I hated having to lie to you, but my dad would have been so furious with me if I disobeyed him. . . . Ethan can do no wrong in his eyes, but I'm a different story."

"You told me my dad was still in jail when you knew he was already out."

She nodded. "It's what my father told me to say. I argued with him about it. You were bound to find out eventually that we'd lied, and I told him it would undo any good impression we might have made. But he wouldn't listen to me." A single tear leaked from the corner of her eye, and she brushed it away.

"Sorry," she said with another sniffle. "I have no right to cry when you're the one who got hurt."

But it was clear that being stuck in the middle had hurt Kimber plenty, too. "You get brownie points for trying to warn me about Ethan, at least," I told her. And, while she'd betrayed my trust by lying about my father, I couldn't help remembering the way she'd calmly accepted what I considered to be my shameful secret.

I didn't want to lose her, I realized with a start. The lie was going to be a sore spot between us for who knew how long, but I didn't know how I could survive in Avalon without a friend.

My decision made, I met her eyes. "If you promise never to lie to me again, then maybe we can kinda start over."

She gave me a wide-eyed, hopeful look. "Really?"

"We can give it a shot."

Her smile was positively brilliant, and there was no missing the relief in her eyes. "Thanks for giving me a second chance," she said, then startled me by giving me an exuberant hug. She sobered a bit when she let go. "I'd better get out of here before your dad comes home. He might not be too happy to see me right now."

I hoped Dad wouldn't be a problem. He'd told me he wouldn't stop me from talking to Ethan, even though he didn't approve, which seemed like a good sign.

"Are you doing anything tomorrow?" I asked. "Because I tried to do some shopping today, and it wasn't much fun on my own."

Her eyes lit up. "Ooh! Shopping is one of my favorite things. And I can take you to all of the *best* boutiques."

"I'm sure we'll have Finn looking over our shoulders the whole time," I warned.

She grinned wickedly. "And this would be a *bad* thing?" she teased. "I got a good look at him before he let me in, and all I can say is, yum!"

"He looks less 'yum' and more 'yikes' when he's in Secret Service Man mode," I warned.

Kimber's grin was undiminished. "All the better. He can be our little secret."

A weight lifted off my shoulders as I grinned back at her.

My dad didn't come home until after seven, by which time my lunch had long been burned out of my system. In other words, I was starving. I'd assumed he'd take me out to dinner, but I wasn't at all disappointed when I came downstairs and discovered he'd brought Chinese takeout. Yay! I'd get to eat sooner.

There wasn't actually a dining room in my dad's house, but he did have a small round table with two chairs hiding in one corner, and that's where we ate. Finn had left as soon as Dad got home, so it was just the two of us. I thought it was kind of cozy, almost homelike. Until Dad started talking.

"So Finn tells me you ran into Ethan this afternoon," he said, and the food turned to ashes in my mouth.

I swallowed, then mentally gave myself a kick in the rear. I should have known Finn would give Dad a full report, especially when Ethan made such a big deal about having something important to tell me. I *should* have spent some time this afternoon deciding what I was going to say to my dad—I was afraid a death threat would make me into even more of a prisoner than I already was—but of course I hadn't wanted to think about it.

"Yeah," I said, trying to sound casual as I shoved another bite of sweet-and-sour chicken into my mouth. It still tasted like ashes, but as long as I was chewing, I couldn't be expected to talk.

Dad leaned back in his chair, and I could feel his eyes on me even though I was looking at my plate.

"Well?" he prompted. "Would you like to tell me what happened? I hear he had something urgent to tell you."

I wasn't eager to tell Dad about what happened. But I also wasn't eager to get killed, so not telling Dad about it probably was a bad idea. I took a gulp of water to help wash the chicken down, then composed myself as best I could.

"On the night that Ethan and Kimber rescued me from Aunt Grace, we were attacked by Spriggans." Fae reserve or not, Dad gasped softly. "Kimber thought they were after Ethan because he's so powerful. But Ethan thinks they were after *me*."

I had left so much out you could drive a truck through all the holes in my story. Don't ask me why I didn't spill the beans about Ethan's role in the attack. I was hurt enough to want to hurt him back, but some instinct made me hold back.

From the look on Dad's face, I could tell he knew I wasn't telling him the whole story. I tensed for the ensuing interrogation, but he surprised me by letting it slide.

He sighed hugely and pushed his plate aside. "I suppose I've put this off as long as I could," he said. "It's time to talk about your status as a Faeriewalker."

"You say that as if you know I am one." I hadn't said a word about it to him, figuring I'd avoid the whole topic until he brought it up.

He smiled wryly. "It became fairly obvious once I brought you home. You haven't even glanced out that front window yet. Most people immediately comment on the view, and it was a sunny day today."

"Maybe I'm afraid of heights."

His eyes narrowed. "Don't be coy." He didn't quite snap at me, but there was definitely annoyance in his voice. "You can see into Faerie."

I shrugged. Being coy, I guess. It was almost like if I didn't admit it out loud, it wasn't actually true.

"And Ethan and his Underground have explained to you what this means?" he prodded.

Another shrug. "To tell you the truth, it doesn't seem like that big a deal to me. Not big enough for all this drama."

"Then you haven't thought about it enough." He was still pissed at me, though I wasn't sure exactly why. "How well do you know history?"

The question startled me. I had no idea what it had to do with the conversation. "Let's just say it's not my favorite subject at school," I answered, because let's face it, history classes are boring, boring, boring.

"Typical American," Dad muttered under his breath. "Have you heard of Richard III?"

I gave him an exasperated look. "I said it wasn't my favorite subject, not that I'm completely ignorant."

"Richard III took the throne when his brother, Edward IV, died. But what he is most famous for is his possible murder of the Princes in the Tower, his brother's sons."

"Like I said, not completely ignorant." I couldn't say I knew much more about it than what Dad had said so far, but I was finding his tone somewhat condescending.

His eyes were like blue spears impaling me, and I gathered he wasn't used to being talked back to. He was going to have to get used to it if I stuck around. Still, that stare was intimidating enough that I felt myself sinking down into my chair.

"Whether Richard killed those boys or not has been a subject of great debate among historians."

He paused, waiting for me to make a smart comment, ready to jump down my throat if I did. I kept my mouth shut, still wondering what this had to do with Faeriewalkers.

"At that time, Avalon was under mortal control, ruled by the kings of England. It was a time of great strife for the Crown, as the houses of York and Lancaster fought over the throne. It was known as the Wars of the Roses, and it went on for more than thirty years. The Fae took sides in the conflict, the Seelie favoring York and the Unseelie favoring Lancaster." He flashed me a smile I might have called bitter. "Remember what I told you about how the Fae don't change. The Seelie to this day wear the white rose of York, and the Unseelie still wear the red rose of Lancaster.

"The Unseelie single-handedly destroyed the house of York by kidnapping the Princes in the Tower and leaving Richard holding the bag, as it were. Because he was suspected of killing those children, he was never able to fully secure the throne, and when he was killed in battle, the crown passed to the house of Lancaster."

Okay, it didn't take a rocket scientist to realize where Dad was going with this. Obviously, a Faeriewalker had been involved in there somehow, but I didn't understand how. I frowned in concentration.

"So there's some kind of spell that can make people just disappear? And a Faeriewalker carried it to the Tower of London and made the kids go poof?"

"No. The Unseelie Fae sent a Faeriewalker and an Unseelie Knight into the mortal world. The Knight cast a series of confusion spells that allowed them to infiltrate the Tower and gain access to the Princes."

"Wait a minute!" I said, sitting up straighter. "I thought Faeriewalkers could just carry magic into the mortal world. They can actually bring *people*?"

Dad nodded. "There is an aura of Fae magic that clings to Faeriewalkers. If the Fae is careful to stay within the Faeriewalker's aura, then he—or she—can enter the mortal world, with all his magic intact. Just as the Faeriewalker can bring mortals into Faerie with working technology."

"So that's what happened to the Princes? The Knight and the Faeriewalker kidnapped them and took them to Faerie?"

"Yes."

"So what happened to them when they got to Faerie?"

Dad looked grim and unhappy. "Mortals cannot survive in Faerie. Not without a Faeriewalker's special magic protecting them. The Faeriewalker abandoned them there, and they died. Are you beginning to see why your being a Faeriewalker is a 'big deal'?"

Yeah, that was getting obvious. No wonder no one knew for sure what had happened to the Princes. They hadn't taken into account the possibility of a magical abduction into Faerie.

"Having a Faeriewalker on one's side is rather like having a nuclear weapon. Even if one never intends to deploy it, the threat is a potent one. Grace wished to win you to her side by force; Alistair wanted to win you to his side by having his children ingratiate themselves to you."

I raised my chin, hating to be reminded of Ethan. "And you?" I asked. "How do you plan to get me on *your* side?"

He smiled at me, leaning over and covering one of my hands with his. "By being your father. By protecting you, and by treating you kindly. And by being honest with you."

I gently extracted my hand from under his, not quite ready for physical signs of affection yet. "I like your way better," I muttered under my breath.

He smiled again, and his eyes twinkled. "I'm rather counting on that."

I went to bed that night cautiously optimistic about my situation. I certainly felt safer, more comfortable, and more free now than I had since I'd first set eyes on Aunt Grace. But I couldn't help wondering if Dad's attitude toward me would change if I stopped doing what he wanted me to do. Would he still treat me "kindly" then? Or would the claws come out? Because I knew he had some, even if he hadn't shown them to me yet.

chapter eighteen

The next day dawned as what I was beginning to think of as a typical Avalon summer day. Meaning it was damp and cloudy with a very un-summer-like chill in the air. I slept in, enjoying the novelty of sleeping in a relatively comfortable bed. The futon wasn't as bad as I'd expected, and the sheets were soft against my skin.

I showered and got dressed, going for another pair of cargo pants, this time with a T-shirt and a hoodie. I was glad to be going shopping again today, because I was going to need some warmer clothes. I'd known it wouldn't be as warm here as in the States, but the damp added an extra bite to the chill that I hadn't been prepared for.

I shoved what I had left of Dad's money—which was most of it—into one of the cargo pockets, then headed downstairs to wait for Kimber. I could tell last night that Dad wasn't thrilled with the idea of me hanging out with "the enemy," but he hadn't tried to forbid it. I gave him major kudos for that.

I'd expected to find my dad downstairs, but instead found Finn, sitting on the living room sofa. He was dressed much like he'd been yesterday, though his jacket was draped over the arm of the sofa, and his dark glasses were tucked into his shirt pocket. I'd been bummed about having him hanging over my shoulder yesterday, but right now I didn't mind the idea quite as much.

"Where's my dad?" I asked as I headed to the kitchen to see if I could scrounge up some coffee.

"At work," Finn answered. "I'm afraid you're stuck with me again."

"I'll find a way to live with it," I said over my shoulder, and I think Finn might have laughed, though it was so short and quiet I almost missed it.

My hopes for a good cup of coffee were dashed when I saw Dad didn't even have a coffeepot. There was plenty of tea, but even if I'd known how to make loose tea, I'd have skipped it. I did eventually find a jar of instant coffee, which I finally decided was better than nothing. I wasn't sure that was true after I tasted it, but I forced it down for medicinal purposes.

Kimber showed up promptly at ten in a disgustingly cheerful mood. I'd never been that big a shopper myself—it was hard to get too enthused about shopping when you were counting every penny, hoping you'd be able to pay the electric bill. But I had to admit, with Kimber, it was fun. She had an awesome eye, and practically everything she suggested I try on looked fabulous on me, if I do say so myself.

Being a practical sort, I stayed focused on buying the basics—sweaters, long-sleeved shirts, and heavier pants, in various blends of cotton and wool. But Kimber was constantly egging me on to buy more extravagant stuff—dresses, skirts, frilly blouses. Like I said, she had a great eye, but though I tried everything on, I just couldn't see spending money on things I'd never get to wear. My "boring" selections annoyed her to no end.

"You have to buy *something* fun," she pouted at me when we left yet another shop without any silk, velvet, or lace in my bag. Finn was already carrying so many bags for me he looked like a very hot porter, but I still had more than two hundred euros left. And I had to admit, the idea of splurging on something completely impractical did have some appeal.

Kimber must have sensed my weakness. "I know!" she said, her eyes lighting up with excitement. "My birthday's next month, and I'll be having a great party. We should start hunting for the perfect dress for you."

I gaped at her. "You expect me to wear a *dress* for a birthday party?"

Kimber stuck her nose in the air, reminding me briefly of her ice-princess act. "It's my party, my rules. And I happen to like dresses."

I remembered the froufrou feathered monstrosity in her closet, and hoped that wasn't the kind of dress she had in mind. I protested feebly as she dragged me into yet another boutique.

If it had been just me, I'd have taken one look at the price tags and turned right back around. But Kimber on a mission was a force to be reckoned with, and I soon found myself in the dressing room with an armful of beautiful, expensive, impractical dresses.

With Kimber's help, I narrowed it down to two choices, but I still wasn't sure I was willing to fork over that kind of money for a party dress.

"I like the blue one best," Kimber said. "It really brings out the color of your eyes."

I made a noncommittal sound. The blue was, of course, the

more expensive of the two choices. Obviously, Kimber hadn't had to pinch a penny in her life.

She made an exasperated little huffing sound. "I'm going to go find something for myself while you think about it. But don't think you're leaving here empty-handed." She shook her finger at me, and I rolled my eyes.

She'd been gone for maybe a minute when I heard a thud from the inside of the shop. I wasn't overly alarmed. Not until the cameo warmed, and I felt the weird, prickly feeling. There was no way that was good news.

I quickly pulled on my street clothes—if I was going to face baddies, I'd rather not do it wearing nothing but panties—and had just shoved my arms through the sleeves of my hoodie when the dressing room door crashed open.

I let out a startled shriek and jumped back as Finn came flying through the door, crashing into the full-length mirror against the wall. The glass shattered on impact, and Finn let out a grunt of pain.

Two men followed Finn in, strolling as if there were nothing unusual going on. One of them stopped to close the dressing room door behind him, while the other advanced on Finn.

They were both tall and muscular, built very much like Finn. They also had the MIB look going, down to the dark glasses they didn't even need *outside* on this gloomy day. I made a wild guess that they were Knights. And that I was in big, big trouble.

I tried a scream, because, hey, that seemed like the appropriate thing to do at the time, but it didn't seem to bother the Knights. Probably the only people who could hear me were Kimber and the shopkeeper, but the Knights would have had to go through them before getting back to the dressing room. I hoped they were okay.

Finn was bleeding from a nasty cut across his forehead, and broken mirror shards had to be stabbing him everywhere. The Knights were between me and the exit, but I made a dash for it anyway, hoping their bulk would make them slow. Unfortunately, it didn't. One of them grabbed me and hauled me against his chest, my feet dangling. He held me to him with one arm around my chest, just below my breasts, one arm pressed hard against my throat. I tried my best to kick him, but it's hard to get a whole lot of force kicking backward, so it didn't seem to bother him much.

"Fight, and the girl dies," the other Knight said to Finn, who had managed to get to his knees.

Finn's gaze darted to me, and the Knight who held me squeezed tighter so I couldn't breathe.

"Don't hurt her," he said quietly. "I won't fight."

The pressure on my throat eased, and I sucked in a big gasp of air. The second Knight advanced on Finn, then pulled back his leg and delivered a brutal kick to Finn's stomach.

"No!" I screamed. Finn had been a pain in the rear, but I had no desire to see him get hurt.

The Knight holding me laughed as his partner hit Finn again. I made another attempt to wrest myself out of his grip, but I was about as likely to move him as I was to move a semi. I couldn't even look away from what was happening to Finn, not with the Knight's arm pressed so firmly against my throat. I could have closed my eyes, but that wouldn't have made things any better. I'd still have heard the impact of fists and feet on Finn's defenseless body, would have heard the grunts of pain he couldn't help making.

The Knight hit Finn again and again, sometimes so hard I

heard bones breaking. I sobbed and struggled and begged Finn to protect himself, but he wouldn't do it. Eventually, he *couldn't*.

Finn lay face down on the floor, and if it weren't for the painful sound of him gasping for air, I'd have thought he was dead. The Knight who'd beat him smiled and pulled a long, thin knife from a sheath hidden in his boot.

"No!" I wailed, although I knew it would do no good. "Why are you doing this?"

The Knight knelt at Finn's side, and even behind the dark glasses, I could feel his eyes locked on mine. His smile was cold and cruel, and I saw nothing even remotely human in his face.

"Leave Avalon," he said to me. "Leave, and never come back. Else, it will be *you* next time."

I screamed as he raised his hand, then plunged the knife into Finn's back. Finn cried out and tried to move. I realized with horror that the knife had pinned him to the floor.

The Knight who was holding me finally let go, shoving me to the floor. Their feet crunched on broken glass as they left the dressing room.

Horrified, I made my way to Finn's side, heedless of the glass. The knife hilt protruded from just above his right shoulder blade, and blood poured from the wound. He was still breathing, though, the air sawing in and out of his chest. I put my shaking hand on him, not sure what to do for him. I'd nursed my mom through a couple of drunken accidents before, but nothing remotely like this. Should I pull the knife out, or would that make things worse?

With a groan of pain, Finn turned his head toward me.

"Oh, God!" I cried. "Don't move!"

His face was . . . ruined. That's the only way I could describe it. I don't know how many bones were broken, but it was a lot. But Knights are apparently made of some really strong stuff.

"I'll live," he managed to gasp at me. "Get help."

I didn't know if I believed his claim, but his words were enough to get me moving. Now covered in blood and mirror shards myself, I stumbled out into the shop.

The shopkeeper was lying on the floor behind the cash register. Kimber, sporting what was soon to be a massive bruise on the side of her face, was helping the other woman sit up. I'd have been relieved to see they were all right if my fear for Finn had let me think of anything else.

"The phone!" I screamed at the shopkeeper, hysteria threatening to take over. "Where's the phone? I need to call an ambulance."

She pointed at the phone, which was practically right in front of my face. I picked it up with shaking hands, but my palms were full of glass, so I dropped it. The shopkeeper had recovered enough to stand, and she reached out her hand.

"Let me," she said. And since I didn't know what number to dial, and couldn't give an address, and probably couldn't dial correctly anyway with my injured hands, I did.

chapter nineteen

The ambulance and paramedics arrived at the same time as the police. I was still shaking, but I had enough brain function to know I was better off staying by Finn's side—even though he could do nothing to help me—than letting the police take me down to the station for a statement or questioning or whatever. The police had arrested my father on a trumped-up charge, and I had no idea whose pocket they might be in. I didn't want to take the chance of losing what freedom I had, so I pretended to be a little more hysterical and hurt than I was. There was enough blood on me to make the act more than convincing.

Kimber and the shopkeeper received a cursory examination by the paramedics and were quickly dismissed as non-emergencies. Finn, however, was a different story. He was unconscious, and had clearly lost a lot of blood.

I rode in the ambulance with Finn to Avalon's only hospital. The paramedics—one Fae and one human—didn't seem anywhere near as worried about Finn's condition as I was.

"He'll be fine," the Fae paramedic said. "If they'd been trying to kill him, they'd have used an iron knife instead of silver."

"And they wouldn't have put it through his shoulder," the human muttered.

The Fae are vulnerable to cold iron, which is what they call pure iron. It doesn't exist in Faerie, where silver is a much more common metal.

I'd gotten a better look at the knife than I'd wanted as I sat by Finn's side waiting for the ambulance. The hilt was some kind of wood, maybe ebony, because it was very dark. But that wasn't what had caught my attention. No, my eyes had been drawn to the ivory rose inlaid in that dark wood. I couldn't help seeing that knife—left behind at the scene of the crime—as a claim of responsibility. Either the Seelie Fae were behind the attack . . . Or someone wanted us to think they were.

There was nothing I could do to prevent being separated from Finn once we reached the hospital. He was whisked off to the Severe Trauma Ward, and I was left with a cranky Fae healer who seemed to think I'd *wanted* to have shards of glass piercing my knees and palms.

I was gritting my teeth, trying to be a brave little trooper as the healer hunted for glass with his evil forceps, when my dad arrived. I was more relieved than I could say when I laid eyes on him.

I think Dad was planning to hug me—or at least give me a comforting pat on the shoulder—but the healer gave him a stay-out-of-the-way glare, and he stepped back.

"What happened?" Dad asked.

I opened my mouth to blurt it all out, then thought better of it. I glanced pointedly at the healer, who seemed to be finished picking glass out of me and was now using magic to heal the wounds. Dad nodded that he understood.

"Is Finn going to be all right?" I asked, even though multiple people had already told me he would. But those Knights had hurt him so terribly, and, because of me, he hadn't even tried to defend himself.

"He'll be fine," Dad reassured me. "We Fae are a hardy lot, and our Knights more so than most."

"What exactly *is* a Knight?" I finally remembered to ask.

"They are a warrior caste, the protectors of Faerie. They're also sometimes known as the Daoine Sidhe. Most of them reside in Faerie and don't set foot in Avalon. But those who live here are the best bodyguards in the world."

"All done," the healer said with a satisfied nod. "You can go home whenever you're ready."

I blinked, startled. No insurance forms to fill out? No bill to pay? And, most puzzling, no police to talk to?

I sent Dad a quizzical look, but he just smiled at me. "Let's get you home and into some clean clothes, shall we?"

I wasn't at all unhappy with the proposition, so I went with him despite my misgivings. On the way out of the exam room, he snatched a hospital gown off the top of a pile on a shelf in the entryway.

"I'll give it back," he assured me when I looked surprised.

I didn't know why he wanted it in the first place—thank God he didn't make me wear it—until we got to the parking lot that adjoined the hospital. Then I remembered the hot little sports car, and realized Dad didn't want me to mess up the seats. It didn't exactly give me a warm, fuzzy feeling, but Dad didn't seem to notice anything amiss as he draped the gown over the seat and held the door open for me.

Okay, I know, if I had a car like that, with tan leather seats, I wouldn't have wanted to get blood all over it either. But I felt sure that if Fae magic could seal all my wounds and save Finn's life, it could probably clean a car seat, too.

Dad didn't question me about the attack again until after we got home and I'd showered and changed. I then sat down on the couch beside him, the ever-present cup of tea cooling on the coffee table, and told him everything I could remember. When I got to the part about the knife with the white rose on the hilt, Dad visibly stiffened.

His lips pressed tightly together; then he let out an angry sigh. "Damn it!" he said. He leapt to his feet and began to pace, and it looked like he was thinking furiously.

"What's going on?" I asked, a bit plaintively, I must admit.

He sat back down, but his posture didn't relax any. "Ethan said that the Spriggans were trying to kill you. But that didn't make sense, not when you were, at least at the time, in the hands of the Unseelie Fae."

I remembered Ethan had said much the same thing.

"And now you've been attacked by the Seelie Fae while you're living with me."

"It was Finn they attacked, not me."

He waved that off. "It was Finn they injured. It was *you* they attacked. And hurt." He put his hand on my shoulder and gave it a squeeze. "Finn is a warrior, and while he might not enjoy being injured in combat, it's part of his job. You have no reason to feel guilty about it."

But I did anyway. I couldn't help remembering how Finn had looked at me and then chosen not to defend himself in order to protect me. How could I *not* feel guilty about that?

"So what does this all mean to you?" I asked my dad. "If neither attack makes sense, then why do you think they're after me?"

He gave me a long, measuring look, one that warned me I wasn't going to like what I was about to hear. "The Fae of Avalon, both the Seelie and Unseelie, want you here, alive and under their influence. But I'm beginning to wonder if the Queens of Faerie have other ideas."

"What?" I cried. Bad enough I had a horde of manipulative politicians hoping to capture me and mold me to their ideals! Now Dad was telling me the Faerie Queens were after me, too? "Why?"

Dad leaned back in the cushions of the sofa, still wearing his thinking face. "The last Faeriewalker before you allied himself with the Unseelie Court. One day, he went into Faerie and never came back. His body was eventually found, beheaded."

I swallowed hard, unable to resist the urge to put my hand to my throat.

"There are those who speculated that the Consul had ambitions in Faerie and might have used the Faeriewalker in an assassination attempt against Mab, the Unseelie Queen. If it's true, the Queens might view Faeriewalkers more as threats than as potential allies or pawns."

I groaned and lowered my head into my hands. This was all just too much to take. My life since I'd set foot in Avalon had been one disaster after another. I wished I had a pair of ruby slippers I could click together to magically transport myself home. Like Dorothy, I hadn't realized how good I'd had it until it all was gone.

"I have to get out of Avalon," I muttered from behind my hands. I didn't like the idea of being bullied into leaving, but if I stayed, I was likely to end up dead. And bring everyone around me down with me.

"No, Dana," my dad said, and he started rubbing his hand

up and down my back. It was probably supposed to be a comforting gesture, but I was way beyond being comforted.

I sat up straight again and stared at him. "You can't seriously want me to stay here now! Not if you supposedly care about me. Or are you hoping to use me to try to take over Faerie just like that other guy you told me about?"

My father's glare was furious enough to stop the words in my throat, and for a moment, I thought he was going to hit me he was so mad. His cheeks flushed red while his lips pressed together so tightly they turned almost white.

"I have no ambitions in Faerie," he said through gritted teeth. "I've made Avalon my home, and I have every intention of staying here."

I believed him, even though he was obviously very ambitious in Avalon. "Then why do you want me to stay when my life is in danger?"

"Because you can be protected here in ways that are not possible in the mortal world. If you leave Avalon, that might be enough to satisfy the Seelie Queen—you are, after all, technically a member of her Court. But I doubt Mab would let you go even then. After all, it's always possible you'd come back someday. She will send agents into the mortal world after you, and they will pursue you for the rest of your life. Don't think that just because these agents would have to be human means that they cannot kill you. Or your mother. Or anyone else who becomes dear to you."

I wished I could argue his logic. But even if I only believed *half* of what he said, it left me up the proverbial creek. Unfortunately, I still wasn't convinced I'd be any safer in Avalon.

"I think it is time for me to have a meeting with both Alistair and Grace," Dad said.

I'd had too many nasty surprises today to react much to the announcement. "I thought they were the enemy."

He lifted one shoulder in a half shrug. "In that they want to manipulate you for their own causes, yes. But they are both extremely powerful. I don't believe either one is cold enough to want you to be killed, but even if they were, they wouldn't want it to happen while they still had a chance of winning your loyalty."

And wasn't *that* a rousing endorsement.

"Do you think either one of them would want to challenge the Queens?" I asked.

Dad shook his head. "Alistair was born in Avalon and has lived all his life here. I can't believe he'd have any ambitions in Faerie when his platform is all about the Fae severing their ties with the Courts and becoming 'true citizens of Avalon,' as he calls it. And Grace . . . has other reasons not to want to live in Faerie."

"Such as . . . ?"

Dad didn't answer.

"Since it's my life on the line, I think I have a right to know," I argued.

His expression turned to one of distaste. "Lachlan."

I waited a beat, but that seemed to be all he planned to say on the subject. "What *about* Lachlan?"

Dad's lip curled into a sneer. "My sister has a certain . . . attachment to Lachlan. One that is not sanctioned even in Avalon, but one that would cause her to be completely shunned in Faerie."

In other words, Grace and Lachlan were a couple. At least sort of. I couldn't help remembering how Lachlan had spoken about her, with a kind of reverence almost. I doubted their relationship was exactly a partnership between equals.

188 • jenna black

Dad shook off his distaste for Lachlan. "I expect the healers to be finished with Finn within the next several hours. I will arrange a meeting with Alistair and Grace, and I will make certain you are well defended while I'm gone."

I narrowed my eyes at him. "Shouldn't I go with you? I have a pretty big stake in all this."

Dad started to say something, then changed his mind. He thought about it a little more, then fixed me with a level gaze. "I promised I would be honest with you, and so I will be. You do, of course, have the biggest stake of all in what we decide. But, my dear child, you really have no say."

I gaped at him.

"Honesty isn't always pretty," he said. "You are young and untried, and you don't begin to know the extent of your powers. I'm also your father, and have legal custody."

"My *mom* has legal custody." And oh my God, did I owe her an incredibly supersized apology when—or, gulp, if—I ever saw her again. Right now, I'd happily nurse her through the aftermath of a bender, while pulling up our roots and moving *and* trying to keep her problem secret from my friends. That all sounded so easy when compared to having two Queens of Faerie trying to kill me.

"Believe me, Dana," my father continued. "As far as Avalon is concerned, my claim on you is undisputed. Your mother isn't here, but I am. That's all that would matter." He reached for me, but I twitched out of his grasp.

"You don't get to touch me and act all paternal. Not after that speech!"

He raised his eyebrows. "Would you have preferred I lie to you? Because although I long ago turned my back on the Courts of Faerie, I was a key player there once upon a time, and one does not survive long without learning to lie with frightful facility."

I didn't fool myself into thinking he wouldn't turn that skill on me in a heartbeat if he thought it would profit him. Hell, for all I knew, everything he'd told me today had been a complete fabrication. But the ugly truth was, if he wanted to keep me here, he could. That was one thing I was certain he wasn't lying about.

Without another word to my father, I stood and walked away, climbing the stairs to my room while my father planned a meeting between all three of my would-be puppet masters. And you can bet the first thing I did when I got to my room was take off the white rose cameo, and toss it into the nearest trash can.

chapter twenty

It was a very long afternoon. After talking to my father, I sat in my room brooding for longer than I'd like to admit. The phone rang on and off, and although I was sort of tempted to eavesdrop, I was probably better off not knowing.

Finn made it back from the hospital at a little past six o'clock. I didn't much want to hang out with my father at the moment, but I *did* want to see Finn, to reassure myself that he really was—miraculously—okay.

Saying he was okay was overly optimistic. I could tell by the careful way he walked and the tightness at the corners of his mouth that he was still in pain. Even Dad could tell, because he quickly urged the Knight to take a seat. Finn sank down onto the sofa gratefully.

"Are you well enough to guard her?" my dad asked. I guess his compassion only went so far.

Finn shrugged stiffly. "Not if I'm escorting her around the city. But in the house with the added protection of your spells, I can manage it."

"Can't you find someone who isn't hurt?" I asked Dad, biting my lip as I looked at Finn. I hated the thought of him possibly having to defend me when he was already injured. I wasn't sure I could bear a repeat of this morning's nightmare.

"I can manage," Finn repeated before my dad could answer. "I wouldn't say that if it weren't true."

Dad nodded his agreement and turned to me. "Even at less than a hundred percent, you won't find a better guardian than Finn. Besides, I'm meeting Alistair and Grace for dinner and strategic planning in less than half an hour. I wouldn't have time to find a replacement."

I didn't bother to argue. I prefer to save my energy for battles I can win.

Dad left about ten minutes later, and I wondered what I was supposed to do for dinner. I'd skipped lunch altogether, and though Dad had called me to come down for afternoon tea, I hadn't taken him up on the offer. I was famished.

Finn levered himself off the sofa, and I winced in sympathy.

"Please don't get up!" I said, although he was already on his feet. "Do you need something?" My mind kept flashing back to the sight of his beaten and bloody face, to the knife stabbing through his shoulder until the tip was buried in the floor. And as brave and strong as he was, he hadn't been able to completely muffle a scream when the paramedic had pulled the blade out.

"I'm not an invalid," he said, and proceeded to amble toward the kitchen.

I was horrified when he started pulling food from the fridge and I realized he meant to cook. That answered my question about dinner.

"You are *not* cooking," I told him in a voice I'd used on my mother when she was too drunk to be allowed near an open flame.

His response was to arch one brow at me while he continued gathering ingredients. It looked like he was planning on spaghetti and meatballs, based on what he'd pulled out so far.

"I've been cooking since I was about six," I told him. "I can handle making spaghetti. Please sit down."

My voice cracked a bit, to my embarrassment. But after what he'd gone through today on my account, it made something deep inside me ache to see him doing this for me when I could do it myself. I had come to Avalon partly in search of someone to take care of me, to let me be the child I'd never gotten the chance to be. Funny how now that I had the chance, I wanted nothing more than to take the reins back into my own hands.

Finn put down the green pepper he'd been examining and turned to face me, leaning a hip against the counter. "I've been cooking since I was six, too, and that was a lot longer ago for me than it was for you."

"But—"

"If you'd succeeded in having me sent home, I'd be in my own kitchen cooking my own dinner right now."

I swallowed hard a couple of times, hating the fact that I felt like crying over something so stupid as who was going to cook dinner. I'd made it through the attack and its aftermath without bursting into tears; surely I could hold them off now.

Finn took a couple of steps toward me, and his voice gentled. He actually had a very nice voice—deep and kind of sexy—on those rare occasions he chose to use it.

"Dana, I appreciate your concern for me," he said. "But the truth is, you were hurt far more than I was."

That opened the floodgates, and the waterworks started no matter how hard I tried to hold them off. I covered my face with both hands, still trying for all I was worth to force the tears back into my eyes. Finn nudged me, and before I knew it I found myself in the living room, sitting on the sofa, a real linen handkerchief pressed to my eyes as I bawled like a stupid baby.

Finn didn't say anything for a long time, letting the most violent waves of emotion settle. I was still sniffling and hiccuping when he finally spoke.

"I'm a Knight of Faerie," he said. "I have been a Knight since I turned eighteen, and that was . . . a while ago. I have been run through with swords, shot with arrows and with bullets, tortured in ways I will not describe to you. It is my job, and knowing full well what that job entails, I choose to do it."

"But they could have killed you!" I protested, trying to wipe away the last of my tears with the soaked handkerchief.

Finn actually grinned. "So could the ones who ran me through, shot me, et cetera. In fact, most of those fully intended to kill me, whereas the Knights today did not." He turned serious again. "Do not grieve for my pain. But *do* recognize your own, and let me take care of you."

I shook my head. "So is cooking dinner part of your job description, too?"

"It is tonight. Let me do this one small thing to help atone for having been used as a weapon against you. Please."

Back in the good old days, when I lived with my mom, I'd gotten used to winning ninety percent of our arguments. Let's face it, my will was just flat out stronger than Mom's. As far as I could remember, I hadn't won an argument in Avalon yet. And Finn was playing dirty with that whole atonement thing.

"Fine!" I said with poor grace.

But Finn smiled, and I figured I must have done the right thing.

Finn wasn't exactly ready to challenge Chef Ramsay for supremacy, but he was surprisingly good. Even with the Fae eyes, which always struck me as mildly feminine, he had the manly-man look of a guy whose specialties came out of cans and freezers, but I had to admit, he seemed at least as at home in the kitchen as I did. I can't say I was comfortable letting him wait on me, but I managed to bite back every protest that tried to escape my mouth.

He was back to his usual taciturn self, but since I now knew he was capable of something resembling a conversation, and since I still had a lot of questions about the attack, I decided to grill him while we were eating.

"Did you know those two Knights?" I asked him.

He deliberately stuffed a meatball in his mouth so he couldn't answer, but I just tapped my fingers on the table, waiting for him to chew and swallow. If he'd hoped the delay would make me drop the question, he was in for a sad surprise.

"Well?" I prompted.

"Yes."

"Yes, you knew them?"

He nodded, then shoved more food in his mouth. I was obviously going to have to work for it if I was going to get information out of him.

"So since you knew them, you were able to identify them to the police, and that's why no one asked me any questions?" That still seemed a bit . . . off. There's no *way* I would have escaped a chat session with the police if this had happened in the United States.

"It's not a police matter," Finn said when he finished chewing.

"What? How can that possibly not be a police matter?" My voice had risen almost to a shout, but I forced myself to quiet down. "What kind of backward, crazy-ass place *is* this?"

His lips twitched, but it was a sorry excuse for a smile, even if he did find my outburst amusing.

"It's not a police matter because the Knights are from Faerie. I'm sure they were back over the border before the police even got to the shop."

"Well, aren't there Fae on the police force? Can't they go into Faerie after them?"

"Can the U.S. police force chase criminals into foreign countries?" He obviously knew the answer, because he didn't pause for a reply. "The chances of getting someone extradited from Faerie are approximately nil. Which is why they could afford so brazen an attack."

I let my fork clatter on my plate. "So let me get this straight. Anyone from Faerie can just waltz into Avalon, commit whatever crime they feel like committing, and then waltz back into Faerie? And no one can do anything about it?"

"That's overstating it. Getting into Avalon isn't a simple thing. We have to guard the borders against the various creatures of Faerie who are not permitted to enter. But if the person wanting to enter is Sidhe, and there has been no specific order issued to prevent them from entering . . ." He shrugged. "Your food is getting cold."

Great. Now I had *two* Fae fathers in Avalon. I was still hungry, though, so I picked up my fork and took a few bites before I went on the attack again.

"What about *leaving* Avalon?" I asked. "I'd have to go through immigration to get out. What about those Knights?"

"You go through immigration to get *into* England, not *out of* Avalon. There is no immigration process in Faerie. Now let me finish eating in peace."

He'd probably talked more during this dinner than he had in the last week. I stopped with the questions, but I was still thinking furiously. If the Sidhe could come and go from Faerie whenever they pleased, then my life would be constantly in danger. I'd have Finn to guard me, of course, but today had proven that one guy—no matter how strong and magically gifted—wasn't always going to be able to keep me safe. When that Knight had grabbed me today, I'd been about as useful as some horror-movie scream queen.

"Do you think you could teach me some basic self-defense?" I asked Finn when we'd finished eating and were clearing the dishes.

He raised an eyebrow at me. "No amount of self-defense would have helped against the Knights," he told me. "Had your father had any inkling that Knights might be sent against you, he would not have let you leave the house without a considerably larger retinue."

Not what I wanted to hear. "I'm not asking you to turn me into some kind of super-ninja. I just don't want to feel completely defenseless."

"But against Knights, you are."

"That's not the point," I said, wondering if he was being deliberately obtuse. "At least if I had some clue how to defend myself, I'd know how to *try* to get away. Besides, at the rate I'm making enemies, I could easily be attacked by someone other than a Knight."

For the first time, Finn looked like he was considering the

idea. He crossed his arms over his impressive chest and gave me an assessing look.

"It is against the Knight's code of conduct to share our training with someone who is not a Knight." I opened my mouth to protest, but he cut me off with a gesture. "*But*," he said, "with your father's approval, I can arrange for someone else to give you some basic instruction."

There was a hint of a grin on his lips, and it made me suspicious. "Do you have someone particular in mind?" I asked.

Finn looked almost smug. "I do. And I can almost guarantee he'll provide you with just the motivation you need to harness your inner warrior."

"And exactly what does that mean?" I asked, beginning to think I might not like getting what I asked for.

"I'll let you find that out for yourself."

I swear, the mischievous twinkle in his eyes held just a touch of evil.

Dad didn't get back until almost ten—it must have been some dinner meeting. I was sitting on the couch with Finn at that point, watching a weird British sitcom where I only got about a third of the jokes. Finn didn't exactly yuck it up either, but the faint smile on his face every time the laugh track went off suggested he was enjoying it.

Even in the few hours we'd spent together tonight, Finn's condition had visibly improved. He moved much more easily as he rose from the couch to greet my dad. The two of them had a brief conversation before Dad thanked Finn and sent him on his way.

Dad opened what turned out to be a liquor cabinet and poured himself a healthy dose of what I think was brandy. He swirled it around his glass, but didn't immediately drink.

"I'm guessing from the look on your face and the fact that you immediately dove for the booze that things didn't go so well?" I asked.

His expression lightened, and he snorted softly before taking a small sip of his brandy. He gestured me to the sofa, and we sat on opposite ends.

"It went about as I expected," he said. "We all immediately agreed that it was imperative we work together to keep you safe. And then we spent the next three hours arguing over how best to do that." He laughed, shaking his head and taking another sip of brandy.

It didn't sound particularly funny to me. "So what did you decide?"

"We decided that we'd talk more tomorrow."

I groaned. "You have *got* to be kidding me."

His smile was wry. "We are all politicians, my dear. Coming to a consensus will take some time and energy. We *did* agree that we need to arrange a safe house for you." I must have looked alarmed, because he continued hastily. "Not that you aren't safe here. You're just . . . too accessible."

"To who?"

He shrugged. "When you have enemies as serious as yours, it is best that those enemies not know where you are."

Gee, I was so glad Dad was still being open and honest with me. Did he think I didn't notice that he didn't answer my question?

"Don't worry," he said, taking another sip of brandy. "My

home is as good a place as any right now. It's just not the best permanent solution."

I didn't say anything, because I was beginning to feel the bars of the gilded cage rising around me. I was already under a sort of twenty-four-hour watch, and I saw the little freedoms I had now—like going shopping—slipping away. If they put me someplace where no one else could find me, then I'd be even more in their power. They'd be cutting me off from the outside world.

It was a depressing thought, but if I had any hope of arguing the Big Three out of it, I had to have better fuel than "I don't want to be hidden away in some secluded location like a princess in a fairy tale." Right now, that was all I had, so I decided to keep my mouth shut. Maybe after a good night's sleep, something would come to me.

I started to force a yawn, and it turned into a real one very quickly. Dad gave me a look of paternal sympathy.

"You've had a long day," he said. "Perhaps you should get some sleep."

"Yeah, I guess so." I swallowed down another yawn.

There was an awkward moment, as neither one of us seemed to know what to do. It wasn't like I was going to kiss him good night or anything, but there was still an uncomfortable feeling like I should make some demonstration of affection. I think Dad felt it, too, but was just as flummoxed by it as I was.

"Well, good night," I finally said.

"Good night," he replied with a formal bow of his head. "Sleep well."

And I supposed that was about as affectionate as we were going to get.

chapter twenty-one

I couldn't sleep. I felt exhausted from today's ordeals, but my mind refused to shut down and let me escape for a few hours. Tonight, the futon felt as hard as I expected a futon to feel, and I tossed and turned restlessly. I had come to Avalon in part to get away from my mom and her drama, but I think in part I'd also hoped that I would find in Dad the parental care and guidance I was missing in Mom. I had wanted someone older and wiser to help me make sense of my life and plan for the future.

You know that old Chinese proverb about being careful what you wish for? Man, did I ever understand it now.

I shoved the tangled covers away from me, sitting up and turning on the light. If I wasn't going to sleep, then I had to find something else to do, or else I'd be lying there making myself into a nervous wreck until morning. I glanced at the clock and saw it was almost one A.M. Which was prime time in the United States. Maybe I'd get lucky this time and my mom would answer the phone. You know what they say about the third time being the charm.

I held my breath as I dialed, hardly believing how badly

I wanted to hear my mother's voice, even if it was all drunk and sloppy. Even if she screamed and yelled and then burst into tears, which I would usually try to avoid at all costs.

I almost gasped when I heard the click of the call connecting. But the voice that greeted me was not my mother's.

"Hathaway residence, may I help you?" the woman said, like I was calling a business or something.

My heart gave a nasty thud in my chest. Oh my God! What did it mean that someone other than my mom was answering? Was she hurt? Sick? Dead?

My whole body was one aching knot of tension, and I could barely manage a whisper, my throat was so tight. "Where's my mom? Is she all right?" Oh, please, please, please let her be all right! I couldn't bear it if something had happened to her because I'd run away.

"Dana?" the woman asked. I still didn't recognize her voice.

"Yes."

"This is Frances, your neighbor?"

I recognized her now. Frances, who made a point of looking down her nose at my mom and made everything she said sound like a question.

"What are you doing answering our phone?" I demanded. "Where's my mom?"

"Don't you worry, Dana honey. Your mom's just fine. You gave her a nasty fright, you know?"

The last thing I was in the mood for right now was being lectured by our nosy, snotty neighbor. I wanted to crawl through the phone and shake her.

"Please tell me where she is," I begged, and I guess I sounded pathetic enough that Frances decided not to continue the lecture.

"I imagine she's somewhere over the Atlantic right about now."

"What?"

"She's going to Avalon to find you. I'm watering the plants while she's gone."

My mind reeled, though not so much that I couldn't entertain the cynical thought that Frances was in our house to snoop. If Mom was on a plane right now, then she'd only been gone a few hours, and the plants would hardly need watering yet.

"Mom is coming to Avalon," I repeated, though I knew I'd heard correctly.

"Yes. She'll be there tomorrow. She's real worried about you, sweetie."

Ugh. I didn't know Frances anywhere near well enough for her to call me "sweetie." Hell, I didn't know *anyone* well enough for that. But if I tried to correct her, I'd just be on the phone with her longer.

"Thanks for taking care of the plants," I said. "And if my mom checks in with you, please tell her to call me at my dad's house."

I hung up before Frances could answer. To hell with social niceties. My mom was coming to Avalon!

I could hardly believe it. First off, I could hardly believe she'd been sober enough to plan a trip like this at the last moment. Second, I could hardly believe she was just planning to show up out of nowhere. Shouldn't she have called before taking such a drastic action? I hadn't had any trouble finding Dad's number, so she shouldn't have, either.

Of course, if she'd called before yesterday, she wouldn't have found me here. It made me wonder if my dad had spoken with her and neglected to tell me about it.

I turned off the light and lay down again, though I was no closer to sleep now than I had been before. I stared at the ceiling and wondered how badly I'd underestimated my mom. I'd fully expected her to get depressed and mopey because I'd left. I'd expected her to feel even more sorry for herself than she had before. Never in a million years would I have expected her to come after me.

Maybe a miracle was actually going to happen. Maybe my running away had finally been the splash of cold water in the face that made her realize what a mess she was making of her life. Maybe it would be the push she needed to get help and stop drinking.

I don't know how long I lay there like that, wishing, hoping, praying, begging the universe to let it be true, but eventually I managed to fall asleep, and I didn't wake up until after ten in the morning.

Finn looked almost back to normal the next morning when I came down for breakfast only to find my father already gone for the day. Even the shadows of the bruises were gone from his face, and he didn't move like a man in pain anymore. I was glad the Fae heal so fast. It helped me feel a little less guilty about what had happened to him yesterday.

I did a double-take when I saw the stranger slumped in the love seat next to Finn. I knew on first sight that he was related to Finn somehow, because they both had the same amazing green eyes, but that was where the obvious resemblance ended. Where Finn's hair was golden-blond, the stranger's was dyed jet black, and where Finn was built like a Mack truck, the stranger was lean and wiry. He was also a lot younger than Finn, and he did not have Finn's conservative taste in clothing. A faded black T-shirt clung to his chest, and his legs were poured into tight black jeans. Unlaced black combat boots spilled out from under those jeans, and the short sleeves of the T-shirt showed off the Celtic armband tattooed on his biceps. To top it all off, he had about fifty earrings in his left ear, and his hair swept across his brow, dangling almost in his eye.

I'd never been a big fan of the bad boys I'd met at school. They were always so full of themselves, and they thought acting like jerks made them cool. However, from a distance, they sure were nice to look at. And a *Fae* bad boy . . . Totally drool-worthy.

Finn smiled at me as I stood gaping in the doorway. "Your father gave the okay for your self-defense lessons," he said. "This is Keane." He gestured toward tall, dark, and surly. "He'll be your teacher."

Keane didn't straighten up from his slouch, and the look he gave me was . . . unfriendly.

Finn smiled even more broadly, obviously enjoying himself. "If you can overlook the attitude," he said, "Keane is an excellent teacher."

Keane stared up at the ceiling like he was praying for strength. Call me crazy, but I had the feeling he wasn't overly enthusiastic about this gig.

"Oh, stop sulking," Finn said to him, but there was obvious affection in his voice. "Teaching her some basic self-defense won't turn you into a conformist Knight clone like me."

Keane snarled at him, but Finn was unimpressed.

"Are you two related?" I asked, though I'd already worked out for myself that they were. It wasn't just the eyes, either, though I couldn't put my finger on it.

Finn nodded. "Keane is my son."

"Oh," I blurted. "I didn't know you were married." I wanted to smack myself for the naive assumption even before Finn shook his head.

"Knights don't marry," Keane said before Finn had a chance.

"It's traditional for Knights to remain single," Finn confirmed. "Our loyalty is meant to belong only to those we serve. Of course, it's also traditional for Knights not to raise their children." He gave Keane a significant look.

Keane rolled his eyes. "Yeah, you're a real loose cannon."

Finn didn't seem to mind his son talking back to him, smiling in what I would swear was genuine amusement. "Keane has never been very fond of the institution of Knighthood. He has broken with family tradition and declined to enter training as a Knight. I think he's afraid the condition is contagious, and if he works with a principle I've been hired to protect, he will somehow—"

"Knock it off," Keane grumbled, and despite the tough-guy thing he had going on, he looked embarrassed. Obviously, he had some problem with the idea of teaching me, but I had no idea what. Maybe he just didn't like the idea of fighting with a girl?

Keane pushed to his feet, shoving his hands in his pockets and not quite meeting my eyes. I remembered Finn telling me my teacher's attitude would inspire me to violence, and I was beginning to see why. The attitude was going to get very old, very fast.

"Let's go," he said curtly, then headed for the front door.

I didn't budge. "Go where?" I asked.

Keane took his hands out of his pockets, but only so he could cross his arms over his chest and glare at me. "I'm the teacher, you're the student. You do as I say, no questions."

Geez, what an asshole. As far as I was concerned, bad boys should be seen, not heard. Behind me, I heard Finn swallow a laugh.

I knew Keane was trying to intimidate me with that glare of his, but with Spriggans and Faerie Queens trying to kill me, even the most intense glare just wasn't that scary. I took a few steps toward him and returned his glare with one of my own.

"I don't know what your problem is," I said, poking him in the chest, "but—"

It happened so quickly, I barely even saw him move. One moment, I was poking him in the chest; the next, I was lying facedown on the floor, one arm twisted up behind my back, Keane's weight keeping me pinned to the carpet. Somehow, he'd managed to do it without hurting me, but the shock left me dazed and breathless.

"My problem," he hissed in my ear, "is I don't like the kind of clientele my father whores himself out to."

Okay, *asshole* was too nice a word for him. I struggled a bit, but he just pushed my arm up until it hurt. I gasped, and he let up.

"If you had the guts," he continued, still whispering in my ear, "you could get me off you any time you wanted. But you're not going to do it just by squirming."

I raised my head as much as I could from that position, glancing over to Finn. He was looking out the window, acting as if he couldn't see what was going on right in front of him. I guessed that meant he wasn't coming to my rescue.

"Come on, Dana," Keane said, no longer whispering, but still talking into my ear. "Think about what parts of your body you can move in this position. What can you reach me with?"

"So this is all part of the lesson?" I asked. Apparently, he was serious about the "no questions" bit, because he gave my arm another push. "Ow!" I protested, but this time he didn't let up.

"Concentrate," he said. "What can you move?"

I really hated to give in, but my arm was starting to throb. I'd humor him and his delusions of grandeur until I was free. Then I'd tell Finn what I thought about him for siccing this psycho on me.

I wriggled around a bit, trying to figure out how to move, but I was thoroughly pinned. Keane might not be as meaty as Finn, but he was no lightweight, either. The only thing I could move much was my head.

"So I'm supposed to head-butt you?" I asked through gritted teeth.

"If that's the only thing you can move, then it's the only weapon you have."

I'd kind of hoped he'd let go after I gave him the answer he was looking for, but he didn't. "Well?" I prompted. "Can I get up now?"

"I think you'll have trouble doing that until you get me off you," he said, sounding drily amused.

"You mean you actually want me to head-butt you?" I asked incredulously.

"Unless you'd like to spend the rest of the day getting up close and personal with the carpet."

I hesitated. I'd never deliberately hurt anyone before in my life—even when I'd kneed Ethan in the cave, I obviously hadn't done it hard enough to slow him down for more than a second—and I was pretty sure that if I head-butted Keane, I was going to hurt him, since the only thing I could hit was his face. But apparently, Keane wasn't big on patience. He pushed my arm even higher up my back, and the pain was going to go from annoying to torturous any moment now.

Gritting my teeth and hoping he knew what he was doing, I jerked my head backward. The back of my skull smacked into his face, but I hadn't been able to bring myself to do it very hard.

Keane laughed at me. "Is *that* the best you can do?"

A growl of frustration rose from my chest. Okay, fine. If he wanted me to hit him with my best shot, I would, and I wouldn't feel guilty about it afterward.

This time, I jerked my head backward with all the strength I could muster, which, considering how pissed I was, was a lot. There was a loud bang and a cracking noise as my head hit against something hard. Keane howled in pain and let go of me, leaping to his feet.

I scrambled to stand up, my heart suddenly in my throat. Pain reverberated through my head, but I knew my skull hadn't taken as much damage as Keane's face. All well and good to tell myself he'd been asking for it, but he was now bent over double, his hands clasped to his nose. Had I broken it? I winced in sympathy and reached out to him.

"I'm so sorry!" I said. "Are you okay?"

I should have remembered that Keane's dad was in the room, and that if I'd really hurt him, Finn would have come running. Keane dropped his hands back to his sides and stood up, smirking at me.

"I'm fine," he said. "You hit my shield spell, not my face."

My jaw dropped open, and right that moment I'd really have liked another shot at him.

"Lesson One," Keane continued. "If you're going to fight someone, you have to be willing to hurt them, or you might as well not bother. Now come down to the garage. I've got some mats set up down there, since you don't have a shield spell yourself."

I turned to glare over my shoulder at Finn. He was rubbing one hand across his mouth, trying to hide a smile.

"Thanks a lot," I growled at him. Maybe later, I'd see the humor in the situation, but not right now. I considered changing my mind about learning self-defense, but that would be too much like letting Keane win.

Finn shrugged. He was no longer smiling, but there was still a twinkle in his eyes. "His methods are, shall we say, unorthodox, but he's a good teacher. He'd have made a great Knight, if he'd wished." There was no missing the pride in Finn's voice.

"So, are we going to have a lesson?" Keane asked, "or are we going to shoot the shit?"

Turning my back on Finn, I met Keane's challenging gaze. "Next time, I won't hesitate," I promised him.

He nodded his approval. "Glad to hear it. Now move your ass."

Man, I wished I hadn't asked for this. Made it hard to complain about it, even if I wanted to. Figuring this was going to be one hell of a long morning, I followed Keane down into the garage.

I was right about it being a long morning. Keane would make the stereotypical drill sergeant seem like a gentle soul. He was arrogant. He was condescending. He was insulting. But damn it, he was good. He showed me all the places on the human body that were most vulnerable to attack, and what parts of my own body made the best weapons. Then he made me use those weapons, and if I didn't hit hard enough, he made me pay for it.

By lunchtime, I was so exhausted I could barely move, and I ached all over. One problem with hitting hard—it *hurts*. But there was no way I would admit that to Keane, so I stifled all my complaints. I'd be lucky if I could get out of bed tomorrow once all the bruises and muscle aches really had a chance to set in.

I expected Keane to leave now that our lesson was over, but apparently Finn couldn't let him out without breaking the extra wards my dad had put on the house after yesterday's attack. Oh joy, we were stuck with him all day.

Shortly after lunch, the doorbell rang. It was the first time anyone other than Kimber had visited this house since I'd taken up residence. My nerves tingled, and my pulse raced. Did I dare hope this was my mom?

I started toward the spiral staircase, but even though Finn was all the way across the room from me, he made it there first.

"Stay here!" he ordered, and my eyes widened when I saw that he'd drawn a gun. Keane was sitting in the living room, looking bored and put upon. He showed not the slightest interest in Finn's defensive measures.

The electric sensation of Finn's magic prickled across my skin, even though I wasn't wearing the cameo. He was in full bodyguard mode now, ready for anyone, human or Fae. He made his way down the stairs and into the empty garage with predatory grace. I crept down the first couple of steps, ready to bolt if Finn's defensive preparations turned out to be necessary.

Finn peered through a peephole, and his posture didn't relax any. "Can I help you?" he asked, without opening the door.

I didn't have to hear more than "I'm Cathy" before I let out a choked scream and started hurtling down the steps.

"Mom!" I practically fell over myself I was so eager, and my quick descent of the spiral staircase made me dizzy.

"Dana!" I heard my mom shout.

I was flying toward the door, ready to jerk it open and throw myself into my mom's arms. But there was a wall between me and the door, and its name was Finn.

If he'd been human and I'd barreled into him like that, we probably both would have gone down. But he wasn't human, and the impact didn't even seem to rattle him, though I bounced backward and he had to grab me to keep me from falling.

"Let go of me!" I tried to pull free, not with any real expectation that he'd let me go. "That's my mom!"

"Dana? Dana, are you all right?" My mom was pounding frantically on the door now.

"She's fine," Finn said. "Everybody calm down a minute."

"I don't know who you are," my mom shouted, "but if you lay hands on my daughter you'll wish you were never born!"

Yeah, my mom can spout clichés with the best of them. Usually, I would roll my eyes when she did that, but right now I was too desperate to see her with my own eyes.

"I am your daughter's bodyguard," Finn said. I tried one of the kicks Keane had taught me, and my foot made solid contact with Finn's shin. He winced, but I hadn't been cold-blooded enough to kick with the kind of force I'd need to really hurt him. He wasn't the enemy, after all. "And if I open the door for you, it will break some of the protective spells Seamus has put on the house. That would be inadvisable at the moment."

"You have no right to keep my daughter from me!"

"It is for her own protection. There have been attempts made on her life. I'm sure you'd prefer she be as well defended as possible."

Oh, yeah. Telling my mom people were trying to kill me was guaranteed to improve her state of mind. Not!

"I'm okay, Mom," I said before she could throw a fit. "Between Dad's spells and Finn, I'm as safe as if I were packed in with cotton. Please don't worry."

I winced at my mom's wrenching sob. Usually, her tears don't have much effect on me anymore, but there was no denying she had a legitimate reason to be upset. Worse, I couldn't think of anything to say that would make her feel any better. I thought the knowledge that both Queens of Faerie were on my enemies list would drive her completely around the bend.

"Seamus will be home around five," Finn said. "Come back then and he'll be able to put the defensive spells back up once he lets you in. Meanwhile, why don't you go get some rest?"

Mom didn't answer, just kept sobbing.

"Mom, I'm fine," I said in my most reassuring voice. "Why don't you go back to your hotel and call me so we can talk before Dad gets home?"

If we'd been playing out this scene at home, with my mom sitting on a doorstep bawling and otherwise making a public spectacle out of herself, I'd have been so embarrassed I'd want to sink into the floor. But my short stay in Avalon had already changed me. Of all the problems in my life, being embarrassed by my mom ranked somewhere around five million and one.

"Please, Mom," I continued in the same voice, though I sounded more like I was talking to a frightened child than to my mother. "You're here, and I'm safe, and I want to talk to you. Please hold it together and call me. So much has happened since I got here . . ."

I was kind of glad Finn was there, big, solid, and unmoved by my mother's hysteria. If it had been just me, I'm not sure I could have stopped myself from opening the door and breaking my dad's spells. Maybe nothing would have come of it and it would be perfectly safe. But I didn't want to risk both my life and hers testing the idea.

Eventually, she cried herself out. At least for now.

"I'll wait here until Seamus comes home," she said between sniffles, and I couldn't help rolling my eyes. Luckily, she couldn't see me.

"What would be the point in that?" I asked, hoping she wasn't completely past seeing logic.

"We can talk here."

Obviously, more logic was needed. "If we talk here, we'll both get hoarse from shouting through the door. And we'll have an audience. Just go back to your hotel and call me. I'll catch you up on everything that's been going on." I crossed my fingers when I said that, because I knew I was going to have to edit some of the details to keep Mom from completely wigging out. "Then you can come back and see me in person when Dad comes home." And wouldn't that be the cheerful little family reunion?

"Okay?" I prompted when she didn't say anything for a while.

She sniffed again. "I just hate letting you out of my sight for even a moment now that I've found you."

"I'm not going anywhere. I promise."

There was another agonizingly long pause. Then she heaved an enormous sigh.

"All right. I'll go back to the hotel. I'll call you as soon as I get there."

"I'll be here," I reassured her again.

I didn't have super-hearing, so I couldn't tell when she finally dragged herself away except by the fact that Finn's posture relaxed.

"I'm sorry about kicking you," I told him, realizing that had been completely petty of me.

Finn gave me a droll look. "Run through with swords, shot, et cetera, et cetera. Remember?"

I heard a loud snort and turned to find Keane, leaning in the doorway upstairs, looking down with disdain.

"That kick wouldn't have dislodged a five-year-old, much less a Knight," he said. "One wonders if you learned *anything* this morning."

I glared up at him through narrowed eyes. I knew he was goading me, knew I should take the high road and ignore his crack. But I could already tell he was having a bad influence on me.

"One also wonders why you'd want me to break your own father's leg," I said through gritted teeth.

Keane opened his mouth for what was no doubt going to be an unpleasant response, but Finn cut him off.

"Enough, children," he said, but he didn't sound like he was really mad or anything. "Try to confine the hostilities to the practice mat."

Keane didn't strike me as the kind of guy who gave a crap about parental instructions, but to my surprise, he shut up. I had no interest in figuring out why that left me strangely disappointed.

chapter twenty-two

I retreated to my bedroom, leaving Finn and Keane to their own devices. I did not want an audience for the call with my mom. I sat in my room by the phone, watching the hands circle my watch.

Mom hadn't mentioned which hotel she was staying at, and even if she had, I probably wouldn't have known where it was, so I had no idea how long it would take her to get there. It was hard to believe it would take longer than twenty minutes to get anywhere in Avalon, unless you were on foot, but my mom almost certainly would have taken a cab if she wasn't staying right around the corner. Yet the minutes kept ticking away, and still she didn't call.

Maybe she didn't have a room yet. Maybe there was a line at check-in, and that's why it was taking so long for her to get back to me. But I couldn't help being worried. Finn had been savagely beaten in an attempt to get to me. Would they also try to use my mother against me?

I paced across the small room, willing the phone to ring,

panic spreading like fire through my veins. She might not be the perfect mom, and I might not have wanted to live with her—though those old days with her were looking pretty good right now—but I did love her. Just as I knew she loved me. She had sacrificed everything to keep me from getting embroiled in Avalon's twisted political game, and what had I done? Run away from home and thrown myself into the shark-infested waters. How could I have been so selfish?

The phone rang before I could continue beating myself to death with guilt. I practically knocked the phone to the floor in my eagerness to get it, though I dreaded hearing a menacing voice on the other end telling me they had my mother. The caller ID said the call was from the Hilton, but that didn't calm my fears.

"Mom?" I half-shouted into the phone, crossing my fingers like I actually thought that would have an effect.

"Hi, honey," she said, as if she hadn't just scared ten years off my life.

I sank down onto the bed, one hand clutching my chest while I willed my heart to calm its frantic thumping.

"What took you so long?" I asked. "You scared me half to death!"

"Check-in time isn't until three, so my room wasn't ready yet. I'm sorry. I should have called from the lobby to tell you."

I squinched my eyes shut and bit my tongue to keep myself from saying something I would regret. Because if there's one thing I'd learned in years of living with my mom, it was that drunks lie. And she was lying right now.

How did I know? Because I could hear the alcohol in her voice. She didn't slur or have trouble forming words like drunks on TV do—she had a lot of practice talking while impaired, so it took *a lot* of booze to make it obvious to the casual observer. But I wasn't a casual observer, and I was way too familiar with the signs.

When my mom is drunk, she talks a lot slower than when she's not. Plus, there's this kind of sleepy tone to her voice, like she'd just woken up in the middle of the night. That's exactly how she sounded now. All the warm fuzzy feelings I'd been having since I found out she'd come after me drained away.

"You just couldn't wait to start drinking, could you?" I asked, my own voice tight with anger. "As soon as you knew I wasn't dead, you ran for that bottle without a second thought, even though you knew I was waiting for you to call."

"I resent that implication!" she snapped. "I have *not* been drinking."

Ah, the other classic Mom behavior that made me want to pull my hair out. If she was just sitting around the house watching TV, she'd admit to being "a bit tipsy." But if she'd been drinking instead of doing something she was supposed to, she would never, ever admit it. Even when her breath reeked of alcohol, she'd swear she hadn't had a drop, and there was a perfectly good excuse for why she'd forgotten to buy groceries, or hadn't made it to that parent-teacher meeting, or hadn't called the gas company to clear up that little misunderstanding about the bill. Whatever.

It all came back to me in a rush, the reason I'd run away from home in the first place. All my fears about my future were forgotten in the swell of anger and hurt that overwhelmed me. How could I stand to listen to the lies and excuses anymore? How could I keep my frustration from turning me into a screaming maniac? How could I watch her continue to destroy herself one brain cell at a time?

"I have not been drinking!" my mom repeated more loudly when I didn't answer.

How could I have allowed myself to hope even for a moment that my running away might finally convince her it was time to clean up her act? And yet, the ache now forming in my chest and throat proved I'd let that hope grow despite knowing better.

"Why can't you just admit it? You *know* I know, so why can't you just say you're drunk?" Don't ask me why, but somehow, I couldn't help thinking I'd feel better if she'd just confess the truth, stop acting like I was so stupid I couldn't tell.

"We are not having this conversation, Dana. I have worried myself sick over you and flown halfway across the world to come find you, and this is the thanks I get?"

Then, naturally, the waterworks started.

When I was younger, I'd start feeling guilty right on cue when she started crying. Now it just made me madder. I didn't say anything, just sat there with my teeth gritted and my eyes closed, waiting for her to wise up to the fact that her tears weren't moving me.

Eventually, she stopped blubbering, and I heard her blow her nose noisily. I'm pretty sure I also heard the slosh of a bottle being tipped.

"Are you okay, honey?" she asked, as if none of the previous conversation had happened.

I tried to play the same game, but it was hard to force the words through my aching throat. "Yeah. I'm fine. Dad is taking real good care of me."

"Of course he is. Your father is not a bad man. It was never him I wanted to protect you from. It was . . . this place."

"I like Avalon," I found myself saying, just to be contrary.

Mom didn't immediately know what to say to that. Alcohol and witty dialogue do not go together.

"That bodyguard said there had been attempts on your life," she finally remembered, and, oh no, off she went again. "My poor baby." Blubber, blubber. "I *tried* to warn you. I tried to make you see." Sniffle, snort. "We have to get you out of here and get you home."

Amazing how little time I had to spend on the phone with my mother before "home" became a four-letter word. I didn't want to go home with Mom, and I didn't want to stay in Avalon with Dad. If only I could think of a third choice. (Other than getting killed by one of the Faerie Queens, that is.)

I tried to wait out my mom's current fit of hysterics. But if I had to listen to her cry for another minute, I was going to go postal. "I can't deal with this right now," I told her in my flattest, coldest voice. "Call me back when you're sober, and we'll talk."

Mom was in mid-wail when I hung up.

She tried to call back a few times, but I didn't answer. Finn came up after the first time and asked me if he should pick up the phone if she called again. The pity in his eyes when he looked at me made me cringe. Had Dad told him my mom was a drunk? Or—ever so much worse—had he been listening to my phone conversation? He was a nice guy and all, but it wouldn't shock me if Dad had given him other orders that had nothing to do with guarding me.

"Just ignore her, okay?" I asked.

He opened his mouth as if to say something, then changed

his mind. "Very well," he said, then slipped out the door and left me to my misery.

I hid in my room for the rest of the day, trying not to rehash my poignant reunion with my mom. I didn't do a very good job of it, though.

Right around five, I heard the faint sound of the garage door opening, and I realized my dad was home. I was *so* not looking forward to whatever drama was about to unfold.

I'd assumed my mom would spend the rest of the day drinking herself into a stupor, which should have meant I wouldn't have to deal with her again until at least tomorrow. But when I stuck my head out my bedroom door, I immediately heard the sound of arguing voices, and one of them was my mom's. Groan. The idea of remaining hidden in my room was embarrassingly appealing, but I figured it was a bad idea to let them discuss my future—because what else were they likely to be discussing?—without any input from me.

I crept slowly down the stairs, hoping to eavesdrop and get a feel for where things stood before I made my entrance. Unfortunately, their voices were muffled just enough by the walls that I couldn't understand what they were saying. I paused at the base of the stairs, listening intently, but both my parents went silent. There was nothing for me to do but go in blind.

I pushed the door open and saw something I'd thought I'd never see: my mother and my father in the same room.

My mom was seated on the sofa, a glass of amber liquid clutched in her hands, and my father stood with his back to the room, staring out the front window with his hands clasped behind his back. He didn't turn to look at me when my mom shouted my name and sprang to her feet, sloshing a bit of her drink over the rim of the glass. I'm guessing she meant to run to me for a smothering maternal hug, but the look on my face must have stopped her.

"You gave her booze?" I cried at my father's back, and I was so outraged I felt like I might explode with it.

Dad turned to look at me then, and those piercing eyes of his stopped my voice in my throat. There was no magic involved, just the crushing weight of his disapproval. Objectively, he still looked young enough to be my mother's son—she had not aged gracefully—but the paternal authority in his gaze destroyed that illusion and made me shrink back.

"*You* are my daughter, Dana," he said, his voice frosty. "Your mother is not, and is therefore free to make her own decisions."

"Dana, honey," my mom said before I could think of an appropriate retort, "let's not fight. We have a lot to talk about."

The fuzz of alcohol still showed in her voice, but at least she wasn't passed out in the hotel room, and she was close enough to sober to retain her powers of higher reasoning. With her, that kind of limbo state could be the worst of two worlds—drunk enough to be maudlin, sober enough that I couldn't work around her.

I swallowed my bitterness the best I could, crossing my arms over my chest in what I knew was a defensive posture. "Fine," I said, then clamped my jaws shut.

Dad was still giving me his laser-beam stare. "If you plan to participate in this conversation, I expect you to treat both me and your mother with the proper respect. Understood?"

I blinked in surprise. I wasn't sure why Dad was mad at me, but that seemed to be the case. I couldn't find my voice, so I merely nodded my agreement.

"Good," he said with a curt nod of his own. "Now sit down, and let's all behave like civilized adults."

My mom winced, and that was when I realized it wasn't *me* Dad was mad at. She sank down onto the sofa, taking a healthy gulp of her drink. I sat on the other end of the sofa and refused to look at her. Dad, of course, remained standing. I think it made him feel more in charge.

"Your father told me what's happened," my mom said.

I looked at Dad, trying to gauge how much he'd told her, but his expression gave away nothing.

"We were discussing what's best for you now," Mom continued, and Dad's poker face slipped.

"There is nothing to discuss," he said in a voice that suggested this wasn't the first time he'd said it. "You cannot change what's already happened, and now that Dana is an open secret, it is safest for her remain in Avalon in my care."

Mom wasn't so boozy she couldn't manage a first-class glare. "Just because you keep repeating it doesn't mean it's true."

Dad's glare was much more intimidating. "And just because you don't want it to be true doesn't mean it isn't. Can you honestly tell me you're equipped to protect Dana from assassins?"

She clunked her glass down on the coffee table and stood up, swaying slightly. "Can you honestly tell me you have nothing but her best interests in mind?" she countered.

Gee, I was glad we were going to discuss this like civilized adults.

Dad looked stricken. "I can't believe you'd think I would put my own ambitions ahead of our daughter! You know how rare and precious children are to the Fae." His voice was tight and choked, and I could barely recognize the stoic, reserved Fae politician I had first met. "You deprived me of my only child for sixteen years, and now you wish to whisk her away from me when I've only just met her. I won't allow you to do it, and I wouldn't have allowed it even if she'd proven not to be a Faeriewalker."

I was really beginning to wish I'd stayed upstairs. Any idiot could tell they weren't really discussing my options at the moment so much as airing out old grievances. Dad had seemed to take my mom's decision to keep me secret from him with barely a blink, but obviously it bothered him a lot more than he'd let on. I wanted to slink away and let the two of them work things out, but I didn't think I'd get away with it.

"You have no need to 'allow' me to do anything," my mom said. "I am Dana's legal guardian, and you can't stop me." She turned to me. "Pack your bags, Dana. We're leaving as soon as you're ready."

She sounded terribly sure of herself, but even drunk she couldn't possibly believe it would be that easy. Still, I leapt to my feet, hoping this was my chance to escape.

"Don't be ridiculous, Cathy," Dad said, then gave me a stern look that conveyed the message "sit down" without need for words. Reluctantly, I obeyed.

Mom gave him an absolutely withering look. "If you think you can keep Dana here—"

"Then I'm right!" he snapped. "How do you intend to remove her without my consent?"

Mom wavered.

"I want us to work in partnership to protect our daughter," Dad continued, his voice steely. "But if you feel we *must* work at cross purposes, then rest assured that I will file a custody suit before you get halfway out the door. Even were Dana not a special case, I'd have enough grounds to believe I'd win, considering . . ." He glanced down at the glass that still sat on the coffee table.

Mom went pale, and something uncomfortable twisted in my gut. I had, of course, seen evidence before that my father was capable of a certain amount of ruthlessness. But as much as I disapproved of my mom's drinking, it was a low blow for him to use it against her like this.

The look on Dad's face gentled, and he sighed. "I had not intended this discussion to end in threats," he said quietly.

Mom sniffled, and I looked up to see tears streaming down her cheeks. For once, I felt like the tears were a sign of genuine pain, not an attempt to elicit pity. I couldn't think of a single thing to say that would make her feel better, but I impulsively reached for her hand and gave it a squeeze.

"It'll be all right, Mom," I said, though I doubted either of us believed it.

"I'm sorry, Cathy," Dad said. "But I have to do what I feel is right for Dana."

She raised her chin and blinked away her tears. "So do I, Seamus."

She disentangled her hand from mine, putting both her hands on my shoulders and turning me to face her. "I will get you out of here, honey, I promise." Then she kissed the top of my head like I was six, gave Dad one last dirty look, and marched for the door.

I wondered if she realized she'd never once asked me what *I* wanted. I wasn't sure I could have answered her, but it would have been nice to think my opinion counted for something.

"Dana—" Dad started as the door slammed closed behind my mom, but I held up my hand for silence, and to my shock, he gave in.

"I need some time to think right now," I said, not looking at him. "Can we please . . . talk about this later?" I sneaked a glance at him, but whatever he was feeling was hidden behind a carefully neutral expression.

"I understand," he said, and I got the feeling he really did. "Take however much time you need."

I nodded, but my throat was too tight to allow any sound out. I couldn't have told you exactly why I was on the verge of tears, but I was, so I beat a hasty retreat before I could fall apart in front of an audience.

I spent at least an hour alone in my room, hugging my knees to my chest while I tried to figure out what I wanted to do. The likelihood was high that what I wanted would have little relationship to what I actually got, but I wasn't used to not knowing my own mind.

A lot of soul-searching led me to the inevitable conclusion that what I wanted was the impossible: I wanted to live with my mom, but not with her alcohol. And I didn't want my dad completely cut off from my life again. Oh, and I wanted not to have to hide from assassins for the rest of my life.

It was a depressing list of wants, and I was on the verge of having a pity party when a burst of inspiration hit me. There was no way I was getting everything I wanted, but maybe I could manage *some* of it.

Mom had made it very clear she wanted to get me out of Avalon. Dad had already dropped a load of obstacles in her way, but I doubted she was ready to give up. One thing that I was sure she hadn't factored into her plans, however, was the possibility that I might side with my dad and want to stay in Avalon.

What might she promise me, what might she actually *do* if I used myself as a bargaining chip? There was only one way to find out.

I didn't give myself very long to think about it before I picked up the phone, finding the number for the Hilton by reviewing the caller ID log.

Mom sounded distinctly drunker when she answered the phone. "Hello?"

"Hi, Mom."

"Dana! Honey, is everything all right?"

"Yeah, everything's fine." I almost laughed. Who was I kidding? "I have a proposition for you, and I want you to hear me out until I've told you the whole thing."

She hesitated. "Okay," she finally agreed, sounding suspicious.

I took a deep breath before I continued. "There's no way you're getting me out of Avalon without my cooperation."

"Dana!" she protested in a shocked whisper.

"Remember, you promised to hear me out." Well, maybe *promised* was a strong word, but Mom was convinced enough to backpedal.

"All right," she said, voice quavering.

"I'll come home with you, but you have to swear to me on your life that you're going to check yourself into a rehab as soon as we get there. And if you deny you have a drinking problem right now, then I'm going to hang up on you, and I will never come home. Ever!"

I could almost feel it, my mom's desperate desire to feed me the lie once again, tell me she didn't have a problem. But I think even in her booze-addled mind, she heard how dead serious I was. My life in Avalon so far had sucked. But now that Mom was here to remind me what it was like to live with her, I wasn't so sure life at home sucked much less. It was just a different brand of suckage.

"I swear to you on my life that I will check myself into a rehab when we get home. Just please, come home with me. I need you. And no matter what, baby, I love you. You *know* I love you, more than anything else in the world."

I took a long, slow, deep breath, trying to bring my thoughts to order. Could I be sure my mom would keep her promise when I wasn't holding the proverbial gun to her head? Hell no. But maybe, just maybe, this time I was getting through to her. This time she'd actually go to rehab, dry out, rejoin the human race. And if there was even the slimmest chance that my ploy would work, I *had* to try it.

Of course, getting out of Avalon was going to take some doing, even if I cooperated. Actually, at the moment I had no idea how I was going to go about it. But I was determined to find a way.

"Okay, Mom," I said. "I'll come home with you. But I need to take care of a few things first." I wasn't about to tell her the long list of obstacles that stood between me and freedom. She was probably going to continue to drink herself silly as soon as I got off the phone anyway, but there was no reason to add more fuel to her fire.

"You mean your father," she said with a hiccup.

"Yeah, that's a big one," I said.

"If Seamus Stuart thinks he can keep my daughter from me, he's got another think coming!"

Yeah, right. Like Mom was in any kind of shape to take Dad on.

"Please, Mom. Let me handle Dad. I think I know a way to make him see things my way." I did the lying-through-my-teeth finger-cross. "But I need you to lay low for a bit. I have a feeling if he starts fighting for custody, we'd need an army to get me out of here."

Mom thought about it a bit, and I could hear the clink of bottle against glass. I gritted my teeth to keep from snapping at her. If by some miracle my ploy worked, she'd have the rest of her life ahead of her without the pickled brain effect; I could put up with her drinking for a little while longer.

"All right, honey," she finally said, and I let out a silent sigh of relief. "I'm at the Hilton, room 526. I'll wait to hear from you."

"Thanks, Mom. I'll let you know as soon as I have things worked out."

"Don't take too long, honey," she warned. "The longer you're here, the harder it will be to get away."

"I know. I'll hurry, I promise."

We said our good-byes. And then I lay down on my bed and tried to figure out how on earth I was going to escape.

chapter twenty-three

I didn't make a whole lot of progress on my escape plan before falling asleep, stress and the exhaustion of my workout with Keane having stolen most of my energy and brainpower. I woke up in the morning not having moved past step one.

Still in my sleep-addled, pre-coffee daze, I sat up and swung my legs out of bed. That's when my body reminded me that it wasn't used to the kind of exercise it had endured yesterday, nor was it used to being repeatedly bashed against a shield spell and thrown to the mats. I groaned in misery and almost got back into bed.

I spent way more time in the shower than was strictly good for me, but the hot water pounding down against my sore muscles felt heavenly. I was still stiff and sore when I got out, but at least I was able to move.

Silly me, I'd expected that after yesterday's intense training session, I'd get a day off. But when I made my way downstairs in search of coffee, I found Finn and Keane sitting at the dining room table.

They didn't see me at first, and I hesitated in the stairway, surprised at the sight that met my eyes. Keane was smiling. Not a nasty smile, or a condescending smile, but a *real* smile. He and Finn were each nursing a cup of tea, and though their voices were too quiet for me to make out words, they seemed to be having an easy, bantering conversation. Was this the same Keane I'd met yesterday?

Then Keane caught sight of me, and the smile vanished. Didn't that just make me feel welcome? Obviously, he had some kind of a problem with me, but hell if I knew what it was.

"Don't let me interrupt," I said as I breezed past them into the kitchen for a cup of Dad's awful instant coffee. I was going to have to remember to buy a coffeepot and some real coffee if I was going to stay here much longer—which I was, if I couldn't figure out how to get out of Avalon. The kettle was empty, so I took it to the sink to fill it, but when I turned around, Keane was standing way too close behind me.

I hadn't heard him approach, so he was lucky I didn't drop the full, heavy kettle on his foot in my surprise.

"You might want to wait until after working out to put anything in your stomach," he said, smirking at the pleasure of having startled me.

"Getting between me and my coffee is dangerous," I warned him. "And there's no way I'm in any shape for another lesson today."

I tried to push past him but, surprise, surprise, he didn't let me. I wondered if his shield spell was up yet or if a strategically placed knee or elbow would actually hurt him.

"Don't even think about it," he said, and I felt the heat creep into my cheeks. Apparently, I'd been pretty transparent.

"Think about what?" I asked, but he just looked down his nose at me. "You know, I'm not in the army, and you're not my commanding officer. I don't have to have a lesson if I don't want to."

He cocked his head to one side, his face a mask of exaggerated curiosity as he stroked his chin. I saw he'd painted his nails black today—just in case I hadn't noticed he was wicked Fae Goth boy, I suppose. "Is it that you think you've already learned everything you need to know, or that you think you're out of danger today?"

"I can see why you opted out of Knight training," I countered. "They'd have 'accidentally' killed you before you made it to adulthood."

His expression and his body language didn't change all that much, but it was enough to tell me I'd drawn blood. His eyes hardened, and a muscle ticked in his jaw. I should have been thrilled at my victory, but I'm just not that mean-spirited.

"Sorry," I muttered. "Just because you're an asshole doesn't mean I have to be a bitch." Perhaps not the most wholehearted of apologies, but his expression thawed.

"I expect you to fight back with any available weapon," he told me, and I saw something strangely like approval in his eyes. "If I attack you with words, then it's only fair you counter with words."

He smiled at me crookedly, and something inside me warmed. I'm pretty sure I was blushing as I turned away from him and put the kettle on the stove.

I should have known better than to turn my back on him. As I was reaching to turn the stove on—I didn't care *what* he said, he was *not* keeping me from my coffee—he suddenly grabbed me from behind. I tried to counter with my elbows, just as he'd taught me, but he'd caught me by surprise, and I was too slow.

Keane whirled me around and bent down, grabbing me

around the thighs and hoisting me easily over his shoulder. He clamped his arm over my calves, pinning my legs to his body so I couldn't kick. From this position, there wasn't much I could reach that was terribly vulnerable—not with any leverage, that is. I might have been able to reach his privates if I really stretched, but no way I was grabbing him there, no matter how effective it might be.

I reached up and tried to dig my fingers into his throat, but the position was too awkward, and he grabbed my hand with his free hand, pinning me even more securely as he carried me out of the kitchen. I raised my head and cast an appealing glance at Finn as we went by.

"Please call off your dog," I said, but Finn held up his hands in a gesture of helplessness.

"I had to agree not to interfere or he'd have refused to come."

"And that would have been a bad thing?" I asked, but we had already reached the spiral staircase, and I wasn't sure Finn could hear me.

Keane carried me to the horse stall, the floor of which was covered with mats. He then slung me off his shoulder.

I'd expected him to *put* me down, not *throw* me down. Even with the mats, the impact with the floor knocked the breath out of me. I lay there, dazed, for a moment while Keane towered over me.

"Next time, put your arms out like this." He demonstrated, holding his arms out to the side with his palms facing back. "Then slap your hands down when you hit to dissipate some of the force. If I'd been a bad guy, you'd be in deep shit right now."

I sucked in a breath of air. "I'm really beginning to hate you," I said.

"Glad to hear it," he replied with a cocky smile. "Now why

didn't you go for my balls when I slung you over my shoulder? I let you hang low enough to have a shot."

I pushed myself up to a sitting position, ducking my head to hide the blush I was sure colored my cheeks. "Only in your wildest dreams am I touching you there," I grumbled.

He laughed and offered me a hand up. I decided to ignore it, figuring it was a trick of some sort. My muscles groaned in protest as I hauled myself to my feet. They hadn't felt too good *before* Keane had slammed me into the mats.

"If a bad guy grabs you, are you going to be too prudish to touch him there if that's your best chance to get away?" he asked.

My cheeks burning brightly, I managed to meet his stunning green eyes. "Touching a stranger is one thing. Touching someone I'm going to have to look in the eye afterward is another." I jutted my chin out and gave him my most stubborn look. He'd pushed me into doing things I wasn't comfortable doing, but he wasn't going to push me into *that*.

Keane thought about it for a minute, looking displeased. Then he nodded. "All right. I suppose I can see your point. Now, let's work on how to escape various holds, using the tools I taught you yesterday."

It was a weird morning. Since Keane was teaching me how to escape holds, it meant he was constantly grabbing me, holding me against his body. He was an asshole, but he was one hell of a sexy asshole, and I couldn't help being aware of it when his hands were on me. He moved with lethal grace, and the intensity in his eyes said he loved what he was doing—whether because he loved teaching, or because he loved fighting, or because he just liked beating me up I wasn't sure.

I was pleasantly surprised to find myself a fast learner. Keane could still overpower me with frightening ease, but I was making him work harder at it than he had yesterday. Hard enough for a fine sheen of sweat to coat his brow. He should have smelled of nasty, stinky guy, but instead I caught the mingled scents of leather and something unfamiliar, yet faintly herbal.

One time when we were rolling around on the mat, I ended up on my back with my hands pinned beside my head. I was eye to eye with him, the entire front of his body pressed against mine. I felt his breath against my cheek, and I smelled the leather-and-herb scent that was beginning to be familiar—and delicious. His hair hung over one of his eyes, hiding it behind an inky black fringe, but I still felt trapped more by his stare than by his hold. His pupils dilated, and I saw his Adam's apple bob as he swallowed hard.

He did not look amused. He did not look annoyed. None of his usual expressions. Instead, I'd say he looked . . . surprised. He lay there on top of me, looking into my eyes, failing to snark at me for not trying to fight my way free.

"Can we just *pretend* I head-butted you?" I asked breathlessly. "My head aches enough already." It wasn't a lie, either. I didn't know how many times I'd crashed my skull into him this morning, but it was a lot.

His grip on my wrists loosened, and a faint smile lifted his lips. "Fair enough," he said, then rolled off of me, lying on his back beside me just out of touching distance.

I immediately missed the warmth of his body. Of course, it had to be just a rebound thing. There was no way I was interested in this arrogant, obnoxious jerk. No matter how hot he might be.

Still, he hadn't looked arrogant and obnoxious just now.

"Can I ask you something?" I said, staring up at the ceiling so I didn't have to be tempted by his hotness.

"Sure," he responded, and he sounded much friendlier than he had since I'd first met him.

"Is all this attitude stuff just part of the lesson, or do you really have something against me?"

He didn't say anything for a long time. He sat up and wrapped his arms around his knees, not looking at me, the expression on his face thoughtful. I stayed where I was, somehow fearing any movement I made would turn him back into his usual self.

"It's not you, exactly," he finally said. "I just don't like being told what to do." He smiled sardonically. "One of the reasons Knight training didn't work out for me."

I frowned up at him. "I thought you chose not to enter Knight training."

"No, I chose not to *stay* in Knight training." He smiled wryly. "It was something of a mutual decision. I didn't want to blindly follow orders, they didn't want to deal with a troublemaker."

"And what does this have to do with me?"

He blew out a breath. "Nothing, exactly." He turned to face me, crossing his legs.

I was tired of looking up at him, so I pushed myself up into a sitting position. "I don't get it."

He met my gaze steadily. "Why do you think they chose an eighteen-year-old Knight reject to be your teacher?" he asked.

"Huh?" I asked intelligently.

"There are Fae out there who have centuries of experience with fighting and with teaching. I'm good, but I'm not *that* good. So why would your father, who could afford anyone he wanted to hire, choose me?"

"Because you're Finn's son?" I suggested.

"That made a convenient excuse. I bet my father was even the one to suggest it. But there's more to it than that."

"Go on. Spell it out for me." There was a hard lump in my gut, and I clenched my teeth tightly.

He looked away. "Your father had a private word with me before he left for work yesterday. He didn't come out and say it—he's far too subtle for that—but he suggested I might want to 'befriend' you." He made air quotes. "He said you'd made a couple of Unseelie friends, and he wanted to offer you a Seelie alternative."

I lowered my head into my hands, fighting a sudden urge to hunt my dad down and personally show him all the neat tricks Keane had taught me.

"I didn't much appreciate the suggestion," Keane continued in a massive understatement. He sighed. "But it wasn't fair of me to take it out on you. Sorry." He managed another smile. "Don't get me wrong—my teaching methods are never warm and fuzzy, and if you don't feel like smashing my face in when we're sparring, then I'll feel like I've done something wrong."

I gave a little snort of laughter. "Thanks for telling me. And I'm sorry my dad—"

"You don't have to apologize for your father." He pushed to his feet, and I could see the drill-sergeant mask drop back into place. "Now, enough resting. Let's get back to work."

I was sore, tired, and pissed off at my dad for his behind-the-scenes matchmaking, or whatever it was he'd thought he was doing. But despite everything, I couldn't say I was completely unhappy to spend more time in Keane's arms, even if it was just to fight.

. . .

I spent much of the afternoon debating whether I should confront my dad about pushing Keane at me. Based on the brutal honesty he'd already shown me, I knew he'd tell me the truth about what he'd done, and maybe even about why. The question was, did I *want* the truth?

When Dad came home that night, however, I decided his little manipulative tricks were the least of my worries. Because, you see, he'd had another meeting with Grace and Alistair, and the Big Three had come to an agreement as to where I would live, the "safe house" that would supposedly keep the bad guys from finding me.

I had a sneaking suspicion that Mom's threats to take me out of Avalon without Dad's approval had inspired the Big Three to come to an agreement faster than they might have otherwise. I also suspected that I'd have a much harder time escaping from the safe house than from my dad's place. Dad told me they planned to have the place ready as soon as tomorrow, so whatever I was going to do, I'd have to do it fast.

I had two major problems to solve if I hoped to go home with Mom. First, I had to get out of the house. Second, I had to get out of Avalon. The first should be manageable, as long as I waited until Dad was asleep at night. I wasn't getting by Finn no matter what, but Dad could hardly expect me to try to sneak out alone in the middle of the night. Naturally, he would assume I wasn't that stupid. I tried not to think about the terrible things that could happen to me if the bad guys found me wandering the streets of Avalon alone at night.

The second problem was tougher to figure out. How could I get out of Avalon without a passport? Hell, even if I miraculously made it through the border and into England without my passport, I wouldn't be able to get back into the United States without one. I was sure I could arrange to get a new one in London, but that would take time, and Mom and I had to get well and truly gone as fast as possible.

The inevitable conclusion was that I needed my passport. But if I asked my dad about it, that would put him on his guard, particularly when he knew Mom planned to "rescue" me from him.

I was completely stymied. Yeah, I could try searching the house for the passport, but I couldn't guarantee it was here, and my chances of getting caught and putting Dad on high alert were too great. I supposed it was a good thing that passports are hard to forge, but I was finding it rather inconvenient at the moment.

And then I reminded myself where I was: Avalon. The Wild City, the Magic City. If I couldn't forge a passport with technology, might magic do the trick? I remembered the dismal little room in the tunnels that Ethan had taken me to, the one no one would ever know was there because of the illusion spell Ethan had cast. If he could create a wall that wasn't there, could he create a passport?

It was a crazy idea. Even if Ethan really could pull it off, I had to be out of my mind to even *think* about asking him. He was the enemy, after all. Well, maybe not the *enemy* exactly, but he was definitely a lying jerk who had his own—and his father's—best interests at heart.

Then again, he had taken quite a risk approaching me at Starbucks the other day to tell me the truth about the Spriggan attack. Finn had been on a hair trigger, and he could easily have flattened Ethan. And Ethan could have just had his father warn my father. The fact that he'd talked to me personally instead told me he probably really did feel bad about what he'd done.

Bad enough to help me escape Avalon?

I gnawed my lip. Even if he wanted to help me, he might think the same way my dad did, that I was safer in Avalon than in the mortal world. I let the idea ping around in my brain the rest of the evening. Dad couldn't help but notice my less-than-lovely mood, but though he tried to talk to me a few times, he didn't push.

I watched TV with him for a bit, my arms crossed over my chest, my shoulders hunched. I hoped I wasn't laying it on too thick. Probably not, because Dad looked relieved when I finally announced I wasn't in the mood for TV and wanted to spend some time surfing the Net.

When I got upstairs, I closed my bedroom door, then booted up my computer. I'd bookmarked the Avalon phone directory when I'd been looking for my dad, so I had no trouble finding it again. I then held my breath as I entered Ethan's name into the search field. I sighed in relief when his number popped up. Then I kind of laughed at myself, because it was way too early to feel anything even resembling relief. I didn't know what the chances were that Ethan *could* help me, or that he *would* help me. But I was about to find out.

I surfed to an Internet radio station and turned the volume up on my computer. If Dad was spying on me and wanted to listen in on my call, all he had to do was pick up another receiver, but at least with the music blasting he wouldn't be able to overhear me accidentally if he for some reason came to check on me.

I then went through a few repetitions of picking up the phone, starting to dial, then chickening out and hanging up, before I finally punched in Ethan's number. I don't know if I'd have had the courage to try again if Ethan hadn't been home, but luckily he picked up before I chickened out yet again.

"Hello?" he said.

My tongue stuck to the roof of my mouth, and I sat there like an idiot not saying anything. How could I possibly be asking help from a guy who (1) could have gotten me killed by arranging for me to be attacked, and (2) had used magic to try to seduce me for political reasons?

"Hello?" he repeated. "Anyone there?"

Then again, it wasn't like I was just overflowing with options. I cleared my throat, and that loosened it up enough for me to talk. "Yeah. It's me. Dana." I rolled my eyes at myself. I'm sure he recognized my voice without me having to tell him my name.

There was a half-second hesitation before he answered. "Well, this is a surprise," he said in a low mumble I'm not sure I was supposed to hear. "Is everything all right?"

"Um, yeah. Sort of. Umm . . ." Oh, please! Could I sound any more pathetic? "Well, not exactly."

"Sorry. That was a stupid question. You wouldn't be calling me if everything were all right. Are you somewhere safe? Do you need me to come get you?"

"I'm fine," I said, feeling more confident. "I'm at my dad's house."

"Oh."

"Look, you know what a mess I'm in. Your father has filled you in, hasn't he?" Because I couldn't believe Alistair wouldn't have told Ethan about the Queens being after me, not when the two of them had already been coconspirators.

"Yeah, he told me. But I was coming to that conclusion myself. The more I thought about those Spriggans . . ." His voice trailed off, probably because he realized talking to me about the Spriggans wasn't his wisest move.

"My dad says I have to stay in Avalon for my own safety. I bet your dad and Aunt Grace agree."

"But you don't."

"I assume Kimber told you about what happened to Finn the other day?"

"Yeah." I could almost hear the wince in his voice.

"If I stay here, I'll have both Queens after me, and they'll have a lot more weapons they can use against me. If I leave, the Seelie Queen will be satisfied, and the only people the Unseelie Queen can send after me are humans."

"But you won't have any sort of magical protection at all," he reminded me.

"I won't need it if I don't have Fae attacking me." I think I was trying to convince myself as much as him. I reminded myself that if we escaped Avalon, Mom had promised to go into rehab, and that was worth whatever crazy risks I was about to take.

He changed gears. "All right; let's say I buy your reasoning. I know I'm not your favorite person right now, so I'm guessing I have a part to play in this great escape?"

I bit my lip. I'd probably told him enough already to get me in trouble if he blabbed to his dad, but even so, it was hard to make that final leap of faith and tell him what I had in mind.

"Did you ever actually like me, or was the whole thing an act?" I found myself asking, without having had any intention of bringing the subject up.

"Of course I liked you. *Like* you. How could I not? I wish I had *half* your courage."

That startled me. "What are you talking about? I've been a mess since day one!"

He snorted. "You saved Jason's life when those Spriggans attacked. If you hadn't slowed the Spriggan down, I'd have been too late to save him. Not to mention that you had the courage to come all the way to Avalon by yourself."

"That wasn't courage. That was stupidity."

He laughed, but it sounded bitter. "I know you had to defy your mother to come here, and you're planning to defy your father to leave. I have never once successfully defied my father. So that's courage in my book."

"If you say so."

"I do. Now tell me why you're calling. What do you want me to do?"

I considered the ramifications of what he'd just said, and my heart sank a bit. "I was basically going to ask you to defy your father and help me get out of Avalon."

"Tell me what you need, and I'll help as best I can. Defying him behind his back might be slightly easier than doing it to his face." Again, I heard a hint of bitterness in his voice. I hoped that meant his conscience was bothering him over what he'd done to me.

"So you don't think I'm completely crazy for wanting to leave?"

"It's a risk. But then, so is staying in Avalon. As you've already seen."

I believed him. Of course, I'd believed him before and been wrong, so my judgment might be questionable. But he was the only hope I had, so I pushed forward.

"Right now, I can't get out of Avalon because either Grace or my father has my passport. I don't see myself getting it back, no matter who has it. So somehow, I need a fake one that will do the trick. Is that something your magic can do?"

For a long, tense moment, he didn't say anything. I could practically hear him thinking. Now, if only I knew *what* he was thinking!

"I suppose you know this," he said, "but that's a hell of a lot more complicated than creating an illusionary wall."

"Yeah, I figured. But is it possible?"

Another long pause for thought. "It's certainly possible. I'm just not sure *I* can do it. I'm good, but that's a tall order. There are a lot of pages in a passport, and they're detailed. Plus, I'd need an American passport to model it on, because I wouldn't know what one looks like off the top of my head."

"I can get you an American passport," I told him. "My mom came to Avalon looking for me, so we can borrow hers. The question is, can you make the counterfeit one?"

"I don't know."

"But—"

"The only way I'll know is if I try. I can guarantee I'll try my hardest, but I can't guarantee it will work. When can you get me the model passport?"

That was going to be a bit tricky. (Yeah, like everything else was going to be so simple.) The easiest way to get Ethan my mom's passport would be to send him to her hotel. But would my mom actually hand her passport over to some Fae she didn't know? I sincerely doubted it.

Maybe if I called her and told her he was coming?

A chill snaked down my spine. I was currently trapped here in Avalon because Grace had absconded with my passport. I was willing to take the risk that Ethan might betray me, but could I also risk my mom like that? Could I have her hand over her passport to a guy I wasn't sure I could trust?

The answer was no. I was going to have to get the passport myself, and I wasn't going to let it out of my sight while Ethan tried to replicate it.

"I'm going to have to sneak out of the house somehow to get it," I said.

"Not a good idea, Dana."

I bit back a snappish response and went for dry sarcasm instead. "You expect me to get out of Avalon without leaving my dad's house?"

He sighed. "Right. Good point. But I'm not letting you wander around the streets of Avalon undefended. Tell me when you intend to perform your great escape. I'll come meet you. I'm not as powerful as Finn, but I'm better than nothing."

More lip-gnawing was in order. If I was wrong about this, if Ethan backstabbed me, then I was delivering myself straight into Alistair's arms. I wondered if he would change his mind about whatever agreement he now had with Grace and my dad if I were in his custody.

But despite my doubts, I had already made my decision before I'd even picked up the phone.

"I'm going to wait until late, when I'm sure my dad is asleep. Maybe one A.M.?"

"That's good. There will be fewer people in the streets then. Less chance of being seen. I'll be waiting for you. Call if there's any change of plans, okay?"

"Yeah. Sure." Oh my God, I was really going to do this. Was I nuts? "I'll see you then."

"Okay. Hang in there. If things go well, we'll have you out of Avalon before the sun rises tomorrow."

I clung to that hopeful idea as I hung up the phone and tried not to think about just how many things could go horribly wrong.

chapter twenty-four

That night was one of the longest in my life. The hours of the early evening crept by like years, and then, once Dad and I said our good nights, they slowed down even more. I tried calling my mom about eight times to let her know I was coming, but she never answered. I hoped that didn't mean something had happened to her. I also hoped that didn't mean she was too drunk to answer the phone. Getting out of Avalon was going to be hard enough without alcohol entering the picture.

I heard Dad mount the stairs to his bedroom at around eleven. Then after that, nothing.

I decided I didn't want to wait until the last minute to go downstairs. I wanted Dad to have plenty of time to fall asleep again if I inadvertently woke him as I crept down the steps. If he came to check on me, I'd tell him I was having trouble sleeping and was going to make some tea.

Before I left, I fished the cameo out of the trash—lucky for me, Dad didn't have a maid service to empty the trash every day. I stared at the cameo for a long moment, then fastened it around my neck. I wanted nothing whatsoever to do with the

Seelie Court, but the cameo was a gift from my dad. If my plan worked, I would probably never see him again, but at least I'd have something to remember him by.

There was no light under the door leading to Dad's room when I passed by, and none of the stairs made any telltale creaky noises to wake him up. When I was in the living room, I did some more ear-straining to see if I could hear him moving around, but the house was silent.

I stood at the front window with the living room lights off, looking out into the distance. Or at least, trying to. A dense layer of fog blanketed the land at the mountain's base, wisps of it drifting through the quiet streets. I couldn't see the moon or stars, and even as I watched, the unseen clouds spat some drizzle to join the fog. I shivered in anticipation.

I knew better than to make my escape attempt carrying my luggage or my backpack. I hated to leave everything behind, particularly my computer, but all my instincts told me I might be running for my life tonight, and I couldn't afford the extra burden.

I'd put on one of the thick woolen sweaters—or jumpers, as they called them here, which seemed like a silly name—that I'd bought on my shopping trip. I'd left my packages in the wreckage of the shop, but Kimber had collected them for me and had them delivered. My throat tightened as I added her to the list of people I would never see again if I escaped Avalon. This, I reminded myself, was why I tried so hard not to get too close to my friends: it hurt so much more to leave if you let yourself care too much.

I did my best to shake off my gloomy thoughts as I waited for Ethan to arrive. The streets were eerily deserted. A car passed by occasionally, and I saw a horse and rider once, but there were no pedestrians.

Which was why I spotted Ethan so easily, even though he was sticking to the shadows, avoiding the street lights. My heart fluttered in my chest when I caught sight of him, but I told myself that was just nerves, not any stupid lingering attachment.

My watch told me I had fifteen minutes until our scheduled rendezvous, but I didn't see any pressing reason to wait now that Ethan was here. Taking a deep breath for courage, hoping I wasn't making the worst decision in the history of mankind, I tiptoed down the spiral staircase into the garage. I'm sure it would have been okay for me to turn on the lights, but I was too deeply in sneak-and-hide mode to feel comfortable doing it.

Naturally, the garage was pitch-black, but Dad didn't exactly keep it packed with stuff. I found his car by feel, then used its contours as a guide to get me around to the front door without falling flat on my face. The practice mats were still on the floor, ready for my next lesson with Keane; a lesson that would never come. I told myself I didn't care. Keane was just eye candy with a bad attitude. Maybe I'd seen a hint of a more likeable guy under his surly exterior today, but getting involved with him would have been as bad a mistake as getting involved with Ethan had been.

Carefully, quietly, I unlocked each of the locks. I remembered Finn saying that opening the door would break Dad's spells. I hoped breaking those spells wouldn't set off any alarms.

I winced in anticipation as I pulled the door open, but no alarms broke the nighttime silence. I took in a deep breath and let it out slowly, trying to calm my shaky nerves. Then I slipped out of my father's house and closed the door behind me.

"You're early," Ethan said, and it was all I could do not to jump and scream.

I whirled on him, covering my mouth to stifle my gasp of surprise. The last time I'd caught sight of him, he'd been loitering in an alley a little ways down the street. I'd assumed that was where he planned to wait for me.

Ethan grinned at me, the grin that made my stomach do flip-flops. He was dressed all in black tonight—appropriate for skulking around in darkened streets, I supposed—and he'd pulled his long hair back into a club at the base of his neck. Not exactly the Rambo look, but sinister enough to give me a superstitious chill.

"Sorry to startle you," Ethan said, though I suspected he'd done it on purpose. The jerk.

I narrowed my eyes at him. "Yeah, what I'm doing tonight isn't scary enough, so pulling juvenile pranks is a fabulous idea."

He looked more genuinely sorry now, but he didn't apologize again. "Come on, let's get moving. Where are we going, anyway?"

"To the Hilton. Wherever that is."

Ethan frowned. "A car would be nice," he said. "That's going to be a hike."

Great. At least I had on comfortable shoes. "Uphill or down?" I asked, praying he'd give me the right answer.

"Down."

"Phew." I tried to tell myself that was a good sign, that it meant fate was with me. "Lead the way."

The drizzle I'd noticed from Dad's window picked up to a light rain as we started walking. Of course I hadn't brought an umbrella, and neither had Ethan. The wool sweater was keeping my skin dry for now, but even so I was already cold. I curled my hands into fists, then pulled them up into the sleeves of the sweater for warmth.

"If this is summer," I grumbled, "I'd hate to see your winters."

To my shock, Ethan slung his arm around my shoulders and pulled me against him, sharing his warmth. I knew I shouldn't be letting him touch me, not after everything I'd learned about him. It was on the tip of my tongue to tell him to keep his hands to himself. But he was so warm. And he wasn't treating the gesture as some sort of a come-on. He didn't even look at me, just kept walking as if putting his arm around me was so natural it didn't occur to him that I might object.

If everything went well, I'd be out of Avalon by tomorrow, and I'd never see Ethan again. So what did it matter if I sent him mixed signals? What did it matter if I acted like I forgave him even when really I didn't? His warmth fought off the chill, and I should take advantage of it while I had the chance. So I slipped my arm around his waist, making it easier for us to walk, and neither of us said anything about it.

For the record, walking in Avalon sucks. At least, it sucks when you're trying to go up and down the mountainside, because the road spirals, which means even if your destination is only a hundred yards down from where you're standing, you have to spiral all the way around the mountain to get there. Every once in a while, there was a stairway that allowed us to quickly cut from one level of the road to the next level down, but they were way too rare for my taste.

My knees and ankles told me that walking downhill for extended periods of time wasn't really that much easier than walking uphill. It just caused a different sort of pain. And the steady light rain had soaked through my shoes and socks, so my feet had turned to ice.

The Hilton was located at the very bottom of the mountain, within view of the Southern Gate. It looked incongruously modern next to the stately brick and stone buildings that surrounded it. There was even a multilevel parking deck on one side. Ethan and I were no doubt looking pretty bedraggled by then, and I know I, at least, was exhausted.

I didn't have the heart to make Ethan wait for me out in the rain, but I didn't want to take him up to my mother's room, either.

"She's pretty touchy about the Fae," I told him. "There's likely to be enough drama already. I don't want her going all hysterical because you're there."

Ethan didn't like it—I think he was afraid I was going to try to ditch him—but since I refused to get into the elevator with him, he finally gave up and agreed to wait for me in the lobby.

"If you're not down in fifteen minutes, I'm coming up to get you," he said.

"Okay," I agreed, just to get him off my back. It would be kinda hard for him to come get me when he didn't actually know what room my mom was in, but whatever.

I wasn't surprised when my mom didn't immediately answer her door. It was, after all, the middle of the night. Plus she hadn't answered any of my calls, so why should I assume she'd answer the door?

I knocked on the door a little louder, hoping I wasn't waking everyone else on the hallway. "Mom?" I said, not quite shouting, but speaking loud enough to have a hope of being heard. If she was passed out drunk, getting her to wake up could be a serious challenge.

Still nothing, though I thought I heard some movement. I knocked yet again, and this time I was sure I heard someone move.

"Mom? It's me." Like she wouldn't know. Who else would call her "Mom"?

She mumbled something incoherent. I breathed a sigh of relief, both that she was awake, and that the bad guys hadn't gotten to her. I knocked one more time, just to make sure she didn't decide she was dreaming and go back to sleep. She said something else—I think, maybe, "Coming!"—and I heard footsteps approaching the door.

At the same moment, my skin started to prickle and the cameo, tucked under the neck of my shirt, started to heat. Just as my mom's door swung open, I realized what that meant. But it was too late.

Someone shoved me from behind, sending me flying through the door and into my mother's room. I slammed into Mom, and we both fell to the floor. By the time I managed to roll off of her and get to my feet, someone had closed the door and turned on the light.

Dread clenching in my gut, I turned to see who had just ambushed me.

Aunt Grace lounged in the doorway, looking terribly proud of herself. By her side, a disembodied arm floated in the air, holding a gun pointed at my mom. On the floor under the arm—about where you'd expect a person's feet to be—were a pair of shoes. I gaped. Grace laughed and reached into the seemingly empty air. A moment later, the arm and the shoes were attached to a smallish, human-looking guy wearing a hooded black cloak. A cloak just like the one Aunt Grace was wearing.

"The cloaks only work when the hoods are up," Aunt Grace explained, like we were having a friendly conversation. "And they only hide what's behind the fabric, so one needs to keep one's limbs tucked under to be completely unseen. They cost me a small fortune, but they were worth it."

I couldn't think of anything clever and witty to say, so I just stood there staring at the gun, hoping Grace's friend didn't have an itchy trigger finger. I swallowed hard, wishing I'd let Ethan come up to the room with me after all. Then again, I doubted Ethan was a match for Grace, and he *certainly* wasn't a match for that gun.

"What do you want?" I asked, and I was surprised that I sounded almost calm. My pulse was galloping, and I'd broken out in a sweat that had nothing to do with the temperature.

She arched one graceful brow. "Don't you know, dear?"

"You want your very own pet Faeriewalker. Well, let me tell you, your methods of winning me over aren't lighting my fire." Gee, that sounded kinda brave. Now, if my hands would only stop shaking, Aunt Grace might actually believe I was as brave as I sounded.

She gave me a marrow-freezing glare. "Obviously your mother didn't teach you any manners."

I crossed my arms over my chest—more to hide the shaking hands than to be defiant. "Apparently yours didn't either. Or do you consider kidnapping your own niece polite?"

Grace moved so fast I couldn't have stopped her if I'd tried. Her hand flew at my face and landed a bell-ringing slap on my cheek. I gasped, and tears misted over my eyes. My face felt like it had just had a run-in with a truck.

I swallowed the tears as best I could, gritting my teeth and ordering myself not to cry over one little slap. I thought about what kind of pain Finn must have gone through during his encounter with the Knights. If he could endure that without complaint, then I could force myself not to give Grace the satisfaction of seeing me cry.

"I've been wanting to do that almost from the first moment you opened your mouth," she growled at me. "And I would be happy to do it again if you have any more cutting remarks you'd like to make."

I managed to hold off the tears, and I didn't put my hand against my aching, burning cheek. But I wasn't anxious for a repeat performance, so I kept quiet.

"Kirk," Aunt Grace said to her henchman, motioning him toward my mom, who was just starting to come to.

"Keep away from her!" I cried as he bent down toward her, but he ignored me, and with that gun in his hand, I didn't dare make a move to stop him. All Keane's fancy moves were useless when the enemy had a weapon—and a hostage.

Kirk grabbed my mom and shoved her onto the bed. She made a puzzled little "Huh?" sound, but she was still really out of it. Kirk tucked his gun in his belt and flipped my mom onto her stomach, then tied her hands behind her back. When he was done, he took the gun out again and put the muzzle against her head.

"You and I are going to take a walk, dear," Aunt Grace said to me, taking hold of my arm. "Behave yourself, and your mother will come to no harm." With her other hand, she pulled a cell phone out of the handbag that was slung diagonally across her body. With one hand, she dialed a number.

"Cathy Hathaway's room, please," she said pleasantly when someone answered.

The room phone rang, and Kirk picked up the receiver and laid it on the nightstand.

254 • jenna black

"Can you hear me all right?" Grace asked, and we could all hear her voice buzzing from the room phone. "Perfect!"

She pushed me toward the door, brandishing her cell phone. "If I give the order, or if this connection is cut, Kirk will shoot your mother in the head. Don't have any illusions that he won't do as he's told—he's a professional. So you're going to do exactly what I tell you to do at all times. Understand?"

I looked at my mother, lying trussed up and facedown on the bed with a gun to her head. She was absolutely helpless, and this time, I couldn't blame it on the alcohol. Had she been stone cold sober, she'd still be in the same mess. And it would still be my fault.

"I understand," I told Aunt Grace through gritted teeth, because I didn't think a silent nod would satisfy her. There was an almost crazy light in her eyes. I wondered if she was certifiably nuts, or if the power was just going to her head. Either way, it scared the crap out of me.

After one last look at Mom, I opened the door and stepped out into the hallway. Whatever Grace wanted, I was going to have to do it. And hope and pray that she'd let my mom go.

But why should she? an evil little voice whispered in my head. *Once she's got me where she wants me, why wouldn't she just eliminate the witness?* I believed Aunt Grace was crazy enough—or evil enough—to do it. But how could I stop her?

I thought about it frantically as we waited for the elevator, neither of us saying a word. I couldn't even bear to look at her, much less speak to her.

The worst part was that Ethan was waiting for me in the lobby. I might have hoped he could play my knight in shining armor, but he wouldn't know my mom was in danger. If he did something heroic to try to save me from Grace, he might very well get my mom killed.

I was shaking and, I'm sure, corpse-white when we stepped off the elevator into the lobby. But though I glanced surreptitiously around for Ethan, hoping to give him some kind of warning to back off, I didn't see him.

I didn't know how to feel about that. On the one hand, it meant no heroics that would get my mom killed. On the other hand . . . it meant no heroics that would get me away from Aunt Grace.

The doorman gave me a puzzled look as I left the hotel with Aunt Grace. I'm sure he remembered opening the door for Ethan and me, and he probably thought there was something strange about me leaving with someone different—and looking absolutely terrified—but Grace gave him a look, and he suddenly lost interest in us. The cameo hadn't heated, so maybe it had been straight intimidation.

"To the right," Aunt Grace ordered, and I obeyed.

"So where are we going?" I finally found the courage to ask.

Grace flashed me a sly little smile. "To Faerie."

I was so startled and horrified that I stopped in my tracks. "You have to be kidding me!"

She stared down at me with her icy blue eyes. "Do I look like I'm kidding? Now start walking, or I'll give Kirk the go-ahead to have some fun with your mother while you listen."

My head swam, and for a moment, I was afraid I was going to pass out. I forced myself not to think about what Grace had just threatened, instead putting one foot in front of the other.

"Why are we going to Faerie?" I asked in a choked whisper, though I already had an idea. An awful, terrifying, unbelievable idea.

"Seamus told us—Alistair and me—about what happened to your Knight. And Alistair told me what happened with the Spriggans. They are both fools, thinking we can keep you safe and eventually exploit your powers for our own purposes." She shook her head and clucked her tongue. "As if even the three of us together could foil both the Queens of Faerie."

I slowed my pace a bit, trying to postpone the inevitable, but Grace gave me a little push to hurry me along.

"If the Queens wish you dead, then you will die," she said. "Faeriewalkers aren't born every day, and it would be a shame not to get any use out of your unique powers while you are still among the living."

By now I was sure I knew where she was going with this, incredible as it sounded. But I had to hear her say it to believe it, so I kept pressing.

"So why are we going into Faerie?"

Holding the phone precariously with one hand, Grace reached into her purse and opened it just wide enough to show me the gun concealed inside. I know absolutely nothing about guns, but even I could tell this one was a nasty piece of work, so big it barely fit even in that large bag.

"The Fae are hard to kill," she said. "Especially in Faerie, where cold iron doesn't exist."

Yep, she was as crazy as I thought.

"This little baby," she said, patting her purse, "would not work in Faerie, even though it is not cold iron. But, if it is in the hands of a Faeriewalker—or in the hands of someone who is within the Faeriewalker's aura—it will fire. And even a Fae Queen can be killed by a mortal bullet to the head."

"You want to assassinate one of the Queens," I said, and it was only half a question.

"I might try for both," she mused. "I have the power to hold Titania's throne if I take it. Perhaps my first official act as Seelie Queen will be to eliminate Mab. I'm not arrogant enough to think I can hold both thrones, but with Mab dead, whoever inherited the Unseelie throne would be less powerful and easier to work with." Grace gave me an evil grin. "And with you at my side, no one would ever dare threaten me. I will be Queen forever!"

Nope, she wasn't a bit arrogant. I honestly had no idea whether the world would be a better place if she succeeded or if she failed. All I knew was that I was running out of time to come up with a brilliant escape plan. Because we only had another hundred yards or so until we'd be on the bridge and crossing the moat to the Southern Gate.

chapter twenty-five

Rain fell steadily as I trudged miserably toward the bridge that would lead me into Faerie. Grace was so cheerful she was humming under her breath. I kept trying to figure out some way to escape her without getting my mom killed, but I couldn't even come up with a *crazy* idea, much less a sane one.

Because the only delaying tactic I could think of was talking, I decided to ask some more questions.

"Dad said he didn't think you wanted to go back to Faerie," I said through chattering teeth.

"Did he?"

"Yeah. Something about Lachlan." I watched her from under lowered lashes, but she showed no reaction to Lachlan's name.

"For all his ambition and delusions of grandeur, my brother is, I'm afraid, a rather unimaginative person," Aunt Grace said. "If I were to go into Faerie and take up with Lachlan as things stand now, then I would be . . ." She frowned. "I'm afraid *shunned* is too mild a word to describe the reaction, but it's the best I can do. But Seamus forgot that if I went back to Faerie, it would be with you at my side. I will be Queen, and you, my dear child, will be a terrifying enough threat to discourage the rest of the Sidhe from treating me with anything less than the utmost respect."

"So, what, you're going to keep me at your side all the time, like a dog on a leash, in case you feel like shooting someone?"

She smiled that mad smile of hers, her eyes glinting with an ugly humor. "I hadn't thought of it before, but I think a leash would be a wonderful idea. That long white neck of yours would look so lovely with a jeweled collar around it."

I shut up, because I didn't want to hear any more about what she had planned for me. We had reached the bridge now, and my last remaining hopes started dying one by one as we crossed toward the gatehouse.

Grace pointed at a door on the far right end of the gatehouse. A small light at the top of the door cast a faint glow on a sign written in a language I didn't know.

"You see that door?" she asked, but apparently it was a rhetorical question, because she didn't wait for my answer. "That door will lead us directly into Faerie without having to bother with any annoying human customs.

"It's beautifully simple and ingenious. In Avalon, there's a long hallway, which leads directly to the border. On the mortal side of the border, there's nothing but a reinforced concrete wall, so for mortals, it's a dead end. But in Faerie, there is no barrier, so we shall be able to walk right on through. There are border patrol officers stationed in the hallway, of course, but you know better than to make any kind of scene."

Yes, I knew better. Even if Aunt Grace didn't have my mom

as a hostage, I couldn't rely on the border patrol for help. After all, Aunt Grace was their captain. No, it seemed like there was nothing to stop her from whisking me off to Faerie. I hoped if nothing else that it would be warmer there, because my clothes were now thoroughly soaked through, and though I hugged myself for warmth, my teeth chattered more and more with every passing minute.

The parking lot I remembered seeing when I first encountered the gatehouse was nearly empty tonight. There were three cars parked close together right near the ultra-secure official entrance. And there was one other car, a nondescript sedan, parked under a burned-out light near the door to Faerie.

As Grace and I stepped into the parking lot, she seemed to notice the car for the first time, and her footsteps slowed. She grabbed my arm with her free hand, pulling me to her, magic prickling across my skin.

At first, I didn't know what she had seen that alarmed her, but moments later a man stepped from the shadows.

He was tall and very thin, almost frail-looking. He looked like he'd been roused from bed, his long blond hair fastened in a frazzled braid, his clothes wrinkled and mismatched. Even in the dim light of the parking lot, I could tell that his shirt was navy and his pants were black, like he'd grabbed them in the dark and just thrown them on.

I thought he was a total stranger to me, until he stepped into a pool of light and I got a look at his eyes. Fae, of course, but of an unusual shade of teal blue. Just like Ethan and Kimber's. Grace confirmed my guess by speaking, even as she backed away, pulling me with her.

"Why Alistair, what a lovely surprise," she said.

He rubbed his face, looking exhausted. I was almost surprised Grace didn't just run right over him. He certainly didn't look like much of a threat. But of course, I knew that looks could be deceiving, especially here.

"Lovely is not a word I would use to describe it," he said, and he sounded as tired as he looked. He took a step closer to us, and Grace continued to back up. Maybe Alistair would be able to chase us all the way over the bridge and back into the, er, safety of Avalon.

"Don't be difficult about this," Grace said.

Alistair shook his head. "I'm afraid I can't allow you to take the girl into Faerie."

"Why ever not?" she asked, and she sounded genuinely puzzled.

Alistair gave a bark of laughter. "It's too late in the night for games. If you try to go through me, I *will* stop you."

Aunt Grace looked . . . annoyed. Her hand tightened on my arm until I hissed in pain. She didn't loosen her grip.

"Perhaps you'd like to convince Alistair to step aside, dear," she suggested to me, brandishing the phone.

My throat tightened in terror, and I turned pleading eyes on Alistair.

"Please," I begged in my most respectful voice. "She has my mother. She's going to have her friend kill my mom if you try to stop us." I could hardly believe I was in a position of begging someone to let Grace kidnap me into Faerie, but I had no doubt she was spiteful enough to have my mother killed if this grand plan of hers failed.

Alistair's gaze darted over my shoulder and then back, so quickly I might almost have missed it if I hadn't been staring at him so intently. I think it was an involuntary moment of distraction on his part, not a cue for me to look over my shoulder. But I couldn't help looking anyway.

And there was Ethan, standing about ten feet behind us, trapping us between himself and his father. Now I understood why Alistair had "just happened" to be waiting for us. Ethan must have either seen Aunt Grace enter the hotel, or had at least seen her leave with me, and he'd called in reinforcements. But neither he nor Alistair could do anything to help my mother.

"I'm very sorry," Alistair said to me. "I would not lightly put your mother at risk. But I cannot allow Grace to take you into Faerie."

"Why not?" Grace asked. "Why should you care? You have never called Faerie home. You owe no allegiance to anyone there, not even your Queen. Why sacrifice this girl's mother to stop me when what happens in Faerie is no concern of yours?"

The cameo warmed in a way that was becoming sickeningly familiar. For reasons I didn't understand, I felt sure that magical electricity, or whatever it was, was coming from Grace, not Ethan or Alistair. Maybe just because she was so much closer to me. I saw her lips begin to curl in a smile, and I knew it meant no good.

"She's going to cast something!" I screamed, sure whatever spell she was casting would not be pleasant.

I felt, rather than saw, the magic swelling around us then bursting forward, rushing toward Alistair. But I think my shout warned Alistair just in time, because he dove to the side.

My ears popped, and Alistair's car, directly behind him in the line of fire . . . imploded. That's the only way I can describe what happened. It looked like semi trucks had smashed into it from all sides at once. I didn't even want to think about what Alistair would have looked like if the spell had hit him.

Grace looked down at me in such a fury I thought the force of her anger should strike me dead. I was sure she was about to hit me again. Instead, she did something much, much worse.

"Kill her!" she yelled into her cell phone.

"No!" I screamed, but Grace shut the phone with a snarl and hurled it over the side of the railing into the waters of the moat below.

Out of the corner of my eye, I saw Alistair get up, shaking off the effects of the near miss, but all I could think about was Grace giving the fatal order. I didn't even *try* to stop the tears this time.

"That was not the wisest move," I heard Alistair say, his voice calm and unruffled. I wanted to kill him for that calm when my mother had just been murdered because he wouldn't let us go. "Even *you* can't withstand a murder charge," he continued. "Not with three witnesses."

"You have always underestimated me, Alistair. Just like my brother has."

At that point, I was so overwhelmed with grief and horror that I honestly didn't care what else Grace had up her sleeve. Until I found out what it was, of course.

The Fae, even slender, willowy females like Aunt Grace, are way stronger than mortals. Which is why Grace had no trouble grabbing me, lifting me off my feet, and flinging me over the side of the railing to follow the path of her phone.

I was too shocked to scream, though both Alistair and Ethan cried out. I flailed around in the air, trying to control my entry into the water, but when I hit, I was flat on my back. I tried to dissipate some of the force by slapping my arms down, just as Keane had showed me, but it didn't help much.

It wasn't a horribly long fall from the bridge into the moat—not the kind of fall you'd expect to die from, at least—but it wasn't just a little hop, either. The water slammed into my back like a slab of concrete, forcing all the air from my lungs and momentarily stunning me.

That moment was long enough for the murky, muddy water to close over my head and begin to suck me down.

chapter twenty-six

I'm not the world's best swimmer, but I can generally dog-paddle with the best of them. When I recovered from that initial stunned, breathless moment, I started kicking and flailing, trying to get to the surface. I was scared, but not exactly in a panic. Not yet. It was just water, after all.

But for all my flailing, I didn't seem to be finding the surface. My heavy wool sweater seemed to weigh about ten tons, and my feet couldn't seem to move much water in my good walking sneakers. Lungs burning, I pried the shoes off with my feet and was able to kick more effectively.

With another couple of kicks, I probably would have made the surface and been fine. Except one of those kicks connected with something. Something soft and yielding, like flesh. Something that wrapped around my foot and held me.

I broke the hold easily enough, but the terror of being grabbed by something under the water, combined with my increasingly critical lack of oxygen, caused me to try to gasp. I sucked some water into my lungs. And *that* was when I started to panic.

I had to cough the water out of my lungs, but you can't cough if you don't have any air. I clapped a hand over my mouth and pinched my nose shut to keep myself from taking another reflexive breath of water, but the need to cough was overwhelming. I couldn't fight it, even though a small corner of my mind knew that if I tried to breathe, I would die.

The reflex became too much, and I let go of my nose and mouth to gasp in another breath of water.

I was dimly aware of the sensation of hands grabbing my arms, but I was far too panicked to feel any relief or to try to cooperate with my would-be rescuer. I was half-convinced it was a near-death hallucination anyway.

But those hands had a firm hold, and a moment later, I burst through the surface of the water into the beautiful, wonderful, life-sustaining air. Unfortunately, I'd sucked so much water into my lungs that even with the air so tantalizingly near, I couldn't breathe.

The hands that held my arms moved until they were wrapped around my waist, one arm squeezing brutally hard and upward. It hurt, but it also caused a gout of water to come flying out of my mouth and nose. Eww, gross!

I managed a sip of air, but then the coughing seized me. More water left my lungs, burning my throat fiercely on the way up. I got a little more air in, so I was almost able to scream when something once again wrapped around my ankle.

"Damn it!" my rescuer cried, and I realized it was Ethan.

I felt him kick whatever had grabbed me, and the grip loosened.

"We have to get out of the water, Dana!" Ethan yelled at me.

I was *so* with him!

I was still coughing and choking too much to swim on my

own, so Ethan towed me. I blinked water and tears from my eyes and saw that Ethan was taking me under the bridge.

Whatever was in the moat made another grab, and I felt a hair-raising pulse as Ethan threw some kind of magic at it.

"Kick with me!" he commanded, and I did the best I could despite my continued struggle to breathe.

It was an agonizingly slow, terrifying swim. I sensed the moat monster lurking below us in the depths of the muddy water. Waiting for us to show a sign of weakness. Or maybe just waiting for Ethan's magical attack to wear off.

I'd recovered enough of my mental faculties to see that we were heading for the base of the bridge, but what I saw there didn't exactly give me warm fuzzies. There was a narrow concrete ledge that jutted out of the water, but it would take a pretty big reach to grab on to it, and I knew that even if I grabbed it, I wouldn't have the strength to haul myself out of the water.

"Almost there," Ethan said, but though he was trying to comfort me, he sounded scared himself, which was not comforting at all.

A few more frantic kicks, and we butted up against the concrete.

"I'm going to give you a boost," Ethan said, panting with the effort of swimming for both of us—and fighting off unseen monsters to boot. "Grab hold of the edge."

I still didn't think grabbing hold of the edge would do me much good, but I wasn't about to argue. Ethan shifted his grip once again, and in any other situation, I'd have objected to where his hands ended up. But somehow, I didn't think he was trying to cop a feel at the moment.

Ethan pushed me up out of the water, and I reached my hands above my head. They connected with the ledge, but I was still in the water from the butt down. It meant I didn't have to support my full weight as I hung there, but it wasn't enough to give me the strength to pull myself up. If I survived this, I was going to have to spend some time in the gym building up some upper body strength.

Beside me, Ethan lunged up out of the water, his hands grabbing the ledge without any helpful boost. Unless the monster was helping, which seemed unlikely.

"Hold on," he ordered me, then easily pulled himself up and onto the ledge.

His hands had just closed around my wrists when the monster grabbed me again.

"Ethan!" I screamed, kicking wildly.

"I've got you!" he assured me, and started to pull.

The monster had let go with little encouragement the last couple of times, but maybe it saw that its prey was getting away and decided to make a last stand. Whatever the reason, it didn't let go when Ethan started pulling.

I couldn't help glancing down at the water, trying to see the creature that was trying so hard to pull me back in. The water was so murky, and the area under the bridge so dark, that I couldn't see anything under the surface.

Something wrapped around my other leg, and I screamed again. Ethan cursed, but held firmly to my wrists as the two played tug-of-war for me.

A ghastly, dead-fish-white face rose from the water near my legs. Hair like sticky gray spiderwebs flowed all around its colorless head, moving this way and that, not—at least as far as I could tell—affected by any kind of current or wind. My stomach cramped as I realized it was the hair that was wrapped around my legs.

The creature's eyes were as white as its skin, giving the impression that it was blind. But I didn't think it was, because it sure seemed like it was gazing balefully up at Ethan.

"Mine!" the creature said in an awful gurgle of a voice. When it spoke, I saw the double row of needlelike teeth in its mouth.

"Ethan," I whimpered. I would rather have drowned than let this creature have me.

"No, she's *mine*," Ethan told the creature in a fierce, throaty, snarl that sounded barely human. Of course, Ethan *wasn't* human.

The creature hissed, its weirdly grabby hair wrapping more and more tendrils around me.

Ethan's eyes practically glowed in the darkness, and his grip on my arms hadn't wavered, though I was beginning to feel like I was being stretched on a rack. My shoulders were screaming in agony, and I was afraid any moment now, muscles would start tearing.

Ethan said something in a language I didn't know. I guessed it was either Gaelic, or some kind of weird Faerie language. With his words came a soft pulse of power that traveled down my body toward the creature.

The creature hissed again, baring its teeth at Ethan.

"You do not wish to make an enemy of me or my house," Ethan told it through gritted teeth, and the look on his face would have scared anyone—or any*thing*—that had two brain cells to rub together.

With a final sullen hiss, the creature let go of me and sank back into the water. The moment I was free of its grip, Ethan hauled me all the way out and onto the ledge.

chapter twenty-seven

I was on my knees on the narrow ledge, back hunched with strain as I tried to hack up a lung for what felt like the better part of forever. Ethan patted my back and murmured comforting words, but I was too miserable to be comforted.

My throat and nasal passages burned from expelling all that water from my lungs. My chest ached from taking all that water in. And all my joints throbbed from being a tug-of-war toy between Ethan and the moat monster. I was also soaked through and chilled to the bone, my whole body shivering violently.

When the coughs had calmed some, Ethan pulled me against him, wrapping his arms around me and holding me close to the warmth of his body. It was only then that I noticed he was wearing nothing but a pair of pants. Even so, his body felt like a furnace compared to mine, and I curled into myself and huddled against him.

"What *was* that?" I rasped, shuddering at the memory of that awful, evil face in the water.

"It was a Water Witch," Ethan explained. "They are natives of Faerie and at least nominally belong to the Unseelie Court, which is probably the only reason I was able to make her let go. There are dozens of them in the moat, and they will attack anything, Fae or human, that falls in. If the moat were just empty water, then people—and Fae—could enter and leave Avalon at will and the Gates would mean nothing."

I shuddered again at the thought of *dozens* of those horrible things patrolling the moat, hoping for a free meal. Not that I was sure the Water Witch had planned to eat me, but with those teeth she'd flashed, it didn't seem out of the question.

I started to cry, then, for once not ashamed of my weakness. I remembered Grace yelling the fateful order into her cell phone moments before she threw it—and me—into the moat.

"She killed my mom," I sobbed against Ethan's chest.

He held me tight and rocked me. "Maybe not," he murmured. "I called your father after I called mine. He said he'd send Finn to rescue your mother. We can only hope that he made it there in time. I wish I could offer you something more certain, but I think my cell phone is at the bottom of the moat by now."

I sniffled and tried to hope. Finn did this kind of stuff for a living. If anyone could have saved my mom from Kirk, it would be him. But everything had happened so fast, despite my attempts at delay. Would Finn really have had time to get to the hotel before Grace ordered my mother's death?

"I want to go home," I said, though I couldn't rightly say where home was anymore.

"I know," Ethan said. "But the purpose of the moat is to keep people out of Avalon, so there isn't exactly an easy exit. There's a trapdoor in the bridge above us, but my father's going to have to get someone to undo the locking spells on it, and then they're going to have to haul us up somehow. We'll be stuck here for a while."

I was so cold I felt like I'd never be warm again in a million years, and the contrast of Ethan's warmth only made me feel colder. He scooted backward until his back was against the concrete piling. He had to let go of me to do it, but then he patted his lap.

"Come sit on my lap," he said. "I'll keep you as warm as I can."

I thought briefly about what had happened the last time I'd found myself on Ethan's lap, but I shoved that thought to the side. Even Ethan wasn't enough of a player to make a move on me now, of all times.

So I crawled onto his lap, and he wrapped himself around me. His arms surrounded me, and my face was pressed up against his bare chest while his body heat seeped through my sodden clothes.

"Aren't you cold at all?" I asked him.

I felt him shrug. "Not really. We only feel the cold when it's extreme. And as you can probably tell, our body temperatures run higher than humans' anyway."

Yes, I could tell. Every inch of me that was in contact with his body was toasty warm. Unfortunately, there were a lot of inches left, and I shivered nonstop.

"You saved my life," I whispered into his chest.

His chin rubbed across the top of my head. "It was the least I could do."

I thought about the Water Witch, with her milky eyes, razor-sharp teeth, and sticky cobweb hair. Ethan had jumped into the moat after me, knowing there were dozens of those creatures in there. And while they were supposedly both members of the Unseelie Court, they obviously weren't kissing cousins.

He'd lied to me. He'd tried to use his magic against me. And he'd set me up for an attack that could have gotten me killed.

But in the end, he'd risked his own life to save mine, so how could I not forgive him for the bad things he'd done?

"Let's just call it even now and leave it at that," I said. Ethan kissed the top of my head but didn't respond.

"How did you know Grace was about to cast a spell at my father?" he asked me. "You saved his life with your warning."

That thought made me feel a tiny bit less wretched. At least I'd done *something* right. And I was glad to have saved a life, even if I'd needed rescuing myself.

"I could feel the magic building up," I explained, and I felt Ethan go still. I tried to lift my head from his chest to see his face, but he wouldn't let me.

"What?" I asked. "What did I say?"

"You felt the magic," he repeated, and he sounded like he couldn't quite believe it.

"Yeah. At least, that's what I think it is. The cameo my dad gave me heats up, and then my skin starts to feel all prickly. I'm pretty sure that only happens when there's magic around."

Now Ethan pushed me away, allowing me to see his face. Not that I could see much in the darkness under the bridge. But I could see the intensity of his expression.

"I'm going to forget I asked you that question," he said. "And I'm very certainly going to forget your answer. If your father or mine ever asks you, say you heard her muttering something and made an educated guess as to what it meant."

"Why?"

"Because traditionally, the magic has always treated Faeriewalkers like humans, even though they are truly half Fae. But if you could feel it building, that means you have an affinity for it, which means you might be able to train and use it yourself. You are a powerful and frightening enough weapon as it is. If anyone thought you could do magic as well . . ." He shook his head. "Too dangerous. It wouldn't be just the Queens who wanted to eliminate you then."

"But it's only because of the cameo," I protested. "If I take it off—" I reached for the clasp behind my neck, but Ethan's hands closed around my wrists.

"Keep it," he said. "I don't know exactly what it does, but if it reacts to magic, then it's an object of power of some sort and could come in handy someday. You wouldn't have felt the effects if you didn't have a natural affinity for magic. A human wearing it would feel nothing. So we never had this conversation. Got it?"

My eyes no doubt wide as saucers, I nodded. Why would my father have given me an "object of power" if he thought I couldn't access the magic? Had he somehow guessed that I would be unusual even for a Faeriewalker? Or had he just figured that since I couldn't sense magic, the cameo was harmless, just a symbol of my Seelie affiliations? If I couldn't ask him about it, then it seemed likely I'd never know the answer. "And you're not going to tell anyone?" I prompted Ethan. "Not even your father?"

"Tell them what?" he asked, and though he was trying to sound dry and witty, he just ended up sounding nervous.

chapter twenty-eight

The moat had killed my watch and Ethan wasn't wearing his, so I had no real concept of how long we huddled there beneath the bridge, except that it was far, far longer than I would have liked. During that time, I discovered a new pain. My skin apparently didn't react well to Water Witch hair, so there were raised red welts all along the lower part of my legs where she'd grabbed me.

They burned and stung, and by the time Alistair arranged for someone to open the trapdoor that led under the bridge, I was starting to feel the warm flush of fever in my cheeks. They had to haul me up with some kind of harness. I'd have been scared, except I felt too awful to bother with fear. Maybe everyone—including *me*—would be better off if I fell and splatted on the concrete below. But I didn't fall.

Alistair and my father were both waiting for me on the bridge, and they helped the emergency folks extract me from the harness. I locked eyes with my dad as they went to work on the buckles that held me safe. He looked pale and worried, impatient to get me out of the harness.

"Mom?" I asked in a terrified whisper, trying to keep myself from bursting into tears yet again.

Dad gave me a reassuring nod. "She's safe."

I didn't try to hold back the tears anymore. I wasn't up to standing, so when all the buckles and straps were loose, my dad picked me up and started carrying me toward his car, which was hard to miss, sitting in the parking lot in its bright red glory.

"Wait!" I cried, looking over his shoulder at Alistair.

He was watching the rescue workers lower the harness again, but he seemed to sense my gaze on him, since he turned toward me.

"Aunt Grace," I said. "What happened to her?"

Alistair's already thin lips practically disappeared as he pressed them together hard and shook his head. "She got past me." He forced his expression into one of wry amusement, but it didn't reach his eyes. "I was somewhat distracted when she tossed you into the moat, I'm afraid."

My eyes fixed on the door to Faerie, and Alistair's slight nod told me that's where Grace had gone. Why did I expect she wouldn't stay there forever?

I lost consciousness before my dad got me to his car. When I woke up, it was to find myself in a hospital bed. The aches and pains I remembered from before were all gone, but my head throbbed fiercely, and I was sweating like it was a hundred degrees in the room. I moaned and turned to my side.

Finn was sitting on a visitor's chair beside my bed—between me and the door, naturally. I supposed he was back on bodyguard duty, but it felt good not to be alone when I woke up. He was reading a magazine, but he closed it and put it away when he saw I was awake.

My stomach wasn't much happier than my head, and for a moment, I was afraid I was going to puke over the side of the bed. But the urge passed.

"Why am I in the hospital?" I asked Finn as I peeled sweaty strands of hair away from my face. "What's wrong with me?"

"It seems you had an encounter with a Water Witch," he said.

"No kidding?" Whatever was wrong with me, it wasn't amnesia. I wished I could burn the image of that evil face from my brain.

Finn gave me a reproachful look, then continued as if I hadn't spoken. "Prolonged contact with Water Witches apparently makes humans rather ill." He frowned. "Actually, prolonged contact with Water Witches usually leaves just about anyone dead. You were very lucky."

I couldn't help it. I laughed. "Yeah, luck central, that's me." The laughter morphed into a coughing fit. I was braced for the coughing to hurt my chest, but only the headache pain troubled me. "How long have I been here?" I had absolutely no sense of time at this point. It could have been hours or days.

"About four hours," he said, and I was relieved that I hadn't lost more time than that. "The healers took care of your physical injuries."

Oh. That explained why the chest and throat and joint pains weren't bugging me.

"But they can't fix the sickness?" I guessed.

Finn shook his head. "The Fae don't get sick, so our magic isn't suited to curing illness, I'm afraid."

278 • jenna black

In a way, I supposed that was a good thing. Otherwise every sick person in the world would be besieging Avalon. In fact, I bet even if the Fae healers *could* cure illnesses, they wouldn't admit it. I could only imagine the chaos it would cause if a handful of people in one small city could, for instance, cure cancer.

I was already starting to feel exhausted just from the effort of simple concentration, but I managed one more question before I drifted back into sleep.

"How long am I in for?" I asked, not only because I hated being in the hospital—like any sensible person would—but because even with Finn guarding me, I wasn't sure how safe I would be here.

"Probably a couple of days. The human doctors want to keep an eye on you, make sure your fever doesn't get too high."

I acknowledged my sentence with a heartfelt sigh, then rolled over and willed myself back to sleep.

The next time I woke up, it was because someone was gently shaking my shoulder.

"Come on, Dana," I heard Finn say. "Wake up for a moment."

The headache still pounded behind my eyes, and I was sweaty and cold at the same time. I didn't much want to be awake for the experience, but I managed to pry my eyes open.

Finn was sitting on the edge of my bed, but my attention was immediately drawn to the mountain that stood just inside the doorway. The mountain named Lachlan.

I should have been alarmed to see him. He was Aunt Grace's . . . boyfriend? Nah. I couldn't see applying that term to Lachlan. But "lover" sounded so crass. I hated the term "significant other," but I decided it was a fair compromise.

Anyway, I should have been spooked, but I wasn't. Either the hospital had me on some really good drugs, or I figured Finn wouldn't have let him in if he was a threat, or I just couldn't see Lachlan in the role of villain. He *had* been pretty nice to me, even though he'd been holding me prisoner.

Finn smiled at me, but it looked like he wasn't really used to smiling. It looked almost like it hurt him.

"Lachlan is here to relieve me for a while," Finn said. "I wanted to wake you and assure you that you're safe with him. He's no Knight, but there are few who'd be foolish enough to take on a troll. And your father is confident Lachlan will not take you to Grace."

I saw Lachlan wince. "Thanks," I mumbled. I just wanted to go back to sleep. Being sick sucks.

Finn gave me one of his businesslike nods, then headed out without another word. Lachlan came to the bedside to tower over me. He looked . . . very sad. There was a shadow in his eyes that hadn't been there before, and his shoulders were tight with tension and misery.

Tired as I was, I managed to smile up at him. "It's all right, Lachlan," I said. "I know you had nothing to do with what Aunt Grace did." And I felt that truth to my bones. No matter what his relationship with Aunt Grace was, he wouldn't sit by and let her kill someone. Or throw someone into the moat.

The tension in his shoulders relaxed, and he bowed his head. "Thank you." He sighed heavily. "I don't know what's gotten into her." He met my eyes with a pleading, earnest look. "She's really not like that. She's just . . ."

I could forgive Lachlan for being in love with Grace, but I really wasn't open to hearing whatever excuses he had for her bad behavior. I guess he saw that, because he didn't say anything more, just took a seat in what I was already coming to think of as Finn's chair.

That was my cue to return to la-la land, and I was more than happy to obey.

I drifted in and out of sleep for the better part of the day, waking up only when the nurses came to take my temperature, give me drugs, or urge me to eat and drink. I was not in the mood for eating and drinking, and hospital food turned out to be hospital food, even in Avalon. But they threatened to hook me up to an IV if I didn't keep myself fed and hydrated, so I did the best I could.

At one point, I woke up to find a huge bouquet of yellow roses on my bedside table. Turned out Ethan had stopped by to visit while I was sleeping and had chosen not to wake me. Just looking at them—and their cheerful, sunny color—made me smile. Interesting that he'd chosen to send me roses, even if they weren't red or white. I suspected gifts of roses took on a whole different meaning and significance when you were Fae.

By late afternoon, I was finding it hard to stay asleep, even though I felt terrible when I was awake. Worse, I knew the ordeal of dinner wasn't far in the future, because hospitals always seem to feed people early. At least, that had been the case in the American hospitals my mom had landed in a couple of times after drunken "mishaps."

Lachlan was still on guard duty, but neither one of us was feeling particularly chatty, so we were sitting in not-quite-companionable silence when I had my second visitor of the day.

I hadn't seen or spoken to Kimber since the attack at the boutique. I supposed I should have called to check on her—after all, she'd been hurt, too—but my mom's arrival in Avalon had driven all other thoughts from my head. Kimber hesitated in the doorway, chewing her lip in a very un-Fae-like show of nerves. The expression on her face was vulnerable, but I wasn't sure what was wrong.

"Come on in." I beckoned her as I raised the top half of my bed so I could sit up.

Kimber smiled tentatively and stepped through the doorway.

"I'll wait outside to give you some privacy," Lachlan said, and I flashed him a smile of gratitude.

When the door closed behind Lachlan, Kimber came to sit on the edge of my bed. She glanced at the bouquet of roses and raised her eyebrows.

"I see my brother has been here," she said.

I discovered I could blush even with fever-flushed cheeks. "Yeah. I was asleep at the time."

Her eyes glittering with mischief, she reached into the tote bag that hung from her shoulder. "I brought you something better." She pulled out a thermos and gave it a vigorous shake.

It wasn't hard to guess what was in that thermos, and as soon as Kimber twisted the top open, my nose confirmed the guess. As badly as I'd dreaded having to choke down dinner, the scent of the hot posset set my mouth instantly to watering. She poured me a careful capful and handed it to me.

It smelled so inviting—especially since the whiskey scent wasn't overpowering—that I wanted to chug it down instantly, but I hesitated. "Is this allowed?" I asked. "I don't know what meds I'm on, and—"

Kimber gave a haughty sniff. "Hot posset is the best medicine of all."

"Yeah, but some meds don't react well to alcohol." And I

imagined she and I both would get in trouble if the nurses came in and smelled booze on my breath.

Kimber chuckled. "I made it according to the actual recipe instead of spiking it like I usually do. There's one tablespoon of whiskey in the whole batch. Now drink up before it starts to get that nasty hot-milk film on top."

I took a sip and let out an appreciative "mmm." It was as rich and creamy as I remembered, and Kimber had obviously used extra honey this time because it was deliciously sweet as well. I'm sure it was just the power of suggestion, but I swear my headache dimmed as I drank the posset down.

I drank the whole capful in no time flat, and Kimber instantly refilled it. She still had that vulnerable, shy look on her face.

"Is something wrong?" I asked, then took another soothing sip.

She huffed out a deep breath, then smiled at me. "I believe Ethan was right and I was being paranoid." The smile faded, and she stared at her hands. "I was afraid that after everything that's happened, you'd think I led you into an ambush at that boutique."

I was genuinely shocked by the suggestion. Obviously, I'm not the most trusting of people, but I'd never once suspected Kimber had any involvement in the attack, and I told her so.

I hadn't realized just how tense she was until her whole body relaxed.

"Why would you expect me to think you had anything to do with it?" I asked.

She shrugged. "I guess I'm still trying to deal with my guilty conscience about . . . before."

"That's water under the bridge," I told her, and realized all the anger I'd felt when I'd discovered her and Ethan's deception had faded away. I grinned. "I let Ethan off the hook because he saved my life. And you brought me hot posset, so you can't be all bad."

Kimber answered my grin with one of her own. "I told you hot posset is the cure for everything."

Maybe it was the placebo effect, but I felt much better after two cups of hot posset. So much so that I was even able to face my delicious evening meal of rubber chicken, instant mashed potatoes, and mushy peas.

By the time I decided to call it a night and go back to sleep, Finn had replaced Lachlan again, and I was beginning to wonder why neither my father nor my mother had visited me. I supposed it was possible my mom was too drunk. She had, after all, been through quite a traumatic experience. But that didn't explain my dad's absence, and when I questioned Finn about it, he just told me my dad was a busy man. He didn't bother to make that sound like the truth. But no amount of questioning would make him change his story.

My parents didn't visit the next day, either, though both Ethan and Kimber stopped by. (And yes, Kimber brought more hot posset.) I'd half-hoped Keane would come—though probably his attitude wasn't good for my health—but he didn't. Silly of me to expect him, of course. And even sillier to be hurt that he hadn't come. He was just my self-defense instructor, after all, not my friend.

I tried questioning Lachlan about why Mom and Dad weren't visiting, but he was about as informative as Finn. I had a really bad feeling about all this, although when I asked, everyone assured me that my mom was fine.

My dad finally made his appearance on the morning of my third day in the hospital. I was still running a low-grade fever, but I was feeling much better, and the nurse who'd stopped by first thing in the morning told me I'd be free to go home after the doctor examined me one more time.

Finn was on guard duty when Dad arrived, but he hastily vacated the room and closed the door behind him. I didn't like the look on my dad's face, so guarded and almost . . . wary. I raised my bed so I could sit up comfortably, since I suspected we were about to have a conversation I shouldn't take lying down.

I'd been so worried about my mom—not to mention traumatized by my little swim in the moat—that I hadn't taken the time to consider my dad's feelings. But as I looked at him and he didn't speak, I finally recognized the emotion I saw, the one he was trying so hard to guard: hurt.

My gaze skittered away from him, and I hung my head. I hadn't known him very long, and he hadn't even known I'd existed until less than a month ago, but he'd deserved better from me than to have me sneak away in the middle of the night without even leaving him a note. Even if my escape had been successful, Dad would probably have thought I'd somehow gotten kidnapped or murdered right under his nose.

"I'm sorry I tried to leave like that," I said, looking at my hands, which were folded in my lap, rather than at him.

Dad didn't answer. I finally couldn't stand the silence, so I turned to look at him again. He shook his head, and it took everything I had not to turn away in shame.

"You could have died," he said softly. "You almost *did*. And if Grace had succeeded in taking you to Faerie, it would have been even worse."

I dropped my gaze again. "I know. But the three of you were going to lock me away somewhere, and you'd made it very clear I had no say in anything. I couldn't stand to live like that."

"Better to live like that than as Grace's pet in Faerie!" he snapped. "Better to live like that than to die!"

I'd never seen my dad this angry before. It was a scary sight. His face was flushed, his eyes piercing, his fists clenched into white-knuckled fists. I even felt the distinctive prickle of magic in the air, though the cameo was safely tucked into a bedside drawer. I guess I no longer needed its help to sense the magic.

I waited in tense silence, hardly daring to breathe. I didn't really think my dad would hurt me, but he looked like he wanted to in the worst way.

Finally, he let out a harsh breath and unclenched his fists. The magical prickle faded, and some of the angry color faded from his face. He still didn't exactly look happy with me, but at least he no longer looked like he was contemplating killing me himself.

"I have tried as best I can to treat you as a responsible adult," he said, each word precise and clipped. "I've been honest with you when pretty lies might have been more expedient. But it seems I misjudged you."

I winced. Dad was obviously a pro at the parental guilt-trip thing. So much so that I felt like I had to defend myself more.

"It wasn't all because I wanted to get away from Avalon," I said. "Mom promised she'd check herself into a rehab if I went home with her." I stared at my hands as I plucked nervously at the sheet. "You don't know what it's been like, watching her destroy herself. And she's never even been able to admit she has a problem, much less tried to get help. I had a chance to try to save her from herself, and I couldn't not take it."

Dad came to sit on the edge of my bed. I didn't want to look in his face, didn't want to see the anger and hurt and—maybe even worse—disappointment in his eyes. He reached out and covered both my hands in one of his, but I still didn't look at him.

"Dana, my child, I am not a young man. I have lived in Avalon and among humans for centuries. And if there is one thing I know, it's that there is no saving them from their own self-destructive behaviors unless they want to be saved. I can understand why blackmailing your mother into going into a rehab would sound like a good idea to you, but even if you'd gotten away with no complications, and she followed through on her promise, it wouldn't have worked.

"You can't *force* her to dry out, not for any significant period of time. Maybe she would have stayed sober for a few weeks or even months, but she would have been drinking again in no time."

I pulled my hands out from under his. "You can't know that! If she had stopped drinking, she'd see everything she'd been missing because she was drunk all the time and that would give her a reason to stay sober. She's just too out of it most of the time to realize the consequences of what she's doing."

Dad sighed. "I think in your heart you know that I'm right. There was a reason you came looking for me, and it wasn't because your heart was full of hope for your mother's recovery."

Now it was my turn to be mad, and I glared at him. "Don't try to tell me what I think and feel."

His look of gentle condescension made me even madder, but he didn't give me a chance to tell him what I thought of him. "I suspect we will have to agree to disagree on this point," he said. He sat up straighter and wiped the condescending look off his face, changing the subject both with his words and his body language.

"According to the nurse, your doctor will be in to see you within the hour, and then you will be free to come home. I have a lunch meeting, but Finn will take you home and guard you until I'm free. When I get home, we will move you to a more secure location."

Ah, yes. The dreaded "secure location." Otherwise known as a prison cell. I knew better than to argue—this wasn't one I could win—but I crossed my arms over my chest and put on my most mulish expression.

One corner of Dad's mouth lifted in a hint of a smile. "For your foolishness of the other night, you are grounded for the next week. You will remain in the safe house at all times, and if you feel imprisoned, then that's not inappropriate."

I gaped at him. I'd never been grounded in my whole life. Heck, it sounded almost like a *normal* thing. Of course, his idea of grounding me sounded more strict than a human's.

"When the week is up," Dad continued, "you'll be allowed as much freedom as we deem safe."

"And who, exactly, is 'we'?"

"Alistair, myself . . . and your mother."

My eyes widened. "Mom?"

He nodded. "She will remain in Avalon. And she has granted me legal custody." His expression turned grim. "Should you think about running away again, you will find you have no-where to go."

I shook my head. "No way would Mom agree to any of this!" After everything she'd done to try to keep me away from my father and from Avalon, I couldn't conceive of her being party to a conspiracy to keep me here.

288 • jenna black

"Of course she would. She *did*." His expression softened. "All she wants is for you to be safe, and she understands that you will be safer here than in the mortal world."

As far as I could tell, Dad had never lied to me. But that didn't mean he couldn't choose to do so now. I bet he could have been real persuasive in trying to convince my mom that I'd be safer here, but I still didn't believe Mom would go for it.

"If she agreed to this, I'd like to hear it from her personally."

"That isn't possible at the moment."

My heart gave a nasty thud in my chest, and adrenaline flooded my veins. "Why not? What's wrong with her? Everyone keeps telling me she's all right, but—"

"She's fine, Dana. But she hasn't had a drink in almost three days, and she . . . isn't quite herself right now."

My mouth hung open, and I could think of nothing to say.

"It isn't a cure," Dad said. "I have had her declared legally incompetent, and she is now under my care just as you are. I will not provide her with alcohol, nor will I provide her the means to *get* alcohol. But if I grant her her freedom, she'll start drinking again immediately. One cannot cure alcoholism by force."

I thought about this a minute. "You had her declared incompetent and put under your care," I said, and he nodded. I was afraid I knew what that meant. "In other words, she's just as much your prisoner as I am."

"Yes."

I grimaced. I'd forgotten how brutally honest he could be. Emphasis on *brutal*.

"Keep in mind that as long as I have her under my care, she will be sober. I'm sure it's not much of a consolation to you—and I'm also sure your mother will hate me for it—but it is something."

So basically, I was trading both my and my mother's freedom for her sobriety. I wasn't absolutely certain it wasn't a fair trade. Not that I had a say in it. I chewed my lip while I thought it over.

"Dana," Dad said softly. "Even *I* cannot hold you against your will once you turn eighteen, unless you feel like developing a drug or alcohol problem to give me an excuse as your mother did. As much as you may dislike my methods, you will have to endure them only a year and a quarter. And during that time, I'm going to have to convince you to remain under my protection when you turn eighteen. I am not a fool. I will not win you over by mistreating you or your mother. It won't be as bad as you think."

Hmm. A year and a quarter in a gilded prison, and then I'd be paroled. It seemed like a long time when I considered all that had happened to me in Avalon since I'd arrived. But it was also a year and a quarter of enforced sobriety for my mom.

There was a part of me that believed Dad was right, that forcing my mom to stay clean wouldn't actually cure her. But at least it would give her body some time to recover from the damage she'd done to it. And at least for that short time, I would have a mom I could relate to, whom I didn't despise and wasn't ashamed of. I would have the mom I glimpsed ever so briefly when she wasn't drunk, the mom who was witty, and clever, and . . . fun.

No, I didn't have a choice in the matter. Dad had made that quite clear. But I did have a choice as to how much of a pain in the butt I was going to be about it.

I swallowed all my protests and took a deep breath. I could do this. I could accept my fate with dignity and regain my dad's trust. And when I turned eighteen—assuming I lived that long, of course—I could decide for myself whether I was better off in Avalon or in the mortal world.

I nodded briskly. "All right," I said. "I promise to be a good little inmate." If my hands hadn't been outside the sheets, I might have crossed my fingers. After all, it is a girl's prerogative to change her mind, so I might not be telling the truth, the whole truth, and nothing but the truth.

Dad's wry smile said, "I'll believe it when I see it." But he didn't put that thought into words, merely patted my hands in another one of those reserved Fae gestures of affection.

He was almost out the door when I stopped him.

"Dad?" I said, and he turned to me with raised eyebrows.

"Thank you for sending Finn to save my mom." My throat tightened as I remembered once again the terrible pain that had slammed me when Grace had ordered my mother's death.

He looked at me gravely. "No thanks are needed. I proved myself remarkably useless under the circumstances. It was Alistair who delayed Grace, and it was Finn who saved your mother. I did not arrive on the scene until everything was over."

"Yeah, but you live halfway up the mountain," I said, realizing he genuinely felt bad about not being my own personal white knight. "Ethan would have called his own father before you, and I'm guessing you called Finn because he lives closer to the hotel. Right?" He nodded. "So if you'd come running to the rescue yourself, my mom would have died before you got there. You did the right thing."

He smiled at me, but his eyes looked sad. "I know I did. That doesn't mean I have to like it."

I didn't know what to say to that, but I was saved from having to figure it out by the doctor making his rounds.

epilogue

I wasn't shocked to discover that my "secure location" turned out to be underground in Avalon's massive tunnel system. The good news was that I had electricity, running water, phone service, and an Internet connection. The bad news was that I hated the tunnel system with a passion. I hated being without natural light. I hated the claustrophobic feeling that the ceiling might collapse on me at any moment. (Never mind that I knew perfectly well that wasn't going to happen.) And I hated the memories of things that had happened to me underground.

After my week of being grounded was up, I was finally allowed to leave my little mini-suite, though only during the daytime, and only with a bodyguard. Still, it was amazing how free that felt after being confined for the week. It's all a matter of perspective. I even renewed my lessons with Keane, who never once mentioned my escape attempt or my hospital stay. I wondered what that was all about.

My mom was occupying the room in Dad's house that had once been mine. She was still not a happy camper, even after the d.t.'s had run their course. But at least she was sober and semirational.

She reminded me, though, of what my dad is capable of. I'd been reluctant to broach the subject with her, but eventually I had to ask her why she had signed over legal custody to my dad. It seemed like the last thing in the world she would do, and I halfway believed he was lying about it.

"I'm tired, honey," Mom said when I asked. "I'd like to take a nap."

I snorted. If that wasn't the most pathetic attempt to avoid the subject I didn't know what was. "I deserve to know, don't I?" I pressed, though from long experience I knew how hard it was to get Mom to answer questions when she didn't want to.

"I just . . . thought it would be best for you," she said, but she couldn't look me in the eye when she said it, and she couldn't sit still, either. Her hands twitched, she squirmed in her chair, and she tapped one foot against the floor. Some of that was her desperate desire for a drink. But not all of it.

"I can always ask Dad," I bluffed. I knew Dad would tell me the truth. I'd already established that he had no trouble with that whole brutal honesty thing, but I really wanted to hear it from my mom. If I had to keep nagging her for weeks, then so be it.

But maybe the lack of booze weakened my mom's will, or just made maintaining the lie more trouble than it was worth. Still twitching and fidgeting, she spoke while looking just past my shoulder.

"He had Finn bring me here after he took me from the hotel," she said. "He . . . wouldn't give me anything."

Any booze, she meant.

"I got . . . desperate," she continued. "But he still wouldn't help me. Then he brought me all these forms and asked me to sign them. He wouldn't tell me what they were, and he wouldn't let me read them."

I couldn't believe what I was hearing. "You mean you sat here and signed away your rights to me without even bothering to find out what you were signing?"

Her shoulders hunched, and her gaze dropped to the floor. "Not immediately," she murmured. "At first, I refused. But I kept feeling worse and worse, and Seamus still wouldn't help me."

And I guess I was beginning to understand how Dad's mind worked, because I figured out the rest for myself. "He said he'd give you a drink if you signed the papers," I whispered, because if I spoke any louder my voice would crack.

Mom's face was a picture of guilt. "I suspect it wouldn't hold up in a U.S. court of law," she said. "I wasn't in my right mind when I signed it." She grimaced. "To tell you the honest truth, I don't even *remember* much of this, but my signature is on the papers, and I have no reason not to believe I signed them just as Seamus said I did."

My jaw clenched tight and I fought against my anger. I remembered that Dad had had her declared legally incompetent. But he'd obviously taken advantage of that incompetence first. Yeah, I was mad at Mom for what she'd done—and I couldn't help feeling hurt that she hadn't fought for me. But a big dose of the blame fell squarely on my father's shoulders.

When I returned to my underground suite, I decided it was time to lay to rest the pretty illusion that either my mom or my dad would take care of me with only my own best interests at heart. I'd been taking care of myself for years now, and that was the way life was going to be, whether I wanted it to be or not.

Taking care of myself in Avalon would be more . . . challenging than taking care of myself at home. At home, my mom's drinking had given me the freedom to do just about whatever I wanted without having to seek parental approval. Now I had *two* parents to appease—and work around, if necessary.

But I had something now that I most definitely did not have before I'd come to Avalon, something I vowed to turn to my advantage: magic.

No, I didn't know how to use it. And yes, Ethan had made it crystal clear that letting anyone know I could sense it was a bad, bad idea. But if I could learn to harness it, I would have a powerful secret weapon. Maybe even one that would allow me to escape from Avalon and disappear from the Faerie Queens' radar.

As plans go, it wasn't much. I'd figured out during my week of extremely boring confinement that the magic seemed to "like" my singing. I couldn't get through a whole song now without feeling that distinctive prickle, but so far, I hadn't been able to convince it to *do* anything yet.

But I will. I'm smart and determined, and I have every confidence that I will be able to figure this out. (At least, that's what I tell myself.) And when I do, I will use that secret weapon to wrest control of my destiny from everyone else's hands and into my own. Where it belongs.

One girl, two worlds,
and a nightmare that
threatens to end it all...

shadowspell

The new novel in the Faeriewalker series

The Erlking and his pack of murderous
minions have descended upon Avalon.
The smoldering and deadly Erlking
has his sights set on Dana and her rare
Faeriewalker powers—but does he only
seek to kill her, or does he have something
much darker in mind?

**Available
Early 2011**

"A magical book."

—*New York Times* bestselling author
Carrie Jones on *Glimmerglass*

Visit www.stmartins.com/glimmerglass and sign up to receive
a sneak preview of *Shadowspell* when it becomes available.

St. Martin's Griffin
www.stmartins.com